The mercs...
speechless with horror

The thing was hardly human. It began to grunt as a
wild twitching pushed air out of dying lungs. The
entire life force inside Kon's daughter had unleashed
a hurricane of energy inside the small body. The
jerking grew wilder until her arms and legs were
blurs and still it did not stop. Triggered by the deadly
chemical of concentrated death, the muscle spasms
threw the young Cambodian girl two feet into the
air in a violent burst of energy. She flipped and
came down on her stomach, then arched into the
air again. The little girl was dead. But the body
thrashed like a fish out of water.

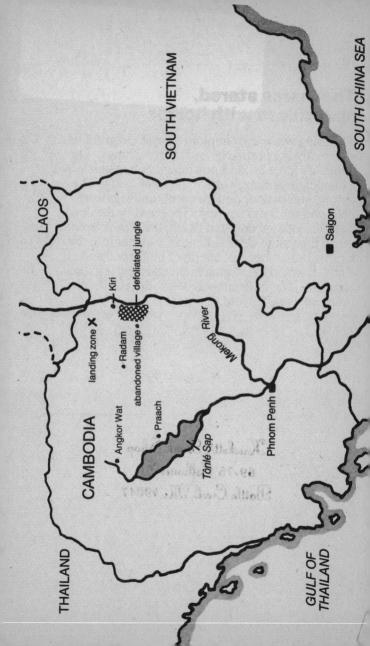

SOBs

RIVER OF FLESH

JACK HILD

Krickett's Book Shop
69-75 Calhoun St.
Battle Creek, Mi 49017

A GOLD EAGLE BOOK FROM

W☉RLDWIDE

TORONTO • NEW YORK • LONDON • PARIS
AMSTERDAM • STOCKHOLM • HAMBURG
ATHENS • MILAN • TOKYO • SYDNEY

First edition July 1985

Special thanks and acknowledgment to
Robin Hardy for his contribution to this work.

ISBN 0-373-61607-4

Printed in Canada

PROLOGUE

Flashback: Vietnam, the final days

1975. Vietnam is being torn apart by the turmoil of the last months of a lost war. The American troops are staging withdrawals. It is not going well for the South Vietnamese forces. In the northwest, along the Cambodian border, troop supply lines and the civilian population are being harassed by a mixed band of Vietcong and Khmer Rouge guerrillas, commanded by General Kon, the notorious Cambodian warlord. Kon's reputation for cruelty and bloodthirstiness, earned in a series of mass executions of villagers and soldiers alike, has fired the fuse of terror throughout the region. Consistently Kon and his company of guerrillas have eluded capture.

In the stifling decay of wartime Saigon, a young army colonel named Nile Barrabas prowled the cage of his routine intelligence duties at Military Assistance Command. He had come to Vietnam years earlier as a captain in the 5th Special Forces Group (Airborne) and had established a reputation as an officer who men would gladly follow to hell and back. On mission after mission, Barrabas had brought Company C in with the lowest body counts among his own men and the highest counts of vanquished enemy. The word went down that if a man wanted to fight a real war, he fought with Barrabas. And Barrabas's men were the meanest, toughest SOBs in the U.S. Army.

Two Silver Stars and a Distinguished Service Cross later, Nile Barrabas had been promoted to the rank of colonel

and transferred to the Military Attaché Liaison Office,
Saigon, in connection with Army intelligence services.

General Kon struck again. A twelve-man patrol from
Barrabas's old command, Company C, was ambushed—
four dead, eight taken prisoner. And the fate of Kon's
prisoners was worse than death.

The rest of Company C, commanded by Captain John
Scott, was now in hot pursuit of the murderous warlord.
Barrabas pulled strings and called in favors until he got
what he wanted—temporary assignment to front-line duty.

Colonel Nile Barrabas had one goal. The death of Kon.

The search for the murderous warlord would be relentless, the pursuit hard, the battle bloody. But the Cambodian murderer would die.

THE BLADES OF THE DESCENDING HUEY snapped the dead
remains of the defoliated jungle into clouds of dust. Captain Scott ripped the bandanna off his forehead and tied it
over his mouth and nose, narrowing his eyes against the
clouds of dust that clouded the air. Spraying the foliage
with Agent Orange robbed the Vietcong of needed cover.
It also made reconnaissance patrols through the dead jungle dirty work.

The Huey's skids touched the earth, and the great bird
settled. As Scott crouched in approach, the man he was to
meet appeared at the open door.

He stood six-foot-two, almost too big for the helicopter
that seemed dwarfed by the man's tall frame. He wore jungle fatigues, with M-16 cartridges belted around his waist,
binoculars and an M-16 slung from his neck. The long
sheath of his Bowie knife stretched down the side of his
pants. The streak of thick whitish hair was the hero's sign,
the banner of his legend. Colonel Nile Barrabas had taken
a bullet in the side of his head at Kap Long. It should have
killed him. Instead, it left his hair almost completely
white—a reminder of his brush with death.

The big man's eyes quickly surveyed the mountain clear-

ing. In the second it took for Captain Scott to raise a
salute, the MAC colonel had sized up the situation and run
out from beneath the Huey's airstream to confront the
fighting men of Company C.

"At ease, Captain—" Barrabas returned the salute
quickly "—and brief me so we can get moving."

The Huey lifted off the ground and was heading back to
Ban Me Thuot. Once again clouds of dead foliage gusted
into the air.

"We found the campsite this morning," said Scott. "It
was a day old, and there were track indications that the
American prisoners were still alive and were being marched
west into Cambodia. We've been going through this defoliated forest now for almost two days, and it's getting the
men down. But the defoliation zone ends about two kliks
farther on when we go down the mountain. There's a village there along the bank of the Ban Do River. The Cambodian border is on the other side."

"What formations are you using?"

"I split the company into two patrols. Lieutenant Cole
takes one, and I head the other. We move forward about
two kliks apart. Five-man point, a hundred meters ahead.
The Rhade guides work the point."

Barrabas nodded, looking across the clearing to the
six Rhade warriors who waited along with C Company for
the command to pull out. The dark-skinned men stood
only a little over five feet in height. Their short-clipped
hair, broad cheeks and large ears elongated with strange
ornaments made their heads look egg shaped. Their bizarre
appearance was further accentuated by the fact that
none of them had upper front teeth. Extraction was a
part of the warrior initiation ceremony. Barrabas had
worked with them often and had the greatest respect for
them. They were consummate jungle guides and fierce in
battle.

"I was going to suggest, sir, that you accompany Lieutenant Cole and his men along the river, while I take the

other patrol through the jungle. We can reestablish contact when we get to the village.''

Barrabas nodded. ''Let's get moving then.'' He heard a voice at his elbow address him in Cham, the language of the Rhade.

''Blah po gia.''

He looked down. A head below him stood one of the Rhade warriors. Barrabas could tell immediately from his brass bracelets and the little *drao*, the medicine bag around the man's neck, that this was a war leader, a *blah po gia*. That meant he had been initiated into the mysterious warrior cult of the Rhade called *mjoa*. It was a religion to them.

Barrabas answered the Rhade in his own language. The Rhade warrior continued. ''We have heard of you, Colonel Barrabas, from our brothers at Mo Nua. You are a great leader, and it will be an honor for us to follow you. But I must warn you of great danger today.''

''What is the danger?''

The Rhade looked down, his forehead wrinkling, as if considering what to say next. From around his neck he snatched his small leather *drao* and held it up.

''I am a shaman who knows the mysteries of the *mjoa*. Lead us and we will follow. But beware.''

The war leader turned abruptly and strode off to where the other Rhade warriors waited.

''What was that about?'' asked Captain Scott.

''The Rhades are a strange people,'' said Barrabas carefully. ''They've been around these mountains a few thousand years, and they can sense things that we have no words for. I don't know how they do it, but I've learned to listen to what they say.''

A sudden wind flung itself through the dead trees, scattering brown leaves. Branches overhead clattered together. There was a silence between the two soldiers. ''Let's move out,'' Barrabas said.

GENERAL KON SQUINTED against the sun that beat down into the village square. He was tall for an Asian—almost six feet, and his high, flat cheekbones distinguished him as a Khmer from Cambodia. With his eyes narrowed and his lips drawn into a cold slash, he surveyed his captive audience.

The villagers gathered in the square, squatting on the dry earth, their wicker hats protecting them from the sun. They faced the black-uniformed general with a mixture of curiosity and doubt. What was a Khmer doing leading a brigade of Vietcong guerrillas? The Cambodian border was only a few miles away, but the Khmer and the Vietnamese had traditionally been enemies for centuries.

Kon had assembled them in the village square, and with typical Vietnamese patience they would hear him out. A ring of soldiers encircling them, their rifles ready for the least sign of restlessness or discontent, ensured that patience.

The hot sun and the buzzing of flies cut the silent tension. Kon let them wait, reading their faces through the thin slits of his eyes. More than half the villagers were women and most, except the very old ones, had young children. There were also old men present. But the husbands and older sons of these people were gone, press-ganged into service by one of the armies that crossed the area from time to time. Since the last army had passed through, three or four boys had moved from childhood into young manhood. Kon would take them when he left. Whether they liked it or not.

He fixed his eyes on a young mother holding an ailing baby in the first row of villagers. They would be useful to him very soon.

Kon began.

"There are devils walking our land," the Cambodian warlord cried out to them. "Devils with white skin called Americans. These devils will bring great evil to us unless we destroy them. The power of these devils spreads far.

There is a sign of their evil magic right here among you!''

Kon strode quickly to the young woman he had spotted a few minutes earlier. He reached down and grabbed the baby from her arms.

The naked infant began to bawl as he held it aloft under the hot sun.

"This is what the devils have done!" Kon shouted.

The child's skin was covered with purplish bruises where blood vessels were visible close to the surface of the skin, and the right arm was little more than a webbed growth. General Kon knew well enough that it was a birth defect. Such things happened frequently, and more often in the past few years. Perhaps it was the strange chemicals the American soldiers used to destroy the guerrillas' jungle cover. Perhaps it was something else.

The cause mattered little. The superstitious villagers would accept Kon's explanation.

"In the great cities these American devils cast their spells. They send out their *hrong*, their spirits, to spread poison to your children even as they lie in the womb...."

General Kon droned on; in half an hour he had what he wanted. His persuasiveness, combined with the hot sun, the empty bellies of the villagers, and the soldiers with the guns, brought enthusiastic response from the throng. They resolved to help destroy the Americans who spread evil. Four teenage boys volunteered to fight under the Cambodian warlord, to rid their land of the spirits who spat poison into the wombs of pregnant women and blighted the land, making it dead and brown.

Kon turned to two of his black-uniformed soldiers standing to one side of the square. "Bring forth the prisoners," he shouted.

Barely had he uttered the order when guerrilla troops pushed the eight American prisoners into the square. Quickly the jeers and shouts rose from the frenzied crowd.

The Americans had been stripped naked, an act of ultimate humiliation in Asian custom. Their bodies were striped with sores, lacerations and bruises, and were covered in drying blood from the beatings they had received. Kon had given them to his soldiers to play with the night before. He did not care what they did to the Americans, as long as they were kept alive. The privilege of killing them he saved for himself.

Soldiers pulled strange contraptions into the center of the village. Large frames of bamboo knotted together, like the barred sides of cage walls. Other soldiers quickly stoked a fire, and the smell of tar rose from a large iron pot.

Kon felt the presence of his second-in-command, a young lieutenant from Hanoi named Nyong Tu, beside him.

"I congratulate you, General Kon," said Tu. "You were at your best today. I have never seen you so impassioned, so persuasive." Tu smiled. Everything General Kon did was reported to Tu's own superiors in Hanoi. The North Vietnamese and the Khmer Rouge guerrilla armies who were fighting to overthrow the government of Cambodia were currently allies. But the situation might change at any time. Still, Kon's success in controlling the minds of ignorant villagers was amazing.

"Yes, it was quite a performance today, wasn't it, Tu?" Kon watched the preparation in the square before him.

The American prisoners were spread-eagled on the bamboo frames and tied down, two to each frame. Several struggled, but only briefly. The guerrilla soldiers butted them hard in the stomachs with their rifles. The prisoners doubled over in agony and were then yanked back upright and strapped down.

"Something is bothering you, General Kon?" Tu was as perceptive as Kon was persuasive. There was something about his tone of voice that was different. A weakness perhaps? A sign of strain? If so, Tu must report it to Hanoi immediately.

"Bothering me?" Kon looked at the Vietnamese officer.

"No, I think not." He paused, then added, "Yes, I was good today. Watch!" He gestured toward the grisly display in the square.

The bamboo frames had been lowered flat to the ground and now the guerrilla soldiers went from prisoner to prisoner fixing long hollow reeds over their mouths. Other soldiers quickly poured bowls filled of molten tar over the contraption. The tar burned into the prisoners' flesh, sealing the reeds into their mouths and closing off their nostrils.

The Americans squirmed and writhed with pain, straining against their bonds. The village square filled with the sounds of muffled screams bursting out of throats sealed by the scalding tar.

When each prisoner had been done, the bamboo frames were lifted again and carried quickly to the banks of the river. The villagers followed, still jeering and pelting the dying Americans with stones and garbage.

The guerrilla soldiers lifted each bamboo square with its human cargo high into the air. The reeds swung from the tarred faces of the Americans like long straws. The soldiers flung each frame into the river and watched as they sank quickly beneath the water.

Only the tips of the reeds remained above the surface.

"They will live a long time like that," said Kon, "breathing through the reeds as their bodies bloat and swell from the water. As the fish feed on them. . . . " Kon and Tu turned and began to stroll back to one of the thatch-roofed houses that served as headquarters. The villagers remained at the riverbank, shouting obscenities at the dying American devils. Kon continued. "It is a horrible thing to be imprisoned like that, in a world of water and immense pain, where one is given neither life nor death. A kind of non-existence. Do you understand what I mean, Tu?"

"You are being poetic, Kon. Or sentimental." Tu hinted that Kon showed weakness with his tone of voice. "Have you no longer the stomach for it? Has your determination weakened?"

Kon shook his head and looked at Tu. "No, I assure you. It is not weakness nor the dissolution of will. It is something else. Something very curious."

"And what is that, General Kon?"

"Their screams excite me. I enjoy killing."

"Then you have only learned to hate the enemy."

"Or perhaps I have acquired the taste. Like wine. Like caviar. The varieties of death one can devise are endless. I hope some day to devise a special one for this Colonel Barrabas, the one our spies in Saigon say is coming for me."

"He is said to be invincible," said Tu.

"I am also said to be invincible." Kon smiled.

The two officers were distracted from their conversation by the sound of hurried footsteps as they approached headquarters. A young soldier stood before them and saluted stiffly.

"Superiors, I report from Fieldwatch Group Two. We have seen patrols of American soldiers passing through the forest. One is descending into the valley. The other follows the river. The white-haired soldier we were instructed to look for is among them."

"Excellent!" said Kon. "Prepare the ambush." He turned from the messenger and looked at Tu. "Now we will kill again."

Tu saw the glimmer of a smile on the warlord's lips.

BARRABAS TOOK POINT along with two Rhades and two enlisted men, leading the patrol east to the bank of the river. The current kept the water free of debris from the defoliated forest. Swarms of flies skittered angrily across the surface of the water.

A few kilos farther the defoliation zone ended, and quickly the landscape of scrub brush and savanah grass on the edge of the mountain changed to green.

The platoon radio operator moved up beside Barrabas. Captain Scott was making radio contact. His patrol had already reached the rim of the valley, had sighted normal

activity in the village of Ban Do and were descending into
the valley.

Barrabas led his soldiers along the river. Half a kilometer farther on the current picked up. Barrabas could see
white water ahead where the river curved through some
light rapids. Then it ran straight, and the forest and river
ended abruptly at a waterfall over a cliff.

The soldiers walked forward to the edge of the cliff and
looked in amazement at the valley that stretched before
them.

The mountain ended with sharp slopes down to a fertile
plain of rice paddies. The waterfall fell in an eight-foot-
long jet, hitting the foot of the mountain in a cloud of
spray. Then it settled back into the Ban Do River, flowing
through the rice paddies and past a small village several
kliks in the distance. The village was little more than a
gathering of thatched huts raised on stilts to keep them
above the river overflow in the rainy season. A road of
raised earth ran above the paddies from the edge of the
valley to the village. Past the village the river veered away
from the steep hill that rose up behind the houses, forming
the other wall of the valley. The golden outline of the gabled roof of a pagoda glinted through the trees on the
hillside.

It looked a little bit like paradise.

Barrabas raised his binoculars and scanned the mountain to the west. The column of Scott's soldiers had already
descended the cliffs and were making their way across the
paddies.

Farther on, some peasants were pushing two oxen away
from the village. They had no tiller, no plow. They seemed
to be in a hurry.

Barrabas quickly trained the binos on the little village. It
was quiet, almost deserted. That wasn't normal. Not for a
peasant village. Then he saw a woman with two small children run from one of the houses and disappear behind it.
Again he shifted his binoculars.

What they were running for was hidden by the last line of houses, but Barrabas would have bet the daily Reno intake it was a bunker.

A trap.

The village was Cong.

And the other C Company patrol was heading right up the garden path.

CAPTAIN SCOTT AND HIS MEN were within a half klik of the village. It had been easy going following the yellow clay road that led between the watery fields. Then the air zinged with bullets that seemed to come from all directions as the guerrillas opened fire from their positions behind concealed earthworks in the rice paddies.

"Perimeter!" Captain Scott shouted. Immediately the men hit the ground, bellies first and fanned out into a circle, shooting at targets that were completely invisible to them.

Since the road rose up from the paddies, they were obvious targets.

"Into the paddies. Move it!" Scott ordered. They backcrawled fast off the road and sank into the shallow water and oozing mud. Now the road covered their backside, cutting the death power of the Cong bullets in half.

But it didn't mean the trap was any less deadly. It only took one bullet to kill, and bullets were clipping across the shallow waters of the paddies like speedboats at Daytona Beach.

Scott unclipped his radio and dialed for help.

BARRABAS DIDN'T NEED to be told.

There was only one thing that was going to save Scott and his men now.

An air strike.

The colonel called up FAC on the patrol radio and spoke slowly in the low voice necessary for clear transmission.

Then he scanned the valley again trying to devise a delaying tactic until the air strike came.

They had two M-60 machine guns with a range of just under a kilometer. The enemy positions were at least that far away. But since they were firing from high positions into the valley, the shots might impress the enemy enough to slow up the firepower aimed at Scott.

Barrabas gave the order and almost instantly his men had the two machine guns set up and spitting bullets.

They tore up the earth and water at a rate of six hundred rounds a minute. The line of fire ended before it reached the Cong positions, but the strategy paid off. The rain of fire pouring on Captain Scott and his men slowed considerably.

There was nothing to do now but wait for the air strike.

Sometimes a soldier fought. Sometimes a soldier waited. It was hard to say which hell was worse.

KON WATCHED from a lookout post above the bunker on the far side of the village as the first Hueys came in over the valley and sent a few dozen 2.75-inch folding-fin aerial rockets slamming into the earthwork positions of his men. Then the big green choppers swerved in at the Cong positions on the other side.

Anger twisted in his gut. It had been a perfect setup. He had told Tu not to give the order to fire until the American soldiers were in the confines of the village. But Tu had given the order too soon. Now the North Vietnamese officer and most of his men were little more than pieces of splattered flesh in the oozing black mud of the rice paddies. Small consolation for the loss of the battle.

Kon could see the American soldiers who had once been pinned in the rice paddies approaching the edge of the village and fanning out to clear it as they entered. More Americans were descending the cliffs and pouring down into the valley.

Kon lowered his binoculars and looked down the ladder into the bunker. The villagers, frightened and quiet, lay piled on top of one another. Kon climbed down the ladder and stepped onto the ground. He pulled a grenade belt around his waist and rounds of 7.62s for his Russian SKS carbine.

His soldiers were returning fire at the Americans as they entered the village but the Americans were fighting back hard. The thatched roofs of the houses on the far side of the village were in flames, and great clouds of billowing gray smoke poured into the sky.

The chatter of autofire was deafening.

It was time to go. In less than an hour, he could slip over the border into Cambodia.

Kon turned and headed for the hillside behind the village where the gabled roofline of the pagoda leaned gracefully above the trees. An idea came to him.

He took a grenade from his belt and ran back to the bunker. He pulled the pin and tossed the grenade inside.

A loud scream came from underground as someone saw the grenade bounce in. It was too late.

The scream died in the explosion.

Then, with an aria of pain, the scene ended with horrible screams.

Kon was certain that the bloody mutilation of the villagers would delay the American soldiers.

He turned and ran for the hill.

THE BEAUTIFUL SUNNY DAY in the green valley was gone forever. It was all too familiar to Barrabas—he'd seen it hundreds of times in his years of duty in Vietnam.

The sky was darkened by smoke from the burning village. The dying sounds of rifle fire and the roar of flames drifted across the paddies.

A half-dozen Hueys chopped at the air in every direction, firing their rockets at the Cong positions and anything else that could have been concealed earthworks. The paddies erupted into explosions of water and mud, and streamers of white smoke crisscrossed the battle-darkened sky.

Air strikes saved a lot of lives. But as usual FAC and the Airborne Battlefield Command and Control Center had sent more than enough. And since the crews had been sitting bored and idle for days, they fought with great exuberance. They fired off every round they had and blew up everything in sight.

By the time Barrabas and his patrol joined Scott's men in the village, it was a mopping-up operation that bordered on mayhem.

The air was heavy with acrid smoke and a soft rain of ash that stung the eyes. The ground was dotted with the bodies of dead Cong, their black pajamas riddled with bullet holes. Women and children ran blindly through the oncoming patrol of American soldiers. Many of them clutched gaping, bleeding wounds and mothers with tears striping grimy cheeks clutched the mangled bodies of dead children.

One thing was apparent to Barrabas. This damage wasn't done by the Americans. The Cong had turned on the villagers in one last frenzied orgy of destruction. There was nothing like war to bring out the evil in desperate men.

Then the colonel saw the reeds sticking above the waters of the river.

He felt sick. He'd seen it once before. It was an execution that bore the trademark of General Kon. He called to the young lieutenant who had accompanied him on the patrol and ordered him to have some soldiers haul out the gruesome relics that lay under the surface of the shallow river.

"Where's Scott?" he asked.

The lieutenant shook his head. "Dunno, Colonel. I can't find him myself, and none of the men in his patrol seem to know where he's gone."

The chop-chop of Hueys and the thunder of rocket explosions diminished as, one by one, the air support headed back to base. But now a new sound filled the air—the sound of a twin-engine Cessna.

Barrabas looked up.

He could see the C-123 coming in from the same direction the Hueys had come. It was coming fast and low over the sides of the mountain with an eighty-yard-wide plume of white spray streaming out behind.

"Agent Orange," said the young lieutenant. "Defoliant. When FAC sends out an air strike, they really give you the works."

Barrabas nodded. Next there'd be helicopters delivering hot pizzas and after that probably a traveling road show with naked dancing girls. And the last thing to arrive would be the medivacs. The living would eat while the wounded died. Vietnam was a war gone wrong.

Already the Cessna had reached the hills on the far side of the village. It would cover a strip ten miles long in less than five minutes. In a few weeks, the valley and the forested hills would be as dead as the forest Barrabas had landed in a few hours earlier.

"I swear there won't be a green thing left in Vietnam when we're finished," said Barrabas. But the pressing concern was the whereabouts of C Company's captain. "Find Scott," he told the lieutenant.

WHEN SCOTT AND HIS PATROL entered the village they had seen the mutilated peasants. Women squatted on the ground crying hysterically, rocking back and forth as blood streamed from their wounds. Around them, their clothes torn and bloodied, little brown-eyed children stood in silent shock.

Maybe it was the death that got to him. Or maybe it was his childhood in the bad side of Detroit that made him ruthless in the face of danger. Scott forgot all caution when an old man came up to him, pointing urgently at the hillside where the roof of a pagoda rose above the line of trees.

Next thing he knew, Scott was climbing the path, his rifle aimed, itching to kill whomever had done this to the villagers.

Finally he mounted the last steep incline and the pagoda stood before him, resplendent in gilt with great carved gables stretching out at each end. Steps led up four sides of the open building.

The war seemed far away. Helicopters droned like distant bees. In the trees, birds chirped in innocence.

Scott moved slowly into the clearing, the snout of his M-16 following his eyes as he scanned the space around him. He was unaware he was being watched.

He reached the steps of the pagoda. As far as he could see the temple was completely empty. He climbed slowly until he got to the top of the steps. It was deserted.

Scott walked carefully forward, past the thick wooden columns that held up the high roof.

He missed it.

Kon flew from behind the column, his wiry body falling on Scott's back and his arms clenched around the American's throat, forcing Scott's head back in a rear stranglehold.

Scott's M-16 clattered to the floor as he reached up to loosen the deadly hold.

As Kon's grip grew tighter, Scott put his right foot outside his opponent's and lowered his body by bending his knees. He turned his head in the tight grip and pressed his chin hard against Kon's inside elbow. With a simultaneous swift bend at his waist, Scott threw Kon over his shoulder in a surprise back flip.

The U.S. captain held on to Kon's arms to follow through with a kick to the head.

But Kon hung on, too, taking advantage of Scott's imbalance.

The two enemies rolled down the steps clutching at each other in a mad wrestle. The desperate fight was fueled by one overriding certainty.

Only one of them would live.

Neither heard the sound of the Cessna flying in low until it buzzed across the clearing, blanketing the forest in a deadly white spray.

The two struggling men were covered in sticky oily liquid.

The noxious reek of chemical poisons clawed at their nostrils and eyes. Scott had the Cambodian general down in a ground counter and was moving his arms into a lock.

He missed the sound of aggressive Vietnamese voices until it was too late.

Rough hands reached out and grabbed him, pulling him back off Kon who quickly rolled out from underneath and pushed himself to his feet.

Four of his soldiers, making a fast retreat from the village, had stumbled on to the scene.

One of them raised his rifle to bayonet the struggling American.

"No!" Kon shouted, slapping down the barrel of the rifle. He began to wipe the sticky liquid from his face and hands. "The death of Barrabas will wait for another day. But we will take this one with us across the border into Cambodia." Kon smiled. "He is a fighter, so his death should be entertaining. I will think of a particularly original one for him."

"AMERICAN SOLDIER go into forest!" the agitated Rhade tribesman pointed to the hillside pagoda barely discernible through the smoky air. The Rhade had come back to Barrabas with information garnered from the villagers. "A peasant man say he go after enemy leader."

In less than a minute Barrabas and four soldiers found the path up the hillside and began the climb.

Sticky defoliant chemicals clung to undergrowth and dripped down from the leaves.

Barrabas tied a bandanna around his mouth and nose and pulled his collar up. Then he pulled gloves from his belt and put them on. He ordered the other soldiers to do the same before continuing into the doomed forest.

The sounds of the burning village, the cries and moans of the wounded and dying, and the chop-chop of more incoming helicopters faded behind them as they approached the clearing in front of the temple.

Barrabas read the scene instantaneously. It was written in dirt. The dry, dusty earth had been wetted by the defoliant. At the foot of the temple stairs was a great rolling imprint where Scott and Kon had landed and wrestled. At the sides of the clearing footprints became visible; too small to be those of Americans. There were signs of a scuffle, and more footprints led off into the jungle. One set of prints was bigger than the others. Scott had been taken prisoner.

"Colonel Barrabas!" a soldier called from the temple. The tall warrior mounted the temple steps.

Impaled on the ornately carved gilt post with a knife was a military dog tag. It was Scott's. At the foot of the post was something else. Scott's combat helmet. The helmet was filled with urine—another of Kon's trademarks, left behind as a sign of contempt.

Barrabas already knew it was over for Scott. Kon and his guerrillas would slip over the Cambodian border and lose their trackers in the labyrinth of trails that led mazelike through the wild uncharted jungle. Barrabas and his men might find the shell that had once been the Scott they had known, some barely living thing defined by a single word—agony.

But he wasn't going to give up easily.

"Let's get back to the village," Barrabas ordered. "I want ground tracking with air support, on the double."

As the soldiers sped down the hill, a different smell began to mingle with the acrid dripping chemical. It was the smell of pizza.

By the time they reached the village the smell was overpowering. So was the sight before them.

A great Kiowa transport copter unloaded enough white square boxes of hot pizza to feed an army, not just a company of soldiers.

Meanwhile, the village burned, peasants wept and children wandered about, their eyes glazed over in shock.

The medivacs weren't anywhere in sight.

This was more than crazy. It was a nightmare. A war gone mad.

Barrabas stood in the circle of hell that had been Ban Do. He couldn't shake the feeling that Vietnam was a lost cause. The war was over. He wanted out.

The days ahead revealed that once again Kon had escaped. Captain John Scott was listed as missing in action.

Barrabas's own war became his future. He did what he did best, fighting as a professional soldier, a mercenary in a dozen wars in as many countries.

But on the day of the bloody battle for the village of Ban Do, Barrabas swore that he would make Kon pay for the carnage he had savored.

1

The *portier* opened the door and eyed the tall muscular man with short, almost-white hair. Giving a brief, almost imperceptible nod of recognition, he moved aside to allow entry. Nile Barrabas walked into the tiny foyer just before the doorway to the festive insanity beyond. The bar was crowded and mad in a way that only the bars of Amsterdam can be on a Friday night.

"Hope you find what you're looking for," a young man at the coat check simpered as Barrabas moved forward.

Merrymakers lined up at the long bar in the first room and danced on the crowded disco floor in the next. There was one element missing from this bar. Women. All the customers were male.

Barrabas gave a mental shrug. The Dutch had a typical happy-go-lucky tolerance for people who were into their own thing. Heads turned as Barrabas passed through the two lower rooms and ascended the stairs to the upper level. He was used to that, too. He stood out in a crowd. It wasn't just his well-honed muscled body or the distinctive white-gray hair, the souvenir of the bullet he took in the head at Kap Long. It was the way he moved. The male animal, proud, strong, confident. People saw a man who belonged to no one but himself.

The clientele in this bar looked at him for other reasons as well. It didn't bother him. He could take care of himself.

Right now he was making a rendezvous for a very special woman. The one woman he'd do anything for. Including keeping an appointment in this place.

At the top of the steep narrow steps a vision in black leather who looked like he'd stepped out of a blue boy magazine blocked the doorway. Barrabas stared him down. He moved out of the way, and the American moved through into yet another room, crowded and dimly lit. There was a bar on one side where a tattooed bartender in a sleeveless leather vest sloshed glasses of draft beer across the bar.

The customers here looked like sailors on shore leave and probably were. Music blared, so loud no one could talk. At the end of the bar he saw the doorway to the last room, the one at the top of the club. He had to stoop down a foot to get through it.

He found himself in a long dark room, lit by a television set high on a shelf on the wall. The picture was on but there was no sound. There were lights on the pinball machine and one dim light over the pool table. Two young men strutted like peacocks with cues in their hands. The player at the table sent the white ball against the far edge, where it ricocheted twice, and popped the orange ball into the pocket. He was good.

The walls were covered with black-light poster relics from the LSD days of the sixties. A poster showing Jimi Hendrix, with the caption Are You Experienced, and a peace symbol, tattered and yellowed with age, were among the assortment.

The music from the other rooms in the club seeped through but not so loud that the men sitting at the tables around the sides of the room couldn't carry on conversations. Not that any of them were trying. Some played chess or backgammon, deeply absorbed by the game boards in front of them. All had the glazed faraway looks that spoke of things smoked and snorted, chemicals soaring through bloodstreams like one-way tickets to oblivion.

Barrabas checked out the room for an alternative exit and saw it on the other side of the pool table.

Then he walked to the corner of the room where the

man he was meeting appeared to be nodding off over a chessboard.

Barrabas slid onto the cushioned bench, bumping heavily into the man. He could feel the steel edge of a gun under the man's jacket. The man looked up, startled.

"Raoul?"

The man nodded. The eyes, dark and sharp, cleared quickly. Already Barrabas didn't like him. But you couldn't always choose the people you did business with. And this was important business.

"I am called that," Raoul said in a high-pitched singsong voice. "Among other things." A thin-lipped smile spread slowly and deliberately across his wide pudgy face. Greasy black hair hung down like a comma over his forehead. His skin glistened with oil, and the air was rank with the smell of almond-scented perfume. The odd little man waved a scented hanky under his nose. His fingers were covered with rings.

"I came for Erika," Barrabas said.

"Ahhhh," said Raoul, nodding his head and looking away to survey the room slowly. He smiled delicately at Barrabas again. "Most unfortunate that Erika couldn't come here. I am not of this persuasion myself. I prefer other pleasures. But I do find these places convenient for some transactions. One can at least do business here unnoticed." Raoul stressed the word "business." He continued. "And should anyone later ask questions, the people who come to a place like this, as you can well imagine, are notoriously hard to find, and usually when asked, suffer a convenient loss of memory. Gay people can always be trusted not to answer prying questions."

"I only came here for one thing," said Barrabas. "Let's do it."

Raoul nodded.

Barrabas felt a hard, heavy object wrapped in cloth shoved into his lap where the table blocked the transfer of goods from view.

"You can examine under the cloth to verify the contents," said Raoul. "Of course, authenticity can only be proved by an expert, but I guarantee. My reputation, you know...."

Barrabas nodded. He dug his fingers through the strips of cotton layered around the object, until his fingertips felt smooth cold stone. The head of a statue. The rest was up to Erika.

"And, of course, you have something for me. A token of your appreciation for this favor." Raoul smiled again.

Barrabas dug into the inside pocket of his leather jacket and drew the envelope out, pulling it down under the table. It was thick. There was something unmistakable about the feel of a wad of crisp American C notes. Barrabas knew the feel well. A decade of fighting as a mercenary in illegal armies that straddled the globe accustomed him to it. He passed it over to Raoul. The hand took the envelope eagerly, the fingers deftly riffling the wad. The envelope disappeared inside Raoul's jacket.

"Very good." The smile was gone now. Raoul looked suddenly preoccupied, eager to be gone. "Erika knows where to find me if she wants more." He stood up, grabbed a fedora from the seat beside him, and quickly left the room with his left arm pressed tightly against his side where the money was hidden.

Barrabas gave him time to leave. The pool player scored a double.

Half an hour later, after a ten-minute walk through the cobblestone streets and narrow canals of the ancient city, past haphazardly leaning town houses that lined the murky canals, Nile Barrabas found himself in the seventeenth-century elegance of the Begijnhof. A Mercedes taxi waited outside the entrance to the courtyard. The driver looked up briefly from the magazine he was reading as Barrabas passed.

A few seconds later he found himself in the courtyard. The noises of Amsterdam disappeared, replaced by the whisper of a light breeze through the flowering bushes in the gardens. For a moment before going in, he stood outside the house and watched. The curtains were drawn back from the tall windows, and candlelight cast flickering patterns on the carved ceiling within. The delicate sound of Baroque string music floated out. And he could see Erika. She stood in the half-light by the fireplace reading something. Then she moved out of view. Suddenly she was back, this time playing with the flowers in a vase by the windows. The sweet yellow light from the candles cast a burning golden glow to her blond hair, and her perfect alabaster features gave her the appearance of a porcelain doll. A tough one, though, Barrabas thought. Unbreakable.

He smiled to himself. Erika would keep arranging and rearranging the flowers in the vase until their bloom was finally gone. The house was always filled with flowers. And every day he brought her another armful from the Bloemengracht.

He bounced the heavy stone statue in his hand, climbed the steps and let himself in.

Erika heard the front door open, left the flowers as they were and walked quickly to the man she knew. His steel-blue eyes caught her with a spark that brought smiles to both their faces. She reached up and circled her arms loosely around his neck, leaning her breasts heavily into his hard muscled chest as she pressed her open lips to his.

Nile Barrabas had been her lover ever since they had met on a tropical beach while on leave from the war in Vietnam. He was a hard man in some ways. Since he'd left the U.S. Army, after his days fighting the Asian war, he'd been a professional soldier. A mercenary. She never knew when or where he'd turn up in her life. Or, sometimes after he disappeared, if he'd ever turn up again.

Some people would say it was a lousy life for a woman. But Erika Dykstra had her own life, too. And, besides, Nile Barrabas was worth it.

He was getting restless again, too. She'd sensed it a few days earlier. She had a feeling this meeting, too, would be short-lived. An envelope waited for him on the table in the hall.

"Mmm, all that for me?" Barrabas said, joking as they drew away from each other. Her eyes were the color of a blue lagoon. She gazed up and threatened to drown him.

"Did you get it?" she asked, widening her eyes. It was her version of a wink.

Barrabas laughed, full and hearty, and disentangled her arms from his shoulders. "Ah, Erika. Back to business. Yes I did. The meeting place was fascinating. I hope this is worth the dough, though."

He put the heavy statue into Erika's waiting hands. They walked to the living room as she carefully stripped off the wrappings. Then she held it up in front of her with her arm half outstretched. It was an object of extraordinary beauty. The soft candlelight highlighted the highly polished red stone. It was the head of a god, the gentle almond-shaped eyes and thick stone lips composed in lines of serenity as it contemplated a Buddhist paradise.

"Damn," Erika said softly. "It's real."

Barrabas looked at her. "For that kind of money I thought you'd want it to be real."

She nodded and sighed.

"The problem is that it's stolen. Sort of. Pillaged is a better word."

"Tell me about it, Erika. Archeological antiques are not a specialty of mine."

She placed the statue on a polished mahogany table where the candlelight glowed onto the face and the highly polished wood threw back a reflection.

"I told you it's from Angkor Wat. Angkor is one of the greatest treasures in the world. It's an ancient city, over a thousand years old, of hundreds of highly carved palaces and temples. And it's a lost city. At least, it was until 1867 when a French explorer stumbled across it deep in the jungles of Cambodia, overgrown and in ruins. It's been restored since then, but there's been a terrible civil war in Cambodia. After the Khmer Rouge rebels won, they closed the entire country to outsiders. There had been reports that the ancient city was damaged but no one knows for sure."

As she spoke she stared at the statue, transfixed by its expression of peacefulness. She turned to look at Barrabas again.

"I made myself a career and a lot of money as a smuggler, Nile. It's one thing to provide assistance to people wishing to avoid export duties; it's another thing to deal in stolen property, and that includes things that belong to the cultural heritage of a country. These things," she said, nodding toward the artifact, "are even protected by the United Nations. Unfortunately that doesn't stop theft. There are historic sites all over the world being hacked to bits to satisfy the appetites of rich European and American collectors. Through my contacts I was offered brokerage on certain artifacts purportedly from Angkor Wat. I didn't know if the offer was real; it is very difficult to smuggle the statues out of the country. But now I do know. Angkor is being destroyed."

"So what are you going to do about it, Erika?"

She looked at her lover squarely and then back at the mesmerizing face of the statue.

"I'm going to Thailand for the next rendezvous. I'm going to buy everything Raoul has to sell. Every piece of Angkor I can find. Then I'm going to hide it in a company warehouse in Bangkok. And when the troubles in Cambodia are over, I'm going to give it all back."

"It'll cost thousands."

"And be worth every cent. To have a thousand years of history wiped out by a few greedy—" Her voice broke. "The money's not a problem, Nile. You know that."

Barrabas put his arm around her, and she leaned against him.

"When do we go?" he asked her.

"Go?"

"To Bangkok."

"Oh God!" Erika put her hand over her mouth and looked at Barrabas in horror. "Oh, Nile, I forgot. I was so excited by the statue. And the taxi's waiting." She pushed herself away from him and ran to the hall. When she returned to the living room she handed him an envelope.

"Airline tickets. They came half an hour before you got back."

Barrabas looked at them. One way to Denver, Colorado. They had been forwarded by an agency in New York. The agency that worked for Walker Jessup. That meant that someone, somewhere, had a war for him to fight. It was time to go. The plane would leave in an hour.

"So I already knew. You can't go to Bangkok," said Erika.

"Maybe I can meet you there. Later."

"Maybe." She smiled, placing her hand softly on his neck. "I packed your toothbrush. And the taxi's waiting." She kissed him.

They didn't say goodbye.

2

"Okay Jessup. So far all you've said is chemical warfare. Fill me in."

As Barrabas spoke, steel doors a foot thick slammed shut behind him. The metallic clunk resounded down the long concrete corridor like a hammer on a kettledrum.

The military guard scanned the faces of the two men. Nile Barrabas, tall and muscular; Walker Jessup, short and overweight. The guard glanced down at the photo ID in his hand. He motioned to another guard standing nearby.

"Corporal Jones, accompany Mr. Jessup and Mr. Barrabas to the inner base. Enjoy your visit, gentlemen." The guard's voice was deadly serious. Guarding one of the nation's top-secret military bases was a fairly serious business.

The two men stepped into the front and back seats of a small electric car the size of a double golf cart. Jessup sat beside the driver. A young Marine took the seat beside Barrabas, and the car glided with a low hum down the long fluorescent-lit tunnel. Jessup turned around in the front seat.

"By the time we get there, we'll be more than a mile inside this mountain," he said.

Barrabas nodded. It was no secret that the U.S. military had bases hollowed out inside the mountains of the Colorado Rockies. The most famous was the NORAD base, which watched the skies for incoming Soviet missiles. But few people knew how many others there were, and fewer still ever saw the inside of them.

Walker Jessup, the Fixer, was one of the lucky few. His

vast bulk filled half the width of the wide tunnel. In Washington, Jessup was known as a guy who could solve problems—no matter who had to be paid off, what had to be smuggled where, or how covert a military or paramilitary operation had to be. And his biggest customer was the U.S. government.

Barrabas knew full well who his ultimate employer was. But it was a discussion he and Jessup would never have. As far as he was concerned Jessup offered him a job, and if the price was right, Barrabas would accept it. Then he and his team of carefully selected mercenary soldiers went into action. The first Soldiers of Barrabas had been legendary in Vietnam. For the second team, there was nothing. No fame, no glory, no thanks. Just a lot of risks and a lot of bucks at the end of it all.

Barrabas knew that he and his soldiers felt the same way about the rewards. It sure as hell beat the soft life; he had only to look as far as Jessup to see where that led.

At the far end of the tunnel, two more armed guards and an open elevator awaited. Once again their ID was checked.

"Security seems a little elaborate to me," Jessup drawled, betraying his Texan origins. "It would be hard for us to switch passengers in the golf cart halfway down a tunnel with one entrance and one exit." The two men and the soldier entered the elevator.

"We have our orders, sir." The soldier inserted a key into the control panel, a red light lit up, the doors closed and the elevator descended. It was impossible to tell how fast or how far down they were going. The elevator had no lights to mark the floors.

"Chemical warfare, Jessup," Barrabas prodded again.

"You heard of yellow rain, Nile?"

Barrabas nodded.

"Well, we're about to get a little lecture."

The elevator stopped and the doors opened onto a spacious corridor that resembled the inside of a modern downtown office building. Two more guards waited.

With one in front and the other behind them, Jessup and
Barrabas were escorted through a maze of hallways until
they stopped before large double steel doors. One of the
soldiers inserted a key in an intercom box and announced
their arrival. The door slid open.

By now Barrabas was ready for anything. Maybe a
motorboat ride.

Instead the doors opened on the balcony of a theater
carved out of solid rock. Instead of seats, a long console
ran along the front. Straight ahead, on the far wall, a bank
of five large screens spread across the curve of the room.
In the pit below a dozen white-coated technicians moved at
light-studded control panels. Banks of smaller television-
size monitors lined the walls, displaying reams of incom-
prehensible data.

"ComSat," said Jessup. "Military satellite control data
center. This is the brain room for all those little tin pods
whizzing around in the atmosphere a hundred miles overhead."

"Mr. Jessup, Mr. Barrabas?"

Two men in white lab coats appeared at their side. One
was tall and gray-haired and stood with a posture that indicated that he had once had military training.

The other, shorter man, carried a very official-looking
clipboard; he addressed them.

"Dr. von Eberhart." He introduced himself with a curt
bow of his head.

"Dr. Green. Jeff Green." The tall one extended his
hand American-style.

"You are Mr. Walker Jessup and Mr. Nile Barrabas, I
assume," said von Eberhart. He turned quickly without
waiting for an answer. "Come along. We have no more
time for introductions."

Dr. Green gave Barrabas a bemused smile when the German scientist turned away. Unspoken recognition locked
between the eyes of the two military men.

Von Eberhart was leaning over the console and glancing

up at the large center screen as the others walked over. Color slides flashed quickly across the screen.

"You've heard of yellow rain?" Dr. Green asked Barrabas.

"A little."

"It is where the story begins," said von Eberhart, staring intently at the screen.

The slide showed a young Asian man in a hospital bed.

"A patient in a refugee camp in Thailand," said Green. The man's body was swollen enormously, and his skin was covered with red running sores and boils.

"Gruesome," Jessup whispered.

"Gentlemen, perhaps some political background is in order," Green suggested. "Since the fall of Vietnam, the Communist government has supported their allies in Laos. However, in Cambodia they have turned against their former allies, the Khmer Rouge. They have invaded the country and installed their own government in Phnom Penh. It is perhaps not a bad thing, since the Khmer Rouge turned Cambodia into little more than a vast concentration camp. The Khmer Rouge still control the countryside in the north. The Vietnamese-backed government controls the south."

Dr. von Eberhart continued. "The Vietnamese continue to push back the Khmer Rouge—as well as helping the government of Laos fight against the rebels. To assist these efforts, the Russians have supplied them with chemical weapons. These are sprayed from airplanes, and the cloud of poison is usually yellow, although it can also be red or white. The natives of Cambodia were the first to call it yellow rain."

"This patient claims he was sprayed in a Vietnamese attack on a village in northwestern Cambodia," said Dr. Green, pointing at the slide on the screen. "The people seen at the camps in Thailand report the standard symptoms. First, an itching and burning in their eyes and on their skin. The air smells like pepper. Then the body swells

up and the bleeding begins from the nose and mouth.
Then. . . .'' The screen changed to a slide of the same young
man in the same bed, taken a few minutes later. This time
his head arched back and his eyes had rolled upward. His
arms had become blurry with movement. He seemed to be
having an epileptic fit.

"Muscle spasms," said Green. "Their vision blurs, and
they can't breathe. We have about six thousand deaths
reported."

"Classic symptoms of trichothecene poisons," von
Eberhart said with satisfaction. "We have also found this
chemical in their blood. And so we know the Russians are
supplying chemical weapons to the Vietnamese."

"We don't know that at all," said Dr. Green sharply.

Barrabas could see there were more than national differences between the open easygoing American and the
stiff German scientist. There was a major disagreement,
and probably professional rivalry as well. It was no
wonder that the public received such confused messages on
issues such as this.

The slide changed again, this time showing a mass of
greenish-blue fuzz.

"Fungus!" said von Eberhart triumphantly.

"Mycotoxins are produced in nature by fungus. They
are highly poisonous, particularly the trichothecenes," Dr.
Green said helpfully. "We know very little about their
effects. But apparently they attack and kill the cells of the
bone marrow, the lymph nodes, the intestines. Veins rup-
ture. The blood will no longer clot. A horrible way to die."

Barrabas nodded. "The way rats die from warfarin.
Bleed to death from internal hemorrhage."

"Exactly," said Dr. Green.

"And only the Russians have the ability to produce such
poisons on a massive scale," von Eberhart said.

"Nonsense," said Green, eyeing Barrabas and Jessup.
"You can make these poisons in your garage with a
seventy-five-dollar mail-order kit. And that's assuming

these poisons are being made at all. We really have no evidence whatsoever."

"Evidence! Dr. Green wants evidence!" Von Eberhart's voice rose in anger and impatience. The slide changed. This time it showed a twig with a few leaves. There was yellow powder on them. "That is evidence. Brought from Cambodia by a refugee. The yellow powder was analyzed and contained high levels of three kinds of trichothecenes. It's quite clear that chemical warfare is being waged in Southeast Asia."

Dr. Green shook his head skeptically. "There are more than fifty kinds of trichothecenes, some natural, some man-made. The three kinds found in this leaf could be either. So maybe the evidence was planted. Maybe the yellow powder is just bee shit, and the fungus grew on it while it was being brought here."

"Dr. Green attended a conference in Russia last year," said Dr. von Eberhart accusingly. "In Moscow."

Green shook his head. "I'm not from Missouri where I have to see to believe. I'm from Nevada, and when I gamble I like to know the odds. Until we have conclusive evidence the odds are against us on this one. All we know is that there are indications that people are being poisoned in Southeast Asia. It could be natural. It could be chemical warfare. Whatever it is, it's getting worse."

"Much worse. In fact, it is a very dangerous situation." Von Eberhart's fingers skipped along the control panel and a new slide came up. It was a satellite photograph of a piece of real estate.

"Cambodia," said Green.

"Exactly," said von Eberhart. "You can see the wavy line, which is the Mekong River. It forms the northern border with Laos before turning south and flowing down through the center of Cambodia and finally into South Vietnam. And just about in the center of the country is Tonle Sap, the Great Lake. It is also the center of the country's extensive irrigation system. In the dry season, which is now, the waters flow south from Tonle Sap into the Mekong and empty into the Gulf of Siam, which is part of the Indian Ocean.''

Dr. Green interrupted. ''What you can't see clearly in this mountainous forested area in the north of the country. Just below the Laotian border, there is a brownish color where it should be green. Dr. von Eberhart, show them the infrared photographs.''

Suddenly the two scientists seemed to have forgotten their differences and hurried to cooperate. The satellite photograph was replaced by one that showed a kaleidoscope of colors. It looked like a paint palette.

''The infrared film measures the heat radiated from objects and reproduces them in varying colors ranging from hot to cold,'' explained von Eberhart.

''The jungles are orange, the agricultural land yellow,'' said Green. ''Urban areas are blue. The rivers are green and also the Great Lake, and the network of irrigation canals.''

Barrabas studied the giant slide projection following Dr. Green's guidelines. Slowly the familiar outlines of Cambodia emerged in the infrared picture.

''The northern area of Cambodia is an area of reported heavy fighting between the Khmer Rouge and the Vietnamese.''

''There's a blue spot there,'' said Barrabas.

''Right. This slide was taken two weeks ago. Dr. von Eberhart.'' Green nodded to the other scientist.

A series of almost identical slides flashed across the screen. The only noticeable difference was the size of the blue spot. It kept getting bigger.

''These are taken by our satellite since then,'' said von Eberhart. ''Notice the change. And this one is the last one we have. Taken yesterday.''

''The blue spot is enormous,'' said Barrabas.

''Almost a hundred kilometers long and twenty-five wide,'' said von Eberhart.

"It grows in the direction of the prevailing winds," said Green.

"So what is it?" Barrabas asked.

Von Eberhart stabbed his finger at the control panel. The screen went blank. The two scientists exchanged glances.

"We don't know," said Dr. Green.

"No idea whatsoever," von Eberhart said, shrugging.

"We know that the jungle in Cambodia is dying."

"Dead, in fact."

"And the death is spreading quickly. Very quickly."

"In a matter of months, it will all be over." Von Eberhart drew his index finger across his throat.

"Over the border into Thailand," said Green. "Whatever's killing the jungle in Cambodia is spreading fast, and we have no idea what it is or if and when it will stop."

"It might be a natural pest or blight or disease."

"But if it is, science has never recorded anything that kills so quickly or spreads so fast. Not even Agent Orange did that."

"So it must be chemical."

"And while Dr. von Eberhart and I may disagree about yellow rain and where it comes from, there is enough evidence to know that some kind of chemical warfare activity is probably involved in this dead forest. But the question is, who is doing it and with what?"

"Even the Russians would not be so stupid," said von Eberhart.

"You never know," said Barrabas. "But now I know what you want me to do. Go in there and find out."

The two scientists exchanged embarrassed glances. Everyone knew what no one was saying. If chemicals could kill a forest, how would they affect people?

Dr. Green spoke first. "We know nothing about your work, Mr. Barrabas." He coughed slightly. "Any arrangements you make will be with Mr. Jessup, of course. But let me just say that we have prepared lightweight protective suits that can travel easily. I will personally instruct you in their use. There is one other very important thing.''

"A matter of life and death," said von Eberhart. "For the whole world. We do not exaggerate."

"You must bring us samples, of course. But should you discover supply depots, even production facilities, you must not attempt to destroy them."

Von Eberhart interjected. "Many of the man-made chemicals used for such things are indestructible. They will exist in nature forever—until the end of time when the sun explodes and the earth is finally destroyed. Even then these chemicals will exist, floating in the debris of space. And sometimes even a millionth of a gram is enough to kill. Or cause terrible disease."

"We are relying on you to help us find out what it is. Then we will know how to deal with it."

Jessup, who had listened in silence for a long time, suddenly cleared his throat.

"Gentlemen, I suggest that very soon we have a look into protective clothing and other provisions. I'd like to speak to Colonel Barrabas briefly, in private."

"Certainly," said Dr. Green. Von Eberhart gave another curt bow. Barrabas and Jessup walked away from the control panel until they were out of earshot.

"Will you go for it, Nile?" Jessup asked in a low voice.

"Geez, Walker." Barrabas rubbed his hand through his short-clipped hair and scratched the back of his neck. "The way they just put it, it looks like someone's got to go in there."

Jessup nodded. "The boys at the top are real worried about it, and I've got total green. Anything you want you got. They'll have the Marines pack up Disneyland and ship it to Rangoon if you think it'll help." His Texas drawl didn't conceal his concern. "You got an action plan off the top of your head?"

"Bangkok. I got some old intelligence connections there. See if I can luck on to some information before I go in. Lee Hatton is still in Majorca with Claude Hayes, picking up the pieces that Spetsnaz left behind. I'll get her over from Majorca to help out in that department. And Bishop is up in Canada. I want him there right away to scout out air support. Meanwhile you put out a call for O'Toole, get Hayes over here and have them round up the other guys. Nate Beck and Alex Nanos are in San Francisco. Billy Two might be a problem. He disappeared somewhere into the Indian lands in the Arizona desert.''

"When can you get to Bangkok?" Jessup asked.

Barrabas looked at his watch. "Tonight." He thought about the perk, something he didn't tell Jessup about. A blond Dutch woman who would be very surprised to see him.

"That long?" Jessup said.

"Tonight, American time, is tomorrow morning for them. Don't worry Jessup. I'll have a whole new day to get started." Barrabas looked at the two waiting scientists who stood to one side, engaged in another heated argument. "Shall we tell the Bobbsey twins I accept?"

Jessup smiled. "Make them so happy they'll kiss and make up."

3

When the crow cawed crazily and flew twice across the lake, Geoff Bishop knew the storm clouds gathering in the northwest heralded a big one. Already he could hear low grumbles of thunder coming over the other side of the mountain. The lake was calm, not a leaf stirred, but the storm was getting ready to blow. A cloud over the sun extinguished the last glint of light on the aluminum skin of the little airplane that floated a hundred feet offshore.

Bishop closed the window most of the way and turned to go downstairs. The big double bed, its sheets crumpled and comforter thrown carelessly back, momentarily tempted him. When the storm came he wanted to climb back into it. With her. A wink of lightning whitened the room. He went downstairs.

As he crossed the living room, he could see her standing on the deck outside the sliding glass doors. Still naked from her swim, she was drying herself. Her body, lithe and firm, was brown from the sun. Years of regular exercise and training in the martial arts had toned her muscles and, if anything, had accentuated the curves of her slender body. Lee Hatton was one of the most beautiful women Geoff Bishop had ever known. And the smartest.

He stood silently at the glass doors. Her back was turned to him while she finished drying her short dark hair. She was gazing past the tall stand of hemlock trees along the shore, watching the clouds roll across the bare rock face of the mountain.

"I'm glad you came," he said.

She turned, laughing, toweling her back and turning her

head sideways to shake water from her ear. Bishop's eyes drifted down to a shadow that fluttered like a brush stroke from the graceful thighs up across the smooth brown abdomen.

"Of course, I came. You came, too, didn't you? I was pretty sure you did."

"Not that. I mean from Majorca."

She winked at him and started to fold the towel. "Don't be so serious." She walked to him and kissed him.

"I am serious."

She turned and walked back to stand at the edge of the deck and looked out over the lake. The sky grew darker. A great tank of cloud rolled over the mountain, throwing the naked face of the rocks into shadow. Still, there was not a ripple on the surface of the water.

Bishop followed her, grabbing her robe from a deck chair and draping it over her shoulders. He put his arms around her waist. "I am serious."

"It's so beautiful here," she said, changing the subject. "You always hear how beautiful Canada is, but I never knew. The loons last night. Laughing out on the water like their lives depend on craziness. In some ways they do, I guess. Are we crazy, Geoff?"

She could feel the broad width of his shoulders along her back, the firm arms encircling her, crossing lightly at her waist.

She reflected on the irony of the circumstances that had brought them together. Geoff was the new boy. An ace Canadian pilot, much decorated in the military and turfed out of his civilian job only to land smack-dab in the middle of the SOBs when Barrabas needed a pilot for a covert operation in Central America. They'd noticed each other the moment they met, in a private airfield in Cristobal, Panama. Noticed was an understatement. While the rest of the SOBs raced on with preparations for the mission, load-ing equipment into the helicopter, counting ammo and breaking down their rifles, Lee and Bishop had locked eyes across the hangar.

A few days later, when the war was over, they flew out of the Honduran hell of the dead dictator's burning death camp. And Bishop asked her to come to his lodge north of Montreal. Lee couldn't make it right away. First, the SOBs made a foray into Siberia to rescue a Russian dissident from a labor camp. It was a mission Bishop wasn't called in on. And he got left out of the action again when Spetsnaz, the Russian military police, came after them at Lee's villa on the Spanish island of Majorca. The result was a lot of dead Spetsnaz and the end of Casa Hatton. Claude Hayes was still there, picking through the dynamited rubble and arranging for someone to buy the property. Lee phoned Geoff Bishop and told him she needed a place to stay.

He guaranteed they'd be alone. They were. She wondered how the other SOBs would react if they knew. They treated her as an equal. They knew she could take care of herself. They'd seen her do it. Liam O'Toole, Alex "the Greek" Nanos, Nate Beck and Billy Two. They were tough guys. Real men. And she knew that they were still protective of her in some ways and always would be. It was part of what they were made of. And Geoff Bishop was the new boy.

"How'd you like the other guys? When you met them in Central America?" she asked.

"You gotta be a little nuts to walk the wire all the time like that. Coming in on the SOBs late in the game, I've missed a few missions, and the rest of you have things in common. You know one another a lot better, so I feel left out sometimes. But that just takes time. I trust them, though. All of them. With my life. And I'd put down my life for them." He looked at her. "Maybe that means I'm a little nuts, too."

Without warning a strong gust of wind blew across the lake, swinging the branches of the hemlocks and tossing the leaves in the mighty yellow birches. Below them, waves came out of the once-still lake and gulped greedily at the shore.

Lee twisted around in Bishop's embrace, freeing her arms to put them around his neck. She kissed him. He breathed her in, her fragrance like sandalwood from an exotic country no visitor had seen.

"This is our secret," she said. "When we're back out there, on a mission, we're just soldiers again. Okay? Please don't ask me why."

He looked down into her eyes. "Okay." He smiled. "If that's what you want."

"Let's go inside." She shivered slightly.

A kerosene lamp glowed softly from the heavy beam of the low ceiling. Lee sank back into the overstuffed couch while Geoff lit the end of a rolled-up newspaper and shoved it into the kindling in the great stone fireplace. It took quickly. The waves of heat swept back over them.

Geoff turned and walked back to the couch. Suddenly he commanded, "Don't move! It's on your arm!"

Lee's eyes registered bewilderment for a brief second. She looked at her arm stretched out along the back of the sofa. It was a tiny red thing the size of a pea with two-inch-long legs, each as thin as a hair.

"What is it? A spider of some kind?"

"Daddy longlegs." The pilot reached down and scooped it off her arm. He walked to the sliding glass door, opened the screen and set the little creature on the deck. As he stood up he noticed a moth flittering about the lamp. With one swoop of his arm he snatched it into his fist. "You, too." He thrust his arm outside, opened his fist to release the insect and quickly slid the door shut again.

"Are you always so kind to your leggy little friends," Lee asked. Bishop sat down on the couch. Lee drew her feet up onto the seat and snuggled her toes against his legs.

He shrugged diffidently. "This wilderness is their country more than it is ours. We build these houses, and they're just great big death traps for all kinds of living things. I remember once, a long time ago, when I was in the Air Force I was waiting in the CO's office. I had been waiting a long time, and I was bored stiff. I saw a bug crawling down the wall, so I squashed it with my thumb." He looked Lee straight in the eyes.

"And?"

"And I thought to myself, I killed it because I was bored and had nothing else to do. And you know what?"

"No. What?"

"I felt terrible. It is that easy to kill."

Lee Hatton could see from the look in his eyes that as funny as it sounded, he meant every word.

"You are nuts." She ran her hand through his hair.

"Since then I swore never to take life, any life, without knowing exactly why." Suddenly he clapped the air in front of him. "Mosquitos, for example." He brought his hands apart and extricated the tiny flattened body from one palm and flicked it on the floor. "Or horseflies, black-flies and deerflies. But never dragonflies or spiders."

Lee watched him, laughing.

He looked at her intensely. "Now I have a question for you. Claude Hayes."

He said the name like a statement. Hayes was another of the SOBs, a black man who had gone from the Civil Rights movement in the American south to guerrilla warfare in Black Africa. He was also the colonel's resident expert on underwater demolitions, guerrilla combat and jungle warfare. He was an eminent survivalist. And sometimes, between wars, he had stayed with Lee at her villa on Majorca. There was a strong bond of friendship between the two mercenaries.

"Claude is a friend, that's all." She smiled. "Jealous?"

Bishop looked bashful. "No. But we've got to work together. I thought I should know."

Lee reached out and played at his lips with her index finger. "Claude has his own interests. His own friends.

Quite different from yours or mine. You've nothing to worry about. He knows about us."

Bishop looked outside. It still hadn't rained. The wind had died down, and the dark mass of cloud had almost passed by.

"I'll be damned. It's passing over."

"Come here." Lee pushed her feet under him and pried him toward her with a teasing smile.

Then the phone on the table behind her rang.

A long ring. Another long. Two short. Bishop's call on the party line. Without turning, without taking her eyes off him, Lee reached her hand over her shoulder, picked up the receiver and gave it to Bishop.

"Hello." The room was silent except for the roaring of the fire.

Then he handed it to Hatton. "Speak of the devil. It's Claude Hayes calling from Majorca."

A look of concern suddenly crossed Lee's face. Claude Hayes didn't phone for the hell of it.

"Claude. What is it?" Silence in the room again. There was a scratching noise on the roof that grew louder. It had finally started to rain.

"Thanks Claude." Lee hung up.

She turned to Bishop. "Barrabas wants me right now. In Bangkok. Claude has to rendezvous with the others in San Francisco."

The phone rang again. Hatton handed the receiver to Bishop.

"Hello." There was a barely audible crackle of another voice on the receiver. "Roger and out," said Bishop, switching to military jargon. He stood up and put down the receiver himself.

"The colonel. I'm for Bangkok, too. Right away. The plane will have us to Montreal in half an hour."

Outside the rain had stopped as quickly as it had begun. On the lake, under the parting clouds, a couple of loons let loose their wild laughter.

"Crazy isn't it?" said Hatton.
Bishop nodded.

LIAM O'TOOLE RANG the doorbell of the quiet suburban house. He heard a long deep dingdong resonate inside the house.

Today his horoscope promised something big would happen to him. If anyone had asked, the Irishman would have stoutly denied giving horoscope predictions any credence whatsoever. But there they were, every day, just above the crossword puzzle he did between his wake-up coffee and his morning shot of whiskey.

He didn't know what the something big might be, but he hoped it had to do with whatever lurked behind the walls of this prim-looking, modest ranch-style house. He had found the address in the latest edition of an adult-only magazine called *Swingers in Touch*.

He pressed the doorbell again. It was five to eleven, and he had to make an important phone call. There would be lots of time, he told himself. After introductions there'd be coffee and cookies, then hints and blushes. If he was lucky and said all the right things, it'd take him an hour to get her to the bedroom. And when he left a few hours later, she'd feel a whole lot healthier and happier than she had when he arrived.

The door opened.

"Hellooo." A short perky blonde answered. She had blue eyes and bright-red cheeks. And yes, indeed, the surprise was very very big. His eyes were riveted. To both of them.

"Liam O'Toole," the red-haired man introduced himself. "I called yesterday."

The blond woman cast her eyes up and down his body in a cool sweep, pausing briefly at the midpoint. Her smile grew wider.

"Mmm, you certainly did," she said. "I'm Susy. C'mon in." She opened the door wider. O'Toole had to squeeze by her to get in. He didn't make it. He felt her body press against him. She breathed heavily. As he looked down at her she cast him an innocent smile.

The interior of the house was as prim and suburban as the exterior. Everything was immaculately clean. Even the plastic runners that ran over the carpets, the rubberized brocade throw-sheets on the couch and the cellophane on the lamp shades.

"Love the artwork," O'Toole said, motioning to the huge matching paintings of big-eyed little girls holding puppy dogs.

"I'm so glad," she said in a high giggly voice. She bore down on him with her twin forty-fives. "I can't tell you how impatiently I've looked forward to meeting you since you phoned yesterday. I get so lonely out here in the suburbs."

O'Toole stepped backward. "I don't usually call a girl up from a classified ad," he said.

"But when you saw mine, you couldn't resist." The outlines of her hardened nipples protruded through the thin knit fabric of her dress. She approached until they brushed against O'Toole's chest. The backs of his legs were against the couch. He couldn't stop her. Sheesh, what'd I do to get her all stirred up, he thought.

"No actually, I mean it's the first time I've ever even looked at a swinger's contact magazine. I found it on the bus."

"That's what they all say." She kept coming at him, a breathless aroused menace. O'Toole tried to step back again. He couldn't. He fell backward onto the couch.

"You said in the ad you wanted a meaningful relationship."

"Isn't this meaningful?" She bent down over him, her hands gliding down his neck, his shoulders, his chest. O'Toole's eyes went wide again. Indeed. Very meaningful. Both of them.

He grabbed her wrists and pivoted her around onto the

couch. She sat sideways on her left thigh, facing him
She didn't seem to know what to do with her right leg
She kept moving it back and forth as if she was runnin
on it.

Her hands resisted Liam's grip as she tried to move he
arms up to reach at him. "I love big hunky redheads," sh
breathed. "You look like the sergeant type. Were you eve
in the army?" Her nails clawed at the lowest button on hi
shirt, then moved for his belt buckle.

"As a matter of fact, that's exactly it. I was a sergeant i
the army. Speaking of which, I've got to make a quic
phone call, then we can enjoy things." O'Toole place
each of her hands on her knees.

"Phone call?" Her eyes were glazed.

"A really quick one."

"Now?" Her mouth was open and she was breathin
hard.

"Sorry. I didn't realize things would get started so fast
It'll just take a minute." He patted her hands and reache
for the white Princess phone on the end table. She grippe
his other hand and massaged it, her eyes glued to it.

O'Toole put the receiver on the arm of the couch an
dialed with the one hand he had left. She began to wet-kis
the other, starting at the wrist and working her way up t
the fingers. O'Toole picked up the receiver. It was ringing
Now she was nibbling on his fingertips.

Someone answered.

The blonde had her tongue out.

"Hello. Walker Agency." A man's voice.

She was licking his palm.

"O'Toole. Checking in."

"Just a moment, please."

"Make it half."

She wasn't stopping at the hand. She dragged hersel
across the couch by climbing up O'Toole's outstretche
arm. She moaned and buried her face into his chest.

The line was still silent.

O'Toole tensed and arched his body into the couch. He couldn't help it. She was going lower.

"Mr. O'Toole." He was back on the line. "We have a code green in for you today."

"Green?"

"That's right, sir. I hope the timing's not bad."

"Could be better. Could be worse." He glanced at the blonde. She was playing with his belt buckle. He hung up the receiver. Code green meant round up the boys. The colonel was back in action. The SOBs had an assignment. He grabbed her hands and gently pulled them away.

"Now?" she said with breathless expectation.

"Sorry, baby. I gotta go to work."

"Work. Work?" She sounded dazed.

"That's right, baby." O'Toole pushed himself up from the couch. "Emergency. I'm really sorry about this."

"Work, now?" She faced him from the couch. The perky eager look had caved in. O'Toole backed toward the door.

"Maybe I'm not your type, anyway," he said, throwing his hands out in front of him. "I'm a serious kind of guy. You know. Movie. Dinner. Holding hands and good-night kisses."

"Oh," she said softly. She sat on the couch and stared off into space. Then she was quiet.

It would have been easier for O'Toole if she had just yelled.

"Goodbye," she said quietly, looking up at him.

"Goodbye," said O'Toole.

He closed the door softly behind him and walked quickly to the street. He didn't blame her for being disappointed. He'd been left in the same position by members of the opposite sex more times than he cared to remember. But he had work to do.

He turned and looked back at the neat suburban house. She was a nice enough kid, he thought. A little fast, but nice enough. Too bad he had to leave in such a hurry.

He hurried up the street of neat suburban houses toward his car.

It was in his chart, all right. Something big was going to happen.

4

Bangkok is a city of water. Built on the low marshy delta of the Chao Phraya River, it is traversed by hundreds of muddy channels called *klongs* that lead deep into the body of the teeming city of three million.

Transportation by water offers a breath of cleaner air, away from the fumes spewed by thousands of cars that clog the main streets of the Thai capital. The *klongs* offer other things, too. Speed, for instance, away from the mad, impossible traffic. And most importantly, access to the obscure, hidden quarters, the underbelly of the mysterious Asian city not often visited by Westerners.

Erika Dykstra pulled her shoulder bag closer to her stomach and hunched her body inward to take up less room. The long narrow water bus, making its way along the Chao Phraya was as crowded and mad as the New York or Paris subway at rush hour. Since the fare was only the equivalent of two cents American, and since the water bus's route took it up the narrow back *klongs* leading past the sprawling slums and into the warehouse districts, it was the preferred transportation for the masses of poor people. Obviously a water taxi would have been less crowded. But she was only following instructions.

She squeezed between two Thai men so she could stand by the open sides where she could breathe more easily. The low flat landscape of Bangkok rolled back from the shore, highlighted by one-story ramshackle warehouses on stilts at the river's edge. The tallest things on the landscape were telephone poles and spindly palm trees tipped by frazzled wigs of leaves.

The water bus turned, slowly in a wide curve, into a narrow *klong*. The opening could barely be seen through the buildings leaning along the river. It was more residential there, if slums could be called that. The houses were made of corrugated tin; some had walls of plastic sheets. All stood on stilts above the water. Children sat in open doorways. On a floating dock below one house a family fished with nets in the filthy water, and an old dog ran back and forth trying to paw a fish out of the water.

The river water had been brown and muddy; this *klong* was scarcely more than an open sewer.

She saw the bus stop ahead, an open-air pagoda on the docks, and pushed her way through the crowd to the front of the boat. The Thai people deferred to the blond Western woman. Some cast her looks of resentment. She was an alien in their territory.

Raoul was waiting for her on the docks. The little Frenchman wore a white suit stretched taut over his plump belly. In the lapel was a yellow rose, and he wore a fedora perched on his round little head. For all his oddness and despite his business, Erika knew Raoul was basically harmless. Her sources had verified it, and no woman could run one of Europe's largest smuggling networks without reliable sources.

"Ah, Madame Dykstra. Enchanted to see you once again." The little Frenchman gallantly kissed her hand. The thick fragrance of frangipani was almost suffocating. "Our destination is merely a short way away. I hope you did not find your journey too discomforting."

"I certainly saw a part of Bangkok I'm not familiar with."

"True, true. Let us call it an experience." Raoul smiled at her, his teeth gleaming. "But even the water taxis rarely come to this part of the city, and any other instructions would have been so complicated."

They walked a short distance along the dock to a small boat where a Thai man with a long barge pole waited.

As Erika climbed in she noticed a glint under the surface of the water. She looked into the *klong*. Giant goldfish, the size of trout, darted about in the brackish water.

"Yes, unbelievable, is it not?" said Raoul. "This *pissoir*, this sewer, is the natural habitat of the goldfish. But is that not often the case?" He sighed wearily. "Precious things are forced to live in circumstances that do not match their outer beauty—or their inner nature."

He raised the handkerchief clenched in one hand to his nose and inhaled deeply. The overpowering odor of frangipani once again floated by. "Goldfish," Raoul continued, "or people with fine tastes, who appreciate lovely things. Like us."

Erika stood with her hand on the railing of the boat. Raoul placed his hand on hers.

"Business, Raoul," she reminded him, moving her hand away.

He appeared slightly embarrassed, but his eyes twinkled. "One must have endless patience in the game of love. And for the game to be interesting the opponents must have strong wills. This man I met in Amsterdam, to whom I gave the statue. He is. . . a friend?"

Erika nodded. "A friend. He's big, he's tough, and he'd be very angry if he thought—"

"I understand completely," Raoul said, raising his hands in the air in a gesture of submission. He smiled broadly. "I am not a fighter. Love must be a game, not a battle. *Voilà! Nous sommes arrivés!* We are arrived!"

The boat drew in against the dock under a low one-story warehouse, and Raoul walked up one step onto the platform. He turned and offered Erika his hand.

She accepted it graciously, and they moved toward the warehouse door. Raoul strode quickly along the platform on short legs and clapped his hands at the two young men who stood outside the wide double doors.

"Ouvrez, ouvrez, vite. La madame est ici." Then turn-

ing to Erika, "This way, Madame Dykstra. What treasures I have for you. *Incroyable!*"

She followed him into the dusty hot air of the darkened house. Immediately she noticed a strange acrid odor that seemed to burn slightly at her nostrils. She coughed lightly as it caught in her throat.

"Yes, I know. The smell is terrible. I can do nothing. It is the chemicals." Raoul briskly closed the doors behind them and flicked a wall switch. A long row of industrial lamps illuminated the warehouse."

The vision took Erika's breath away.

The building contained a field of statues and stone reliefs carved with dancing women, warriors atop elephants, battle scenes and strange gods at war and at play. The treasure of Angkor stretched out before her. She had never imagined that there would be so much.

"How did you get this, Raoul?" she asked in amazement.

"Tch tch, Madame Dykstra!"

"Of course. I'm sorry I asked. I'm just so amazed at the collection you've assembled. These are the finest pieces from Angkor."

"The seller, a powerful man in Cambodia, has assured me that there will be one last shipment. It is ready this week."

"Fine," said Erika. "I will want that as well. I assume that one is included in the price we discussed." Her voice was crisp and businesslike. Inside she felt sick. The ruins of the ancient city had been stripped bare by this looting. Raoul smuggled the artwork over the border into Thailand, but someone very powerful had to be behind it all.

Raoul looked embarrassed. "My client wants another two hundred thousand dollars for the final shipment."

"A great deal of money, Raoul."

"I am only the humble broker. My share is extremely modest."

"I will have to arrange a transfer of funds. I can give you an answer tonight."

"Of course. There is one further thing. Your payments so far have been in American dollars as requested. This has enabled me to purchase certain materials my client requested."

"What do you mean?"

"Barter, Madame Dykstra." The little Frenchman held his handkerchief to his nose again to block out the smell in the warehouse. "My client did not want dollars. They are quite useless in Cambodia, where they do not even use currency under the new regime. He wanted chemicals of a certain nature. For agricultural uses apparently. For distribution to the peasants to improve their crops. To create goodwill and gain their support, I suppose." Raoul shrugged. "Even armies must eat rice. It is nothing to me, except for this terrible smell. Two months ago they were stored here, and the smell has not yet left. But now, for this last shipment, my client has given me different instructions."

"They are?"

"Diamonds. Payment in diamonds. Of course I could arrange to purchase the diamonds myself, with the money you pay me. But on the other hand, were you to pay me directly in diamonds it would avoid. . ."

"I understand." It cost money to convert cash to something else. And conversion would eat into Raoul's profit margin. "I will give you my answer tonight."

"Of course. I trust our conversation about the methods of payment in this transaction will remain confidential."

"You can trust me."

"I feel I can always trust a beautiful woman. Particularly when we are engaged in a transaction such as this where discretion is essential. Otherwise we will both lose our lives. My client is very powerful, and his power extends far beyond the borders of Cambodia." Raoul said it with complete calm.

"I want to return to my hotel immediately."

"It is so terrible that it is occasionally necessary for beautiful things to swim in such poisoned waters."

NILE BARRABAS WATCHED HER walk across the lobby of the luxury hotel. She had a regal bearing, unlike any other woman he had ever known. She was both proud and defiant, and it showed in the way she moved. He also noted the looks that other men gave her as she walked across the room. He stepped back to lean against a column, partially obscured by a potted palm. He didn't want Erika to see him yet. No matter how he did it, it was going to be a surprise for her. He was good at surprises.

She was asking for messages at the desk. He could see from the clerk's response that there were none. She picked her bag up from the desk and turned toward the elevator. Then she stopped. She seemed to be thinking about something. She turned and looked directly at him.

He stepped out from behind the palm.

She ran across the lobby and threw herself at him. He caught her and spun her around as her arms circled his neck, and she planted a kiss on his mouth.

"You! What are you doing here?"

"Business, like you," he said. "Got a room where I can stay for the night?"

"What'll they think of me at the desk if I do?"

"Do you care?"

"Not a bit!"

A short elevator ride later and they were in her hotel room.

"So, how's my favorite smuggler," Barrabas said, pulling her to him once again.

"After a long morning of business in the hot backwater—literally—of Bangkok, I'm exhausted."

"Sometimes I don't think this is any life for a woman."

"I like being a smuggler. The way you like...your work." She avoided the word, pushing away from him and sitting on the bed.

"A mercenary." He said it for her.

"A professional soldier. 'Mercenary' has bad connotations."

"So does 'smuggler.'"

Erika shrugged. "You said you were on business, too."

"A job. Inside Cambodia. In and out again. Nothing I haven't done before."

She asked no more. She didn't want to know the details.

She watched him strip for the shower, awed by his hard body, his muscled thighs and arms, and frightened by the crisscross of scars that climbed from limb to limb. They told his story like an inscription on a monument, and she knew every line by heart.

"How's business with Raoul?" he asked her, changing the subject.

"It's going well. The stuff he has is incredible. Worth every cent—ten times what I'm paying if I sold it on the black market, which I won't. He's got a line on someone in Cambodia. Someone very powerful, who's stripping Angkor Wat and smuggling the statues into Thailand. His contact is willing to make one last shipment, for another couple of hundred thousand dollars. And this time he wants it in diamonds."

"Instead of U.S. currency?"

"I've been paying U.S. dollars. But Raoul has been bartering some kind of chemicals with them and trading them for the statues. Now the Cambodian wants diamonds. What's the matter? You look like you've seen a ghost. Something I said?"

He grabbed her wrist. "Tell me. Tell me everything Raoul said, word for word. It's important."

Erika recounted the meeting at the warehouse with all the detail she could recall.

"This has something to do with why you're here, doesn't it?" she asked.

Barrabas nodded. "I must know the chain, all the links in it that take Raoul from Bangkok to Angkor Wat."

Erika shook her head. "Raoul is a comical little man. But he's as hard as nails, too. He won't give up this kind of information, mainly because he'd be afraid you'd move in on his operation. What are you thinking?'' She could see in his eyes that a plan was forming.

"That if you sweetened the deal for Raoul on condition that you accompany him to Angkor Wat on this last shipment, it might be very useful to me. I have a pilot coming so we can even supply transportation.''

"So at last I get to see Angkor Wat," Erika said, her voice dripping with irony.

"This could be dangerous, Erika. We can use the cover, if you set it up. But you don't need to go.''

"That's not fair, Nile, and you know it. If I set it up, I go, too.''

"We can talk about it later.'' Barrabas headed for the shower.

He turned it on hot, so hot it made his skin red, and let the hard spray beat down on his back to massage the tightness away. Bishop and Hatton were on their way. Bishop could work on flight logistics, getting them into and out of Cambodia. Hatton would help him out on intelligence work. By now, O'Toole should have the rest of the SOBs rounded up and ready to go. He just needed a few more answers. And Raoul, it seemed, was the key.

5

"It's real serious, O'Toole. I've never seen it like this before." Nate Beck's hands were waving around like a traffic cop's on speed. His voice slipped to a whisper. "Nanos has gone nuts. Totally nuts." His hands sank to his sides in a gesture of defeat.

Liam O'Toole exchanged glances with Claude Hayes, the big black man beside him. "Someone's got to get in there and snap him out of it."

Claude Hayes shrugged his huge shoulders. "If it's me, I'll go in there and boot his ass from here to tomorrow."

Nate Beck rolled his eyes. "Jeez, I tell you, nothing works. Look what he's done already. Who knows what he'll do next?"

They were standing by the swimming pool in the courtyard of the LaCresta Apartments, a little place that catered to single folks on the sunny side of San Francisco Bay. It was getting late in the day, and on the roof of the two-story units a giant neon sign cast pink lights onto the dappled surface of the pool: "Kitchenettes, Bachelorettes, Fun!"

"Fun" flashed on and off.

But today the owner of the place was pissed, which wasn't fun at all.

He didn't like the three men standing beside his pool having a strategy session, or the man who'd rented one of his apartments and refused to come out. Nor did he like the smashed plate-glass living-room window in the unit, or the busted television, the broken lounge chair, the ruined coffee table and the telephone that lay on the bottom of the neon-dappled turquoise swimming pool.

"Two minutes," the owner said. He was wearing his undershirt and chewing on a cigar. "You got two minutes to get him out. Then I call the police." He chomped down hard on the cigar to show them he meant business.

"Does he know we're here?" O'Toole asked Beck, ignoring the guy with the cigar.

"Uh-huh. The door's locked and he won't let anyone in. I phoned from the manager's office to tell him what's going on. That's when the phone went into the pool."

O'Toole dug out his wallet and pulled five C notes out. He wrapped them across his index finger and snapped them at the bald guy in the undershirt. "That's for the damage so far. I'll double it if you just shut up, go back into your office and let us take care of things."

The owner's teeth worked overtime on the end of the cigar. He eyed the money for a moment before he grabbed it. "Ten minutes. Then I call the police." He stormed into his office and dropped into the chair behind the desk, where he could keep an eye on them.

"So what's the plan, Sarge?" Hayes didn't disguise the exasperation in his voice. Hayes was big, black and muscular. He had learned how to fight in the guerrilla armies of a half-dozen African countries that had thrown off the yoke of their various colonial masters. Hayes's role in each victory had not been small. A ten-hour flight from Majorca to San Francisco hadn't tired him in the least. It had just made him irritable. "When I'm finished with the Greek," said Hayes slowly, socking his right fist into his left palm in an even rhythm, "he'll have a lot more than a broken heart."

Nate kept pleading. "Look guys, the dame really did him in. It's not his fault. He's in love with her and she tells him to buzz off. Hey, it's hard on anyone's ego. Right, guys?"

O'Toole and Hayes exchanged glances again.

"Guys?" Beck looked from the black man to the red-haired Irishman and back.

The two men turned toward the apartment.

"You kick in the door. I'll do whatever the moment calls for with Nanos," O'Toole said to Hayes.

Hayes nodded. He turned back to Beck who was still standing by the pool. "Don't worry. We'll be gentle."

He tested the knob of the closed door. Indeed, it was locked. He pushed his shoulder against the door and shoved gently. Obviously the doors in a singles apartment-hotel complex were built to withstand such things. But Claude had dealt with recalcitrant doors in the past. He knew that, as the saying goes, third time lucky.

He raised his foot and aimed it just right of the door handle. Then he gave a very solid kick.

The door shattered inward, paused as though deciding what to do next, then fell flat forward onto the inside floor. The handle and a few shards of wood remained securely latched to the doorframe.

Hayes turned to O'Toole. "After you." He waved his hand gracefully.

"Why thank you." O'Toole walked in. Hayes followed.

The entire apartment was painted the same color as the turquoise swimming pool, except in high gloss.

"No wonder he went crazy," said Hayes, looking around quickly.

Nanos was sitting on a plastic chair at the banana-colored Arborite dinette table. He was carefully pouring the remaining contents of a bottle of vodka into a highball glass that he held at eye level. It was obvious he was keeping his eyelids propped up with the greatest of difficulty. Two empty vodka bottles stood on the table. He emptied the third one into his glass and set it down without spilling a drop.

Then he looked up and saw his visitors.

"O'Toole! Hayes!" His greeting was enthusiastic, but when he tried to say something else the words ran off before they hit his tongue. He raised his glass. "To your health, old buddies." He gulped back the vodka in mouthfuls.

O'Toole reached for the glass. It slid easily out of the Greek's hand. Nanos was too far gone to resist. By the time he realized what O'Toole had done, the Irishman was pouring it into a potted cactus.

Nanos grabbed for it, but it was too late. He lost his balance and sat down heavily. His head slumped forward, and he couldn't stop the momentum. His forehead smacked onto the Arborite tabletop. Nanos left it there. "Oh you guys," he said wearily from that position. "Take my drink. Take my girlfriend. Doesn't matter. I'll just be alone."

Hayes looked at O'Toole. "I don't believe it. Nanos the Greek is feeling sorry for himself."

Nate Beck came in the door still worrying. "Is he okay? Jeez, Alex, you okay?" No one answered.

O'Toole was filling a big pot with cold water at the kitchen sink. He walked over to the dinette. Hayes reached down and took a handful of Nanos's hair. He pulled the man's limp head up. O'Toole threw the water.

Nanos spluttered, his eyes opening suddenly. Hayes let go. The head flopped forward again, but this time Nanos had control of his neck muscles and held it up. He looked unsteadily from left to right, from O'Toole to Hayes and back to O'Toole again. Then he looked at Beck. "What're these guys doing here?"

"Colonel's got a war for us to fight, Alex," Nate explained. "We gotta go fast."

"You guys go. I quit. I got nothing to fight for anymore. I'd just be a lot of trouble."

O'Toole pulled a plastic chair up beside Nanos. "Hey, Alex, listen." He put a hand on the man's back and spoke soothingly. "Nate here tells us a dame gave you a bum steer."

"She ain't no dame!" Nanos wailed. "She was the most beautiful girl on the whole west coast...."

"All right, all right," O'Toole said quickly. "I'm sorry Alex. Sorry. Sure she was beautiful. Because you got great taste Alex. You really know how to pick 'em."

The Greek nodded. "Yeah. I do," he agreed.

"Every time, Alex. Every time you come up with a real knockout."

"Yeah."

"And you will the next time, too, won't you."

"You bet I will." Then he stopped, realizing what he'd just said. O'Toole didn't let him forget.

"There you go, Alex. You're over her already." He gave the man a comradely slap on the back. "You've already forgotten all about her. Onto the next. But first, why don't we go fight a little war the colonel has for us."

"But, but..." Nanos was still trying to figure out how his mind got changed so fast.

"Face it, Alex," said Hayes, pulling up a chair on the other side of the table, "she didn't know a good thing when she saw it handed to her on a silver platter. Guy like you! Why there's dozens of women who are dying to tie the knot with you. Dozens more who'd be happy just to slip in the sack. I mean if she didn't see what a great guy you were, then if you ask me, your old buddy, you deserve more than that."

"That's right, Nanos," O'Toole added. "You need to find yourself a real high-class woman. A woman with lots of smarts. You know. A scrapper, like you. There's lots of good women around."

Then Nate Beck decided to be helpful. "Sure Alex, like Lee Hatton."

At the mention of Lee's name, all three men looked up at Beck.

"Lee Hatton?" Nanos said. He almost slurred her name.

"Lee Hatton?" O'Toole and Hayes said together.

"Sure. Well, ah, it's just an example," Beck stammered. "I mean, er, Alex, that's the kind of woman you need. Someone strong...strong and independent. Someone who doesn't take shit from no one. Like you. And someone... someone who knows a good thing when she sees it."

"Lee Hatton." This time Nanos said it slowly as if he was savoring the sound. As if an idea had just come to him. "She's beautiful," he added, jabbing his finger in the air to make a point.

"Beck, what are you doing?" Hayes asked. Then he turned to O'Toole. "Let's nip this train of thought before it goes any further."

O'Toole and Hayes stood up simultaneously. They took one of Nanos's arms and hauled him to his feet.

"Beck, run the shower," O'Toole ordered.

"Real cold," said Hayes.

"Lee Hatton," Nanos repeated the name reverently, his eyes hazed over in a vodka dream.

6

Patpong by night was wall-to-wall white men. Tourists and businessmen from America and Europe, servicemen on leave from Pacific bases all gathered there for a little sin. Overhead, the pink and green and red neon signs advertised the Pussy Cat Pub, the African Queen, the Sexy Bar and the Wagon Wheel Saloon. Little Thai street urchins with liquid eyes begged for spare coins or sold flowers. When they got older they became the men who stood on street corners passing out leaflets to advertise the local strip shows. Or the slender women who sat on stools outside smoky American-style bars.

The noise was unbelievable. The narrow streets were hung with tinsel and colored lights, and jam packed with a motley swarm of three-wheeled taxis, motorbikes and compact cars, all of which spewed pure exhaust into the air.

Patpong was Bangkok's sleaze central, and for five hundred *baht*, or about twenty-five dollars, anyone could buy a dream for the night.

Lee Hatton elbowed her way through the heavy crowds, ignoring the looks and catcalls.

"Hey, lady, where're ya going." The fat man in a leisure suit punctuated his question with a belch. He held a can of Singha beer and smelled like he'd been drinking for a couple of weeks. He reached out and grabbed her elbow. "You don' wanna go down there little lady. You wanna come with me."

He had some buddies with him, and he was trying to impress them with his technique.

Hatton shoved her elbow back hard so it hit him in th
sternum just above his protruding belly. The blow knocke
his air out. He let go of her elbow and tried to suck the ai
back in. Hatton drove the heel of her shoe into the top o
his foot. The air he'd just recovered came out again as
howl of pain. He drew his foot up and hopped on one leg
His buddies laughed at the dancing monkey. Hatton kep
going.

A plane from Vancouver had deposited her and Bisho
four hours earlier. It was a big change from the shores of
blue northern lake, but in fact Lee was more familiar wit
exotic Thailand. As an intelligence officer with the CIA
she had worked under deep cover in Asia for several years
The cover was finally blown in the final stages of a suc
cessful operation. She still had good connections there
though, and that was what the colonel wanted from her
While Geoff Bishop was out looking for available ai
power, Lee had to find out what rumors were current i
both Bangkok undergrounds, intelligence and criminal.

There was one place in the city where the two stream
intersected. The Big Prize Bar. She saw the entrance jus
past a food vendor with a wagon filled with steaming pots
Hatton squeezed past and went in.

It hadn't changed a bit, neither the bar nor the clientele
It was long, low and dark, and at the far end of a sea o
beer-splattered vinyl chairs was a little chrome stage. Thre
Thai go-go girls danced to the latest disco hit like sleep
walkers.

There was a crowd along the bar already, but the table
were only half full. A quick scan of the room told Hatto
what she had suspected. The customers hadn't changed
either. Except that now they weren't active U.S. service
men on leave from Vietnam. They were discharged service
men, the ones who got trapped in Asia and never made i
back. Some could never adjust to America after their wa
experiences. They settled here to anesthetize themselves
trying to dull their painful memories with the daily round

of drinks. Others had the time of their life in Nam, a high they couldn't get over, and they thought if they stayed around the high would, too. Except the battle high gave way to booze, and booze made every guy a warrior for the night.

The guy she wanted was still there, too, sitting at a corner table. He had a glass of beer at his elbow and the cards laid out on the table in a game of solitaire. He was absorbed in it.

"Can I sit here?" Hatton asked, pulling out a chair.

"Sure can." The man gave a quick distracted look and went back to his cards. Very absorbed. Then his mouth opened and he did a double take.

Lee Hatton slid into the seat.

"Close your mouth, Willy, and act like you see me every day."

Willy closed his mouth and looked at the cards in his hand. "What in hell's name are you doing here?"

"You know better than to ask me a question like that, Willy. Why would anyone want to see you?"

"I didn't take it, Lee." Willy drew a card from his hand and placed it in one of the rows on the table. His hand trembled.

"Take what, Willy? Fifty thousand dollars from the covert-operations funds that were earmarked as a bribe for a certain North Vietnamese general. Oh, I don't care about that anymore. No one does really. If anyone did, you'd be dead by now. You know that."

Willy nodded, his head bowed over the game of cards.

"But I figure you owe me, Willy."

"What?" His voice was a timid whisper.

"Information."

Willy nodded over his cards again. "Sure, Lee. Anything. You know that."

"There's been a lot of activity over the Cambodian border. Know anything about it?"

"Everyone knows, Lee. But it's small potatoes. You

won't be interested. Nickel-and-dime jobs. There's an
open field five hundred meters from Ban Non Mak Moon
and a few hundred meters this side of the Cambodian border. People take their goods there. Bicycles. Food. The
Cambodians come over the border and trade. Usually gold
or silver. It's all supervised by the Cambodian government
troops.''

"Government troops?"

"Yeah, the ones who support the Heng government and
the Vietnamese. The Khmer Rouge rebels, that's a different story. They have their own black-market zone. In the
north at Ban Kok Soong. Everyone gets a share. Everyone
stays happy.''

"The black market I want to know about is different.
For bigger items. Lots of money involved. Maybe air
transport.''

Willy nodded once more. He continued his game of solitaire. "I've heard of it," he said. "I heard just enough to
make me not want to hear any more.''

"What did you hear?"

"I heard that sometimes knowledge can be very deadly.
So whatever it was that I heard, I forgot.''

Lee paused. "Like I forgot about the fifty thousand
dollars, Willy. What did you forget?''

Willy swallowed. "I forgot that I heard that someone
very big, very powerful, in the Khmer Rouge wants to take
over the whole show. He controls all the black-market activity in the north and lots of money, too. Where does the
money come from? Some say opium. Some say artifacts
stripped from temples.''

"Is that it? Or did you forget anything else? Like who is
this guy. A name, Willy.''

"Can't give you one, Lee, I swear. I don't know. But
there is something else. I heard a lot of people are out to
stop him. Already people are dead. Here in Bangkok.
Maybe it's a war between black-market rivals. Maybe it's
another kind of war, I don't know. You and I, we've see

both. And we both know what happens to people who get caught in the middle. So I advise you to forget everything, too.''

"I can't, Willy. And I need to know more. I can pay for it.''

Willy was silent. He scanned the cards arranged on the table, looking for a line to place the few remaining in his hand. He couldn't find one.

"Willy, you owe me.''

Willy nodded. He put down his cards and took a pen from his pocket. He wrote an address on a soiled coaster and pushed it across the table to Lee.

"His name's Yang. Chinese businessman. Ostensibly an opium dealer. But he markets something else. Information. No one touches him because he doesn't owe allegiances. But he's very expensive.''

"Thanks, Willy.'' Lee shoved the coaster into her pocket and stood up.

Willy swept his hands together, gathering the cards into a deck. "That's the thing about solitaire, Lee.''

"What, Willy?''

"Even when no one beats you, you still lose.''

"IT IS MORE than a pleasure to meet you once again, Mr. Barrabas,'' said Raoul in a low unctious voice. He stood and bowed graciously over the table. Then he looked at the bevy of young Thai women who lounged on chairs around him, eager for his attention. "Away now, my precious butterflies, I must be alone. Away, away!'' He clapped his hands twice. Two of them pouted, one looked sulky and the fourth threw Nile Barrabas and Erika Dykstra a dirty look. But they scattered, wordlessly and obedient.

The restaurant was called the Peachtree Moon and it was in Soi Cowboy, a district named after a notorious American businessman. It was on the other side of Bangkok from Patpong, but the difference was slight. Soi Cowboy

was a little more up-market, with a patina of elegance, but
the same pleasures were available.

"Please be seated," said Raoul, lowering himself carefully back into his chair. With a flowery gesture of his
hand and arm he motioned toward the departing women.
"A diversion of mine. They are enchanting. Simple, perhaps, like little girls. But even little girls have their charms,
no?" He was smiling generously. "May I order drinks?"
He snapped his fingers without waiting for an answer. "I
was not aware that your friend is also your business partner, Madame Dykstra."

"Raoul, considering the amounts of money involved,
Nile is a partner of necessity. But he's also my friend. And
needless to say, I expect you'll trust him as you trust me.
Both of us have a great deal at stake. A great deal of
money."

"I understand completely," said Raoul. A waiter appeared to take their orders. Raoul called for champagne.

"Erika has told me the pieces are magnificent," said
Barrabas.

Raoul gave a modest bow of his head. "Naturally, I
have my own standard of quality to maintain."

"You have bought only the best, the finest pieces from
Angkor. You must have gone in yourself to choose them.
The city has been closed to the outside world for years, of
course. But perhaps with help from your business partner
inside Cambodia...?"

Raoul smiled graciously. The conversation paused while
the waiter delicately set glass in front of them and un-
corked the champagne. Finally the Frenchman spoke, his
voice ingratiatingly warm but tinged with a warning. "My
friends, you ask me to reveal what must remain secret. But
I detect a direction to which your question may be leading.
Perhaps we could do away with the circling and speak on
the point." He gazed at Barrabas and Erika. Neither his
eyes nor his smile wavered.

Barrabas exchanged glances with Erika. What she had

said was true. The little Frenchman was comical in appearance, almost overbearing in his manner and his elegant talk. But underneath that pudgy exterior was a businessman as hard as nails. Barrabas had little doubt that in certain circumstances, survival for example, Raoul could even be deadly.

"Erika has told me of your offer for a final sale. Two hundred thousand in diamonds is not impossible, but difficult. It is too much to gamble with. And I'm sure you are as aware as we are how often such things do not turn out as planned. Particularly on the final transaction. We're prepared to make a deal, but on one condition. That we accompany you to Angkor to make the selection of the appropriate artifact. And to make payment directly at that time."

"Impossible!" Raoul sipped his champagne. His eyes flashed with anger.

"Then so is the deal," said Barrabas. "We are, however, prepared to sweeten it. For you. It is important to us that we make the selection and supervise payment directly."

Raoul twirled the champagne glass in his fingers. Now he was considering. Finally he shook his head. "I do not think it will be possible. The nature of my Cambodian client is...difficult."

Barrabas and Erika stood to leave. "And yet your client wants diamonds. If the diamonds aren't important to him, fine. If they are, let us know. And let us know the arrangements."

"Permit me to inquire," said Raoul. "To whom shall I communicate the response."

"When can we know?" Erika asked.

"Tomorrow morning. I shall take a water taxi for a tour of the river at ten o'clock, leaving from the Dharavaya docks. I invite you to join me."

"We'll be there," said Barrabas.

The meeting was over. Without further ado, Raoul

snapped his fingers. Instantly the four Thai girls appeared and rearranged themselves on his knees.

Barrabas and Erika took a motor rickshaw back to the hotel. On the way they detoured to the Dharavaya docks. Under streamers of gaily lit electric lights, tour boats and water taxis lined up along the dock. They did a brisk business with the more respectable side of Bangkok's tourist industry. Barrabas left the rickshaw and strolled up to the information booth. He asked about private boats, and the routes they took for a tour of the river. Then he returned to the rickshaw.

At the hotel, he and Erika went directly to the small cocktail lounge off the main lobby. They sat at a table near another American couple who were chatting over drinks. The waiter came, they ordered, and in a few minutes they poked the lemon slices in their mineral water with swizzle sticks. An observant customer, who thought such things important, might have noticed that the couple next to Barrabas and Erika also drank mineral water. It was a part of the discipline of being professionals. When the profession is war, there's no such thing as drinking on the job.

Barrabas sat straight in his chair and said, as if speaking to Erika, "What have you got?" The words were heard by the man and woman at the next table. Lee Hatton and Geoff Bishop.

"It's very fuzzy and it's very dangerous," said Lee as if she was addressing Geoff. She recounted the information she'd gotten from Willy at the Big Prize Bar. "Yang apparently has the rest of the story," she concluded. "But it'll cost."

"You have the address," said Barrabas.

A napkin fluttered to the floor from Hatton's table and landed between their chairs. Barrabas left it there for the time being.

"I'll go," he said. "I have other plans for you two."

Erika took her lipstick from her purse. As she fumbled with her mirror, it slipped from her hands and fell to the floor. She leaned down to pick it up and grabbed the napkin as well.

"Let's have it," said Hatton.

"I want you two to kidnap someone for me," said Barrabas. "And if all goes well, we'll have all the answers we want by noon tomorrow."

7

The sun was bright yellow and trickled down through the leaves of the ginkgo trees onto the street. The pavement was dappled with light and shadow. It was still too early to be oppressively hot. Bangkok's most beautiful moments were in the morning.

Barrabas found the place very quickly, a one-story corrugated tin house squeezed between identical buildings. The narrow door opened in two parts, upper and lower. He knocked. The bottom part opened and a Thai man poked his head out.

"Yang," said Barrabas, looking down at the upturned face.

"Yang no here."

Barrabas pulled out a purple five-hundred-*baht* note and handed it to the man. He snatched it.

"Yang here!" said the Thai enthusiastically, tucking the money into his shirt. He disappeared inside. Barrabas waited for the upper door to open. The head appeared through the open bottom part again, along with an arm that waved him forward.

"Come, come!"

Barrabas stooped and entered, his large frame not easily passing through the narrow space designed for the shorter, smaller Asian body.

He was in a small dark room with an earth floor. There was no artificial light. What light there was came from the ripples in the corrugated tin where the roof met the walls. Enough for Barrabas to see a man on a mattress on the floor. He moaned softly. It was not a sound of pain. It was a conversation with an opium no-where.

Another man sat at a table. In one hand he held a spoon, in the other a lighter. He was melting something in the spoon. A syringe waited on the table.

Neither man paid any attention to the tall muscular white man with the sharp blue yes.

"Yang here." The little man who met him at the door was standing beside a curtain of bamboo beads, holding it apart and gesturing inward.

Barrabas walked toward it, but the little Thai suddenly blocked him. He stuck his hands up under Barrabas's arm-pits and frisked down his body. He found nothing. "You go now," he said.

Yang sat at a table, his face lit by the low glow of a kerosene lamp. He was unmistakable. His Chinese origins made him taller and his face narrower than the Thais. He had a long drooping Fu Manchu mustache that made him look like the villain from a Charlie Chan film.

On the table in front of him were a small scale and some carved wooden boxes. Beside him, incense burned in a brazier of glowing coals. The room was smoky, the air thick.

"Sit," the Chinaman commanded, gesturing to a cushioned stool in front of the table. Barrabas noticed Yang's nails were long and yellow.

The American sat. He waited for Yang to speak first. Silence forced others to speak, and when others spoke, he learned things.

Yang was silent, too. He eyed Barrabas steadily. Finally he said flatly, "I can interest you in something?"

Barrabas nodded, then shrugged. "Perhaps."

"Something to bring sweet dreams?"

He shook his head. "I come on Willy's recommenda-tion."

"Ah. Then you seek information. What do you wish to know?"

"A great deal of smuggling is going on over the Cambodian border. There are rival factions. Someone wants control. Someone very powerful inside Cambodia. I want a name and a place where I can find this man."

Yang said nothing. Instead he eyed Barrabas through the dim light and waited. Barrabas reached inside his shirt and took out a wallet. From it he took an American thousand-dollar bill and placed it on the table.

Yang eyed it.

"I will take this as payment just for hearing the question," the Chinaman said, plucking the note from the table.

With a careless toss he threw it onto the glowing coals of the brazier. The thousand-dollar bill burst into flame.

"And I do that to show you how much it is worth in relation to the information you seek."

Barrabas eyed him steadily. Without averting his gaze, he took the wallet out again. One by one he placed more thousand-dollar bills on the table. Yang eyed the growing pile of money. Barrabas paused at five. Yang looked at him without saying anything, without picking up the money.

Barrabas counted out five more and stopped again. This time he put the wallet back in his shirt.

Yang eyed the American colonel.

He eyed the money.

Then his arm swooped down and collected it. His other arm opened the lid of one of the wooden boxes. The money disappeared inside, and the lid was quickly closed.

Yang clasped his hands together and with both elbows comfortably on the table, rested his chin in his hands.

"Somehow valuable artifacts from Angkor Wat, the greatest treasures of the ancient city, have been plundered, the plunder finding its way into Bangkok from where it will undoubtedly find its way into private European collections. A Frenchman is broker. But such an arrangement requires assistance. Power assistance, from inside Cambodia. Naturally such assistance requires payment. This payment has been made in the form of agricultural chemicals." Yang paused momentarily, examining Barrabas's eyes. Barrabas didn't move.

"But you know all this," Yang continued. "I know you know because my business is information."

"A name, Yang. And a place where I can find him. That's what I paid for."

Yang raised his hand to stop Barrabas. "You have paid and you will receive. There is a very powerful man in Cambodia. He was a general in the army when the Khmer Rouge controlled the government in Phnom Penh. Their reign was bloody. They emptied the cities, turning them into wastelands, and enslaved the populations, forcing them to farm the country with their bare hands. Then the Vietnamese invaded. They control the southern part of the country, and the puppet government of Heng Samrin that sits in Phnom Penh. The Khmer Rouge have been driven to the jungles. To the mountains in the north. To the dead cities that they themselves created."

Yang paused to throw more incense onto the coals beside him. The air filled with the thick smell of camphor. Yang breathed deeply before continuing.

"The Khmer Rouge have many secrets, not least of which the identity of their leaders. All the world knows the name of Pol Pot. But it is a mere illusion that he is powerful. There is another. A leader who is far more powerful, far more deadly. He is a warlord, and his headquarters is in the north of the country near the Laotian border, in the dead city of Kiri."

"And the name of the warlord?" Barrabas waited for the final piece of information to fall into place.

"He is very dangerous. But just as dangerous are the agents of Heng Samrin who wish to stop him. Even the Frenchman's life is in danger. The name of the warlord is . . ."

Yang spoke, but not the name. Not even words.

He spoke blood.

A slow trickle suddenly ran out each side of his mouth, soiling the long mustache. Yang looked at Barrabas, his eyes glazed in death, the last sparks of fast-diminishing life asking questions of the soldier. But Barrabas had no answer. Not for the knife that had flown over his shoulder and pierced the Chinaman's throat.

The crude expulsion of Yang's last breath grated dreadfully from the open throat, spraying blood through the flapping skin of the mortal wound.

Barrabas threw himself low and to the right. As he went into a crouch he reached and grabbed the Browning HP pistol in the holster strapped to his left ankle. It was an unpretentious little gun, but the 13-round mag gave him an obvious advantage. Simultaneously he spun around to face Yang's attacker, just as the second knife was thrown. The one intended for him.

It thudded into the edge of the table and twanged.

Barrabas fired. Twice.

The man in the doorway yelped and grabbed his shoulder as 9mm parabellum tore up the woodwork and sent splinters flying. Knicked him.

Now to stop him.

The attacker disappeared into the front room, the bamboo curtain clattering and dancing in terror behind him.

Barrabas threw himself through the doorway in pursuit, twisting around the doorframe, his finger pressing halfway down on the HP's trigger.

Too late.

The front room was assaulted by white sunlight invading the opium den from the wide-open door. The attacker was gone, but Barrabas had seen enough to recognize him. It was the guy who'd been moaning on the mattress when he walked in. A quick look about the room told the rest of the story. The door man and the guy who'd been melting heroin in a spoon were Yang's security. They'd been taken in by Yang's murderer, too. And paid for it. They lay dead in lakes of their own blood, their throats slashed.

There wasn't time to feel sorry for them.

Barrabas ran out the door into the sunlight-dappled street. His quarry had a fifty-foot head start now, his feet licking the pavement at the end of the block. Barrabas shoved the HP into his belt and tore after him.

The street ended in a T with the cross street crowded with shoppers carrying food home from market and vendors selling food from steaming pots under brightly colored umbrellas. One direction lead back to downtown Bangkok. The other led to a nearby *klong*. Barrabas had scouted out the area before his rendezvous with Yang. But the attacker was nowhere to be seen in the thick crowds.

Barrabas noticed that the uniform shuffling movement of strolling people had been disturbed in the direction that led toward the *klong*. A few Thai women were looking over their shoulders in annoyance, as if someone had rudely jostled them.

They turned their heads back only to encounter a second rushing figure, this one bigger, taller and harder than the Asian who had just slipped through. This one had white skin, white hair and blue eyes that saw nothing but the chase. This one was Barrabas.

Angry shouts followed him as he zigzagged through the dense crowds of shoppers with his elbows out. Puddles of water left from the morning rain splattered out in all directions, raising the chorus of curses sent after him even louder. He could see the man running pell-mell ahead of him now. The distance narrowed from fifty to twenty feet. He was closing in.

Panicked by the excitement, a brown-and-white speckled goat bleated its way into his path. He veered to avoid it and confronted a little girl in a purplish dress bathing her baby brother in an enamel bowl on the street. He braked but couldn't stop. So he propelled himself up and leapfrogged over the tiny astonished child.

Some people on the street were throwing things at him

now, peeved at being twice disturbed by the hunter and the hunted. Bits of fruits and vegetables flew through the air after Barrabas as he burst out of the fringe of the crowd and came to a stop at the edge of the *klong*.

The dirty black canal, which had been empty only an hour earlier, was filled with small boats that were similar to kayaks, ten feet long and propelled by petite Thai women who sat in them holding long barge poles. The boats were stacked high with fruit and vegetables. The *klong* had become a floating marketplace.

Yang's murderer was halfway across. He stepped from boat to boat, crushing fruit and vegetables underfoot and rocking the flimsy-looking crafts up and down in the water. As he passed, a cacophony of curses went up from the women in the boats. They raised their barge poles out of the shallow water to hit him. But he was too fast. The long wooden poles swung through air. Angered into a fever by the audacity of the escaping man, the old women kept swinging their poles back and forth, screaming madly.

It was one thing for a lightweight Thai man to run across a thirty-foot-wide *klong* by leaping from boat to boat. It was another thing altogether for a big American to do it. For one thing, Barrabas wasn't sure if the little boats would hold his weight or just capsize. It took him a second to decide. He had no choice.

But this time the old women in the boats saw him coming. And they had their barge poles ready.

Between leaps from boat to boat the long wooden poles came driving at his legs. He jumped high as they whooshed by underneath. Every time he landed on another boat he felt the soft squish of vegetables underfoot and the heavy dip of the little craft.

He was halfway across when the attacker reached the other side. The boat he landed on pitched down into the filthy water that washed up over his feet. The woman at the other end of the boat bounced up into the air, speechless with fury. He heard a solid whack, and dull pain shot down his left arm from the shoulder. If he hadn't been moving fast enough to deflect the blow, it would have broken his arm.

He was six feet from the escaping killer and onto the penultimate boat. Whoosh! He jumped to avoid another swinging barge pole, which shattered the air inches under his feet, then threw himself forward at the feet of the attacker in front of him.

He caught the guy in a midair tackle, sending him head forward in a fall on the far dock of the *klong*. He heard a splat as the man's face hit the boards. The escaping murderer began wriggling and twisting his legs to pull out of Barrabas's grip.

From the corner of his eye, the American saw a barge pole toppling through the air toward the back of his legs. He rolled fast, which forced him to let go of his captive. It was either that or broken legs.

In a flash Barrabas was up as the escaping assailant pulled himself onto the dock. His face dripped blood from lacerations suffered in the fall. He took off down the street. Barrabas jumped three feet of water and landed on the dock, his forward momentum throwing him into a run.

While the other side of the *klong* had been frantic with shoppers, this side was deserted except for a pair of Buddhist monks with shaven heads and saffron robes.

Yang's murderer was nowhere in sight.

"STILL, I DO NOT UNDERSTAND why it would be necessary for you yourself to personally assume the dangerous journey to Angkor Wat," Raoul murmured to Erika, squinting against the reflection of the morning sun on the river.

The flat landscape of Bangkok stretched away from the riverbanks on both sides of them, the low profiles of thatched roofs relieved by distant rows of utility poles. The river was wide there, perhaps a quarter of a mile, and the water only mildly dirty. Its light muddy-brown color contrasted greatly with the noxious black liquid of the *klongs*

Erika leaned back against the cushions of her seat and felt the fluid movement of the private tour boat as it slid along the water. They had instructed the driver at the front of the boat to dispense with the guided tour. She saw a motorboat leave a dock on the distant shore and speed across the river.

"Whim, Raoul." Erika feigned boredom, as if the Frenchman's question no longer interested a woman who had made up her mind. "Perhaps just a whim and a longing to see Angkor Wat, which is difficult when Cambodia is closed to the outside world."

Raoul sighed with frustration. Erika spoke again. This time her voice was hard.

"My friend and I are investing a great deal of money. We are not prepared to let it slip through our fingers. Make the arrangements or there's no deal."

"It is too difficult," he replied, obviously torn between the lure of profit and whatever obligations or conditions he had with his patron inside Cambodia. He looked out over the river. "That motorboat. Strange. It looks like it's coming this way."

Erika followed his gaze, then turned away uninterested.

"Explain why it's so difficult, Raoul. Too difficult for two hundred thousand dollars worth of diamonds."

"With the greatest respect, Madame Dykstra, and without impugning your motives, were I to take you and your partner with me it would perhaps endanger the confidentiality of my source."

"In other words, you're afraid once you show us the way, and we meet your contacts, we'll move in on you and push you out as middleman."

"Exactly, my dear."

Erika nodded. Barrabas had been right in guessing why Raoul was reluctant to make the arrangement.

The sunlight on the water faded abruptly as the boat moved into the cool shadow cast by the overhead bridge.

Just as suddenly, the motorboat they had seen speeding away from shore a few minutes earlier roared up behind the tour boat and swooped alongside. The two-foot wake rocked the wooden Thai craft and jarred Raoul back into his seat. His mouth fell open in astonishment and fury. Three men dressed in black and wearing black face masks grabbed the gunnels of the boat. They climbed aboard. A fourth attacker also jumped into the boat and ran forward to the driver. The motorboat sped away down the river.

Raoul and Erika froze.

The men had guns.

The boat slipped into the darkness under a bridge.

8

Barrabas walked to the first corner and looked both ways down the street. The two Buddhists were entering a large white stucco temple. It was the only open door on the street.

Barrabas approached the entrance. Arches lined with gold supported an elegant pagoda roof that tapered off with long slender gables of wood. The glazed tiles on the roof gleamed like sun pouring onto water. The scent of incense emanated gently from within, along with the low steady murmur of Buddhists chanting quietly at prayer.

He went inside.

Ahead of him, in the main hall of the temple, a giant gold statue of Buddha contemplated eternity. It was surrounded by banks of low-burning candles. The temple was half full of monks and ordinary Thais, busy at prayer. They paid no attention to the tall American.

Barrabas moved to the side of the temple. Outdoor light poured through an arch on the other side of the temple. Drops of blood led across the tile floor in the direction of the arch. He slipped behind a long row of kneeling Buddha statues and walked quickly and quietly to the open doorway.

On the other side he found himself in a courtyard filled with magnificent flowering trees. It was as quiet as the sunlight, save for the merry chirping of colorful birds that flitted about the shrubbery, oblivious to the chase below them.

The line of gold Buddhas continued down one side of the courtyard to a temple on the far side. There, a mammoth red stone statue of Buddha reclining on his side was sheltered under a gold arcade. The statue was half a block long and two stories high. Halfway down the courtyard, one of the statues of the kneeling Buddhas was smeared with a bloody handprint.

Barrabas moved through an arch until he was under the roof of the arcade. He flattened himself behind the head of the giant reclining Buddha. There were more speckles of blood on the floor.

The enormous stone rump of the statue jutted out, affording a hiding place somewhere down between the legs. The blood led in that direction.

Barrabas pulled out the HP and slid slowly forward. He kept his back against the statue until he came to the curve of the rump. He reached down, slipped off his shoe and tossed it up over the rump. When he heard it fall on the floor behind, he pivoted around the curving stone with the HP barrel up.

The killer had turned to follow the noise of the shoe and was backing up in terror. He backed right into Barrabas.

The soldier grabbed the man's left wrist and wrapped his left arm in an iron grip around the Thai's neck. Then he shoved his arm under the man's armpit, pushing his elbow out and away from his body. He shoved the barrel of the HP tightly into his diaphragm. Then he squeezed the Asian's head back, putting pressure on the throat. Dark clots of blood striped the man's face where his fall had cut him.

"You speak English?" Barrabas growled.

The man jerked his head rapidly. Yes.

"One bad move, I blow a hole through your heart. Understand!"

The prisoner jerked his head again. Yes.

"Who are you working for?"

"I am Cambodian. I work for Sit Sret." Sit Sret was the Cambodian secret police. It meant the man worked for the Heng government and the Vietnamese.

"Why did you kill Yang?"

The man squirmed. Barrabas pushed the barrel of the HP harder into his diaphragm and pulled back on the neck. "Answer!" he ordered.

"Yang talk too much, know too much. You know too much, also. And the Frenchman Raoul. We are ordered to kill Raoul and all who are with him. You and the blond woman. We see you with Raoul."

"Who is 'we'?"

"Sit Sret."

"How many?"

The man shook his head. He didn't know.

"Why must you kill Raoul?"

"Because he work for Khmer Rouge. For the warlord."

"The name of the warlord, what is it?"

The man shook his head rapidly. "Not your business."

Barrabas pulled the hammer back on the HP and the click echoed in the empty temple. "The name," he said. Barrabas voiced an ultimatum, but he wasn't prepared for the answer.

"His name is Kon. General Kon."

The white-haired warrior's blood froze. The name of his ancient enemy reached through the years like an arm of death. Kon. The road from Vietnam had led him through a dozen wars in as many countries until it had finally brought him back to the deadliest opponent he had ever faced. He had a score to settle. Fate was giving him the opportunity.

While he absorbed the name of his adversary, he didn't notice the Cambodian agent move his right arm slowly, almost imperceptibly back.

"When will the Sit Sret kill Raoul?" Barrabas demanded.

Again the man squirmed without answering.

Barrabas shoved the HP harder into his diaphragm.

"This morning. An ambush. On the river," the prisoner sputtered. Without warning he shot his arm forward. A long dagger slid from a brace, projecting out beyond his small hand and locking in place. Simultaneously he arched his arm up over his right shoulder toward his captor's face.

Barrabas jerked to his left but felt the sharp blade slice down the side of his neck. There was pain and the sudden liquid warmth of blood. It was only a surface laceration, but the counterattack had dislodged the HP.

Losing the angle for a safe shot, Barrabas dropped the gun and swiftly drew his hand up to grab the assailant's wrist. The American was bigger and stronger, but the Asian was wiry and slithered from his hold. He pulled forward, swinging their clasped arms over his head, and twisting out of the neck lock. Now the two men were face to face.

The colonel jerked hard on the man's arm, pulling it forward. He heard the snap as the bone left the shoulder socket. The Asian had no time to feel the pain. Barrabas rammed the man's arm toward his own body. The sharp thin point of the dagger disappeared into the killer's chest.

The Asian hunched forward, stiffened, his eyes bulging in surprise. He fell forward, driving the knife in deeper. A coarse sigh of air left the man's lungs. His body went limp, falling forward against the American.

Barrabas lowered the body slowly to the floor.

He straightened, wiping his hand on his pants and looking at his watch. It was a few minutes after ten. Erika and Raoul had begun their tour down the river.

Death was waiting for them somewhere en route.

Barrabas ran through the temple to the street.

Fast!

THE FOUR GUNMEN worked quickly and efficiently. One pointed his rifle at Erika, while two grabbed Raoul and pulled him from the seat. The helpless Frenchman sputtered in panic until a cloth was pulled around his mouth and tied at the back of his neck. The men worked quickly as light at the other end of the tunnel grew larger. Raoul's hands were tied behind his back.

In the dim light under the bridge, Erika could make out the faces of slum dwellers at the doors of their pathetic shelters as they silently watched the tour boat go by. They seemed unaware of what was happening. Or uncaring.

Suddenly the wooden seat frame beside Erika's head burst into a shower of splinters.

She jerked forward, thinking the poor onlookers were throwing things at the boat. In seconds she knew she was wrong.

The firing of a gun echoed like hollow thunder through the concrete tunnel. The black-garbed attackers on the boat appeared startled. The one guarding Erika grabbed her by the shoulder and threw her to the floor of the boat. She heard rising hysterical screams coming from women in the slum houses and saw orange tracers coming from a platform. Bullets slammed into the hull of the boat and tore at the wooden deck.

Raoul was thrown to the floor, his eyes locking momentarily with Erika's. Then they rolled upward into his head and suddenly closed. He had passed out.

Meanwhile the men in black were under attack. They crouched with their rifles up. One returned fire in the direction of the tracers. The tunnel sounded like a train was passing through it. The bullets smacked into flesh. A wild scream rose from the darkened dwelling and a dim form fell from the platform, plunging into the muddy waters of the river with a great splash.

Feet thudded onto the wooden deck. The attackers, Asian men in street clothes, were landing on the boat. The great opening of daylight at the end of the tunnel yawned ahead, throwing the scene into high visibility.

The driver of the tour boat suddenly dived into the water and began swimming toward shore. The Asians attacked the black-garbed gunmen with knives. In the close quarters of the boat it gave them an advantage. The combatants locked in hand-to-hand struggle, just as the boat burst through the end of the tunnel into blinding daylight.

An automatic rifle landed on the deck eye-level with Erika. She reached for it. One of the Asian men was struggling arm to arm with an attacker from the motorboat. His foot ground into Erika's outstretched arm. She pulled back, wincing in pain. The little Asian jerked his hand out of his opponent's grip and swung a knife sharply upward.

It connected, piercing the left shoulder of the man in black. The knife came back and the Asian prepared to stab again. Erika reached for the rifle on the deck in front of her once more. She grabbed it by the barrel. This time she pushed herself up from the floor and gripped the rifle firmly with both hands. There wasn't time to turn it around and fire. She swung the butt of the weapon hard against the ankles of the Asian. He yelped in pain and tipped. The man in black whipped out his arm. A fist connected with the Asian's face. He grappled madly for balance, lost it and toppled over the edge into the water.

The man in black held his hand tightly over his bloody shoulder wound. He shot a quick look at Erika. "Thanks," he said quickly in English. Then he turned to his masked comrades, who were still fighting.

Another of the attackers in black emitted blood-curdling shrieks as he grabbed an Asian attacker by the arm and with casual ease flipped the man over the edge of the boat. He turned to the next Asian, doing a standoff dance sideways along the deck, hands out. The opponent had his knife out and slashed sideways at the man's stomach. They edged down the deck toward Erika. She still had the rifle. She looked at it. It was some kind of automatic. She had no idea how to fire it. She gripped the barrel again and swung. She connected. Cold steel rifle butt hits head. The Asian attacker stopped. Blood spurted from a major head wound, turning his hair red.

He fell into the water and disappeared beneath the surface.

From redhead to dead-head.

Right in the path of yet another fast-approaching motor-boat.

This time, Erika recognized the person in it. Barrabas was aiming the craft for a tight sideways landing against the tour boat. He used his knee to hold the steering wheel because his hands were busy. The right one held the Browning HP. The left one steadied it.

Two pops and the barrel flashed. One of the Asian attackers, his knife poised over another of the men in black, fell back into the water like a tin soldier.

Barrabas's boat crashed against the side of the tour boat, rolling it high into the air on an angle. Erika grabbed a seat to hold on with one hand, and with the other grabbed the unconscious Raoul by his lapels to stop him from slipping off the deck. Her eyes met Barrabas's for a second.

He was busy with the fight. He jumped onto the deck of the tour boat, swinging his arms out with the HP clasped tightly in his hands. He fired again, twice. The last Asian, fighting in the driver's seat with one of the disguised attackers, slumped over the steering wheel.

The attackers in black had already started to flee. They retreated to the far side of the boat, where the motorboat waited for them on the other side. It closed in on them quickly, and the four disguised men jumped for it.

Barrabas went for Erika. He knelt beside her as she propped up Raoul and removed the gag from his mouth. The Frenchman had regained consciousness, but his eyes still showed shock and confusion.

Barrabas quickly began to undo the knots at his hands.

"What the hell was that all about," Erika said. "It was a little more than I expected."

"I am shot. I am wounded!" the Frenchman sputtered, patting his plump body up and down as if he expected to find holes.

"No, you're not, Raoul." Barrabas helped him to his

feet and lowered him into a seat. "You're fine. And very lucky. But that's the kind of trouble you get when you're involved with General Kon."

Raoul eyed Barrabas with astonishment. "You know!"

"I'm a businessman, Raoul. Money talks. Or at least it buys talk. I listen."

"Ah, Monsieur Barrabas, Madame Dykstra." Raoul fanned himself with his hand. "You have saved my life. How can I repay you?"

"Take us to Angkor," said Erika.

Barrabas nodded.

Raoul looked from one to the other in disbelief. "Why do you still ask me for that?" he said, as if to dissuade them once again. "I could not possibly ask for better bodyguards. You would be doing me the favor, not I you!" The Frenchman shrugged, and looked at them again. "Why not," he said. "If that is all, it is yours."

9

On the far shore of the river, the men in black jumped from the motorboat and ran to the back of the waiting van.

The door swung open and a big black man stood there. Claude Hayes.

"What in hell was going on out there? I could hear the shots all the way over here, so let's move ass 'cause the cops heard, too." His disappeared to the front of the van and climbed behind the steering wheel. The masked men jumped in the back of the van and closed the door.

The first to take off his mask revealed a mop of thick red hair that belonged unmistakably to Liam O'Toole. "We had some help out there we hadn't counted on. If the colonel wanted to scare the little Frenchman into doing him a favor, I think he got what he wanted.

"He sure as hell looked scared. He went into shock and passed right out." Lee Hatton, who a few minutes earlier had been slipping Sit Sret agents into the water, pulled off her mask and shook her head to loosen her hair.

The other masks came off as Hayes put the van in gear and drove it quickly through the Bangkok traffic. Nate Beck and Geoff Bishop began stripping off their black overalls. Hatton went for Alex Nanos. The Greek had taken a knife in his shoulder.

"Let's get this fixed up," said Lee, stripping the shirt off Nanos's shoulder. The man winced slightly as she pulled the cloth away from the wound.

The main body of the SOBs had arrived from San Francisco barely a few hours earlier. They were hardly off the plane when O'Toole had outlined his plan. Frighten Raoul with an attempted kidnapping. Barrabas would arrange the rescue, and if all went well, Raoul would be cornered into making Barrabas an offer he wanted to hear. The SOBs had not counted on the Sit Sret attack, and they were still in the dark as to who their attackers had been.

"Baby, I wouldn't let anyone else take care of this," Nanos said to Lee as she examined the knife wound. It was the first time any of these guys had called her "baby," and she wasn't sure she liked it.

"Hold tight," she told him as she swabbed his wound with alcohol and wiped away the clotted blood. He breathed sharply when the alcohol found its way into the tender muscle. He stared intently at Lee's face as she worked away.

When she started wrapping the shoulder she noticed Nanos was looking at her. "What's the matter with you, Alex?"

"Nothing," the Greek said, shaking his head. "I just think you're an angel."

"You're weird, Alex. You sure you feel all right? I'm going to swab that wound again. Maybe there was some kind of drug on the blade of the knife." She reached for the alcohol swabs.

Hayes zigzagged the van through the traffic while the other mercs stripped down and changed into street clothes.

"The leisure-suit brigade," quipped Bishop.

"Yeah, we look like real-estate agents from West Palm Beach," Nate added. He turned to Nanos. "You okay, Alex?"

"She's beautiful!" Alex motioned at Lee. She pulled hard on the bandage. Alex winced. Beck swallowed. He never thought the Greek would take his comment about Lee Hatton seriously. The Greek was nuts. Yesterday he was the last of the brokenhearted. Today he was playing with fire.

A few minutes later the van parked in front of the hotel, and the five SOBs piled out.

"Do we get a chance to crash for a few hours?" Beck asked as they crossed the sidewalk to the front doors.

"First the lecture," said O'Toole. "Barrabas will be here in a few minutes. We rendezvous in the penthouse suite immediately."

The red-haired Irishman walked in the big front door first. Nanos ran forward and with his good arm held the door open for Lee. She looked at him, surprised.

"Weird, Alex. Weird." She shook her head as she walked through.

Alex looked at Nate, who was coming in behind her. Beck shrugged. Nanos shrugged too. Bishop and Hatton were coming up the steps. Nanos eyed Bishop warily. He turned into the hotel, letting the door close behind him.

A FEW MINUTES LATER a rickshaw taxi deposited Barrabas and Erika in front of the hotel.

"How did you know Raoul would change his mind?" Erika asked as they entered the hotel lobby.

"Raoul's not the kind of operator who likes to owe favors," said Barrabas. "Ultimately, arranging for us to land at Angkor Wat comes cheap. We even supply the air transportation. It was just a matter of putting Raoul in a position where he had to agree to it."

They crossed the lobby and waited by the bank of elevators. Finally a soft ding announced an arrival. They entered, and Barrabas pressed the button for the top floor. Erika reached over and pressed the number ten for her room.

"Nile, sometimes I think you can spin webs around a spider. I didn't know what to think when those men with the knives attacked the boat under the bridge. For a second I thought they were part of your plan. Suddenly it got a little too deadly."

Barrabas put his arms around her and held her close to him. "Getting the information from Yang's killer was a real break. We got to the Cambodian secret police before hey got to us. We were all marked to die. It also means hat I can go directly to the source of the problem in Cambodia, instead of trying to track the Khmer warlord down hrough Raoul. I want Bishop to fly into Angkor with Raoul, though. We'll use the rendezvous for our exfiltra-:ion from Cambodia.''

"What'll Raoul do when Bishop and I show up without you?''

Barrabas shrugged. "He'll have no choice. Just as he'll have no choice when the SOBs are waiting at Angkor for a ride out. Raoul's smart. He knows something's going on. He's going along with it right now because he thinks he's getting a free bodyguard out of it as well as free shipment of material out of Angkor.''

"And the possibility that whatever it is we're doing, he can somehow turn it to his own advantage and make some money out of it.''

"Right.''

The elevator stopped at the tenth floor, and the doors slid open. Erika pushed herself away from her lover and started to leave. Barrabas reached for her arm.

"Why don't you come up to the briefing. You've met them all in Sri Lanka.''

Erika put her hand up to hold the elevator door open.

"Not Hatton and Bishop." Then she added, "They've got something going, haven't they?''

"Not that I know. Why do you say that?''

"Intuition. Does it matter?''

Barrabas paused before answering. "Sometimes it's not good to have those kind of personal attachments in this business.''

"That's why I don't want to go to your briefing, Nile.'' She lifted her hand and stepped out. The steel door slid closed, and the elevator resumed its ride to the top.

The American warrior leaned back against the wall deep in thought. The mission as assigned was to go into Cambodia to get information and samples of chemical agents

from the dead forest. Through his own resources, and a
little bit of luck, he'd already got all the information he
needed. He was sure his old enemy General Kon was behind it—as sure as death is for keeps. He had scores to settle with Kon. Lots of them.

But that wasn't the mission. The mission was for the
SOBs to go in there and run around like a bunch of botan-
ists with butterfly nets.

The elevator stopped and the doors opened. By the time
he walked through them he'd made his decision.

BARRABAS ENTERED THE PENTHOUSE SUITE just as Lee Hatton began her briefing. The colonel signaled to her to continue and took a seat behind his other soldiers. As he sat he
noted the white bandage around Nanos's left shoulder.
That was a problem. And without Billy Two they were already short one man.

Lee held a plastic case the size of a shoebox in her hands.
She opened the flap and began pulling out shiny foil
material. It was followed by a mask with goggles and
canister.

"We can thank the space industry for inventing this,"
she said. "It's a chemical-protection suit that provides
total coverage and it weighs about seven pounds."

She shook the material until it unrolled into man-size
coveralls, complete with boots and a hood. "The colonel
briefed us earlier today on the assignment. We're not sure
at this stage what kind of chemicals we might run into, so
we're going prepared. These suits will give us a bit of extra
weight and bulk, but it shouldn't be a problem if you
figure your life depends on it. Because it does."

She threw the suit on the table. "There are different
kinds of chemical agents that might affect us. First, defoliants. Maybe they're using these to kill the forest in
Cambodia. It probably won't disable us, but exposure may
have long-term effects. So we'll cover up when we go in.
But the defoliation agent may carry antipersonnel chemi-

cals, too. These could be blood agents, choking agents or blister agents. There's no specific treatment for these except washing yourself off quickly and breathing fresh air. These might help." She held up two glass capsules. "Amyl nitrate. Crush them and put them under your mask for a few quick snorts. Gives you a great rush. If you're drifting into unconsciousness, they'll bring you right back. Each of you will get an individual decontamination kit that will contain a few vials of amyl."

Hatton held up a small metal box. "This is the decon kit. It also contains alcohol swabs and a variety of syringes. The most dangerous chemicals are the nerve agents. Even a small drop on the skin can sometimes cause horrible death. People exposed to it feel dizzy and start vomiting. Their skin breaks out in blisters, their eyes, gums and fingernails start to bleed. They begin to salivate profusely. Their hearts pound inside their chests like they're going to explode. They can't breathe. Then the nervous system goes. They start flapping and twitching like fish out of water. Eventually all the internal organs swell up. Death follows."

Hatton stopped and looked at the mercs. They were giving her their full attention. "There are different ways of spreading these chemicals," she continued. "Yellow rain is sprayed from airplanes. It can also be orange or red or white. The nice thing is you can see the airplanes coming. Cover up. Immediately. Other gases can be delivered by rockets. A small explosion from a big weapon probably means it's delivering chemicals. There are a few other ways to avoid contamination. Look around. If you see oily liquids on the surface of water or on leaves, it might be the chemical carriers. Also look for dead animals—or no animals at all. Now, if you do get contaminated, I'm going to show you how not to die."

Hatton surveyed the medical equipment on the table in front of her. She opened a decon kit and held up two syringes. One was yellow, the other green.

"This," she said, holding up the yellow syringe, "is atropine. Atropine is effective against almost all nerve agents. Each kit contains three syringes. Take all three within one minute of contact with a supposed agent."

Then she held up the green syringe. "This is called TAB, a mixture of three different antidotes including atropine. Unfortunately the Russians have already come up with one nerve agent that atropine won't help. They may have others. TAB was found in a captured Russian decon kit, and seems to work against most of the new agents. But it's dangerous. It's still experimental and has serious side effects. For one thing, it affects short-term memory. You'll have no attention span."

Nate Beck slugged Alex Nanos across his good shoulder. "Hey, we'll never notice with Alex."

"Shut up, will ya. I'm trying to listen." Nanos pushed back.

"Guys, it's serious so listen up," Hatton told them. "You may also suffer from hallucinations and spatial and coordination distortion. In other words, you won't know where you're going or what you're shooting at. TAB is the last resort. If I or the colonel feel we've made contact with an unknown agent, or if you have no relief from symptoms after the atropine, take both TAB syringes in your kit immediately. And one last thing to keep in mind," Hatton concluded, "recovery time from nerve-agent contact is up to three months in hospital and there may be permanent liver and kidney damage. Think about it. Colonel?" Lee Hatton looked at Barrabas. He stood up and walked to the front of the room.

"Thank you, Lee. Your advice is always appreciated, and I always hope we don't have to use it."

Hatton joined the men seated in front of the colonel. A large map of Southeast Asia had been tacked to the wall behind him.

"O'Toole briefed all of you on the assignment," their leader began. "We're going into Cambodia to investigate a possibly defoliated jungle and chemical-warfare involvement in the north-central region of the country. We have to bring back samples to the U.S. government to analyze. Initially we thought the Vietnamese army, which occupies southern Cambodia, was using Russian-supplied chemical weapons against the Khmer Rouge rebels. Now it looks as if the Khmer Rouge may have developed some of their own chemicals."

Barrabas took a long pointer from the table. He walked to the map and aimed it at a long blue line that wandered from the northeast portion of Cambodia to the southeast. "The Mekong River," he said. "Some of us are familiar with it in another country. It flows through the highlands in the north near Laos down to the broad flat rice paddies in the south, before veering off into South Vietnam." He traced the line of the infamous river with the pointer. Jumping west with it, he outlined a circular patch in the northern part of the country.

"This is the area of defoliation. Almost a hundred kliks long and twenty-five wide. And here—" he pointed to the northeast "—is where we are going in about twelve hours. The city of Kiri." He looked at his soldiers. "If you agree," he added.

Barrabas moved back to the table to address them. "I explained this mission *as assigned*. But since then I've filled in a few of the missing pieces of information. The person behind the defoliation—and possibly other chemical weapons—is a Khmer Rouge warlord named General Kon. I figure he has the means to manufacture some extremely lethal chemical weapons. When the Khmer Rouge took over Cambodia in 1975, they captured the entire scientific-research establishment of the country. Perhaps they're using these people to create the weapons. In 1979 the Vietnamese invaded Cambodia and pushed the Khmer Rouge out of the southern part of the country. Kon's headquarters is in Kiri. It's a gamble. But if we go in there, chances are we'll get Kon, the chemicals, and maybe bust up the whole organization while we're at it."

"Is that the same General Kon who tore up South Viet
nam when we were there?" O'Toole shouted from his seat

"I can't make a one hundred percent positive ID on that
Liam. But the pattern fits." Barrabas nodded.

"Then, let's go for it," the Irishman said without hesita
tion.

A fast murmur of agreement came from the other men.

"Colonel," a long slow voice rose from the side of th
audience. It was Claude Hayes. Hayes rarely had much t
say, but when he did talk he usually made a lot of sense
"I'm all for getting in there and cleaning this scumbag ou
once and for all. But how are we going to find him if he'
in a city. We aren't set up for urban warfare. And let's fac
it. Five white-faces and a black guy wandering aroun
Cambodia aren't likely to be mistaken for tourists."

"Good point, Claude. It's true we'll have to infiltra
the city. And Kiri used to have a population of about
hundred thousand people. I say 'used to' because it's
dead city now. All the Khmer Rouge controlled cities ar
dead. They drove the entire population into enslaved labo
in the countryside. So my feeling is that we won't have
problem locating relevant activity inside Kiri and deacti
vating it."

The mercenary leader picked up the pointer again an
walked back to the map.

"Bishop, what have you found for us?" he asked th
Canadian pilot.

"Colonel, best I could do is an old Twin Otter used b
some guy who was running booze into Burma. That's
twin-prop beast. But it's a good bet because it's similar t
the planes the Cambodian air force had both before an
after the Khmer Rouge takeover. It might confuse them i
they see it going over, but it's not sophisticated enough t
raise any suspicions about an outside force."

Barrabas nodded and pointed at the map. "Tonight a
2400 we parachute into here." He pointed to the Laotia

border. "The Mekong River flows through the center of Kiri. We go overland an hour until we hit the highway running along the Mekong. It'll take about another hour to get to the city. We take care of Kon. Now the hard part. Getting out."

He moved the pointer slowly across the map from Kiri westward. "All we have here are trails of packed earth used by peasants. We'll commandeer a vehicle, or if we have to, go on foot until we get to the highway, here." The pointer landed in the north-central region. "From there we go by car, jeep, truck, whatever we can find and appropriate. We'll be traveling through Khmer territory, and the roads are usually as deserted as the cities, except for checkpoints. We have to travel two hundred kilometers to our exfiltration rendezvous at the ruined city of Angkor Wat." Barrabas aimed the pointer at a spot not far from the Thai-Cambodian border on the west side of the little country. "In two days' time," he concluded. "Any questions?"

All of them, shaking their heads, looked at one another.

"Looks like we make a lot of it up as we go along, Colonel," Nate Beck, the least experienced merc, commented.

"That's what being a mercenary is all about, Nate. Resourcefulness. I doubt if any of your computer expertise will be put to use this time around, but we may be running into some complex, even dangerous chemical equipment. So be prepared for it."

Barrabas paused again, waiting for final comments.

Finally Nanos said it. "I sure could use a good sleep, Colonel."

"You got it, Alex. Report back here at 1800, all of you, for final briefings and preparations. One last thing, though. Lee, what's the story on Alex's shoulder. You know the policy on that."

She nodded. The policy was that wounded men didn't go. "The dagger didn't go in deep. And the weapon had a very thin blade meant for piercing, not slashing. He was lucky. He'll be sore, but he shoots with his right."

Barrabas nodded. "Should I take him?"

"Depends how badly you need him, Colonel. We're missing Billy Two as it is."

"Nanos?"

"I'll be all right," the Greek said firmly.

The chief looked at him. "Okay," he said. "You go."

The men stood up and got ready to go to their rooms.

"Enjoy your beds, boys. You won't see another one for a few days," O'Toole teased them.

"I'd enjoy it a lot more if I had someone to share i with," said Nanos. Bishop saw his eyes move toward Lee.

"You're on a diet," said Beck.

"Man, I can never get enough."

"We noticed," said O'Toole. "Come on, rest time boys, move it." The voice of the ex-sergeant was a command, not a joke. The men moved.

Talk time was over.

The war began at midnight.

10

The sun rose high over the flat Cambodian landscape, pushing the temperature to over a hundred degrees. The rice paddies had been virtually cooked down to shallow fetid puddles. The heat brought thirst to the throats of the peasants who toiled in the paddies. The warm dry wind, blowing down from the northern highlands, gave no relief.

A long cavalcade of jeeps and military trucks drove down a highway on the long earthen dike that traversed the land. One of the peasants looked sideways from his work, carefully maintaining the steady, monotonous chopping with his hoe in the stagnant water. He could not stop. The men who watched him, watched all of them. And the men had guns. Angka Loeu, the Organization on High, was the faceless, bodiless authority in Khmer Rouge-occupied Cambodia. And Angka Loeu disliked slackers, even when the sun was high overhead, the temperature 102 degrees, and work had begun at five o'clock in the morning.

The peasant watched the cavalcade roll by. Clouds of dry brown dust from the dike mixed with the wind. He and a thousand others had built that dike with their bare hands. He and the others who had been driven from the cities by the Khmer Rouge, forced into the countryside to scratch irrigation ditches from the soil with their nails, to carry the earth to the dikes with their arms. It was a hard life for a man who had once been an architect. But that was in the world as it had been before the Khmer Rouge won the civil war. The world that he and all the other peasants toiling in this field had once lived in. The world they would never see again.

As the convoy passed, the peasant who had once been an architect saw something that was so painful it was as if a dagger had been plunged into his heart. He saw a red Mercedes with a white convertible top. Like the one he had once owned in Phnom Penh. Perhaps even the same one. Now, it was undoubtedly driven by an emissary of Angka Loeu. Or perhaps, in a car as luxurious as that, Angka Loeu himself rode. Whoever—or whatever—the Organization on High was as lofty as its name.

The hot wind from the north caught the dust raised by the wheels of the passing vehicles and blew it off the dike into the paddies. It mixed with the sweat dripping down the peasant's face, coating him with grit and tickling his throat and nose. He sneezed quickly and stifled it as much as he could, lest one of the guards along the perimeter of the field notice. It was possible for Angka Loeu to consider even a sneeze to be a sign of slackness. Angka Loeu was merciful. Angka Loeu gave two warnings. The third time, execution was swift, if not always painless. The peasant who had once been an architect turned back to his work, chopping with his hoe at the weeds in the muddy water.

In the back of the red Mercedes, General Kon sat back and relaxed. Beside him, on the seat, his little daughter slept, wrapped in blankets. He put his hand out and patted the sleeping child gently. Then he gazed at the passing landscape.

The high earth dike gave him a panoramic view of the rice paddies, which stretched into the distance on both sides of the road. And as far as his eye could see, peasants toiled, their backs hunched over, hoes in hand.

It was a view of the revolutionary world of the Khmer Rouge. It was a society where everyone was equal. If that meant they were equally miserable, equally hungry, equally oppressed, so be it. The people of the city had many lessons to learn.

Running his hand down the smooth red leather of the seat, Kon's mind wandered briefly back to his days as a student in Phnom Penh and Paris. So many years ago, before he became a guerrilla soldier in the Asian wars. How they had laughed and made fun of him. Because of his face, because he was awkward, because he was serious. They had pushed him around, shouting "Fight us. Fight." Instead he had turned and walked away from them as they hurled their epithets. "Coward," they had called him. "Weakling!"

All the cruelty, the ridicule, the humiliation he had suffered at the hands of his schoolmates was remembered and carefully stored away for future use. Because even then, he knew that someday his time would come. He had been sure of it.

And it had, as many of his former classmates found out, to their displeasure. To their great pain, in fact. Most of them were dead now. Those who were not toiled in the fields, hoes in hand.

And Kon rode across the plain in the Mercedes, an emissary of Angka Loeu. He smiled at the joke. The Organization on High did not exist. But it was a skillful propaganda tool. Everything was done in the name of the all-merciful Angka Loeu. Kon was merely an instrument of the benevolent organization. It was impossible for anyone to rebel against an authority that did not exist. Impossible even for the Vietnamese, who had turned against them, to destroy a leadership they could not find.

General Kon enjoyed his power. No one laughed at him or humiliated him now. Nor would they ever dare to laugh or humiliate anyone whom he loved. There was only one such person—his daughter who slept on the seat beside him.

The long convoy of cars turned from the top of the dike onto a paved two-lane highway and approached the outskirts of the city. They stopped. The convertible roof of the red Mercedes slid back, exposing its occupant to view. Then the cavalcade proceeded.

The slow procession was a ceremony Kon repeated

often. It brought back memories of the day the Khmer Rouge won the civil war and drove the people from the cities. The sick and the wounded had been expelled from the hospitals, the wealthy from their mansions and villas, monks from temples, and merchants from their stores. They were herded into the streets, a stampede of desperate frightened humanity.

Surgeons pushed from operating theaters still wore their gowns, the old and the disabled were pushed along in hospital beds, pregnant women gave birth on street corners. Their voices rose in a great babble of terror and confusion. Their protests were met by a chatter of bullets. What Angka Loeu commanded, no man denied. They learned that lesson or they died.

General Kon's Mercedes entered the city. There the same hot dry wind blew in from the highlands, but not on long lines of waving spectators, turned out to cheer the arrival of an emissary of Angka Loeu. It whistled down empty boulevards, gnawing at the rusting hulks of televisions, sewing machines and air conditioners strewed about the streets. Chrome hospital beds lay overturned on the pavement, the wheels in the legs spinning as the wind skipped by. The heavy metal doors of dead cars creaked in the breezes. Rotting mattresses vomited their stuffing.

These were the disintegrating remnants of the lives of the people who had once lived here. Their prized possessions, packed hurriedly when told they must leave their city, were abandoned when the guns of Angka Loeu told them they would not be returning.

Along the boulevard, trees withered from thirst. Clumps of charred paper rustled across the pavement from the remnants of the huge fires in which they'd burned the books of the libraries and universities. Purple-and-red notes of useless Cambodian paper money swirled about in the breezes.

The bright and unrelenting sun glinted on the bleached

bones scattered here and there, at intersections, outside houses, in piles under trees.

The boulevard narrowed and the cavalcade slowed as it entered the older part of the city, built in the style of the French who had once gone there as colonists.

Shutters hung at odd angles from smashed upper windows. Ragged curtains blew from the gaping holes. The sidewalks were littered with shards of glass and crockery and broken furniture. Through all this Kon rode in his Mercedes. He stood erect, in a military posture, like a great emperor inspecting his domain, the Kingdom of Death.

The line of cars and trucks turned abruptly, entering a great square. On one side, a bridge led across the Mekong River. On the other three sides the square was flanked by great buildings. Deserted pagodas with graceful golden roofs stood beside empty banks with columned porticos. Finally, on the far side was the first building in the city to show signs of life. It was a once-elegant hotel, its facade swathed in the red flags of the Khmer Rouge.

The cavalcade circled the square slowly, and ground to a halt outside the entrance to the hotel. Two lines of Khmer Rouge soldiers stood at attention in an honor guard, their black uniforms crisp and clean.

Kon stood erect still, as if massive throngs cheered his arrival. The square was silent except for the sounds of the car engines.

Soldiers ran quickly from the hotel and opened the door of the Mercedes. Kon turned stiffly and stepped down. He strode through the honor guard and up the steps into the hotel.

The lobby had once been elegant, befitting its first-class ratings. Now everything belonged to Angka Loeu. The great crystal chandeliers were dark, and light was provided by portable spots that cast an eerie glow across the dirty carpets. The sofas and easy chairs, once carefully placed for the relaxation of hotel guests, spilled forth their stuffings. Khmer Rouge soldiers had cut away the leather seats to make shoes. Metal boxes of ammunition were piled high against the walls. In some places, the walls themselves had disintegrated, where portraits or the patterns of the wallpaper had been used for target practice. The floor was littered with shell casings.

Commander Ly strode across the ruined room to greet his superior.

"Welcome, General Kon, to Kiri." Ly inclined his head in a bow. "The scientists have informed me their work is completed. Their leader awaits you here. And we are ready for the executions."

"Excellent. And the Vietnamese army?"

"They are approaching quickly from the east. We believe they will attack tomorrow."

"Then the scientists have finished just in time. Make sure their families are with them outside. I will speak to their leader now."

Commander Ly led Kon from the lobby into a large high-ceilinged room. The floor of inlaid wood was scuffed beyond recognition, and the wall of glass doors that led onto stone balconies overlooking the square had been destroyed by grenades. Another huge chandelier, blown from the ceiling by the explosions, lay smashed on the floor. Boxes of Red Cross supplies and bags of rice were piled along the walls and in the corners of the room.

Kon took no notice of the havoc wreaked by the armies of Angka Loeu.

A middle-aged Cambodian man in a white smock stood by a table at the back of the long room. The fingers of his left hand tapped nervously on the table, as he watched Kon come rapidly toward him.

When the warlord was in front of him he bowed his head and clasped his hands together as if in prayer. "General Kon, it is a source of great pride to inform you that in our fervent wish to perform our duty to Angka Loeu, the scientists of the university, working with the scientists of the Agricultural Research Station have successfully completed the task that Angka Loeu set before us."

His voice trembled slightly as he spoke. He handed Kon a narrow wooden box. The warlord undid the clasp and opened it. Inside, nestled in a bed of cotton, was a test tube filled with a brilliant-blue liquid.

"This is it?" he demanded, taking the tube from the box and holding it up to the light.

The scientist nodded. He bowed again.

"And there is enough here?"

"General Kon has already seen what this chemical can do when sprayed in the jungle. It has unusual properties. It is a nerve agent to animal life and a defoliant to plant life. It is also water soluble. We sprayed only a small area of jungle. Rains and runoff have spread the poison until now a strip a hundred kilometers long and twenty-five wide is dead. The sample you are holding is one hundred times more concentrated, more potent. A tiny drop, smaller than the end of a needle, will kill a man almost instantly. The quantity you demanded is here."

The frightened scientist cast his eyes down, as he pointed to a twenty-gallon steel drum on the table behind him.

"Excellent!" Kon walked to the drum and caressed it with fascination. "And what will be the effects of this if it is poured into the Tonle Sap?"

The scientist, shamed by his complicity, struggled with his reply. His voice was low and awkward in his throat. "As it is the dry season, it will flow into the Mekong River and the other tributaries of the Great Lake. All life on the low-lying plains and in the rice paddies fed by the waters of these rivers and the irrigation canals will die. Cambodia, South Vietnam, Thailand. It will enter the saltwaters of the Gulf of Siam, then the Indian Ocean...."

"Yes?" Kon prompted him to continue.

"Diluted by the ocean waters, the effects will not be as lethal farther from the shores of Southeast Asia. But this chemical is indestructible. Eventually its molecules will spread to all the waters of the world. Many sensitive species of plants and animals will die. Those more resistant will suffer.... " Again the scientist's voice trailed off, pained by his understanding of the enormity of what he and his colleagues had done.

"Will suffer what?" Kon prompted him, forcing the nervous man to say the words.

"Sickness. Disease. Cancer. Genetic mutation."

Kon turned away, cutting the man off. He paced a short distance into the room. His voice was dreamy as he savored the words he spoke. "A chemical that is indestructible. A chemical that integrates itself with life, becomes life, changes life, for a thousand generations afterward. A chemical that weds with the genetic structure of life itself."

The scientist spoke, on the verge of weeping. "Great Kon, we the scientists of the university and the research station have labored for you to produce this. We have done as you commanded. You promised us our freedom. And for our wives and children."

Kon turned sharply, his thoughts broken by the pathetic man's words. "You shall be released," he said.

"General Kon, there is one further thing...."

"What is it?"

"The researcher and the young woman. They meant no harm."

"They are criminals!" Kon raised his voice and held the scientist with his eyes. The man squirmed. "Angka Loeu has forbidden all physical contact between the sexes outside of marriage, and marriage or even discussions of marriage may not be initiated without the permission of Angka Loeu."

"But General Kon, the young are sometimes foolish...."

"And were warned. It is forbidden to make love. And they must pay the penalty for disregarding Angka Loeu's merciful warning. I will hear no more. Join your comrades in the square outside."

The scientist left the room, his head hanging low and his

shoulders stooped under the great weight of guilt. Kon turned back to Commander Ly. "Everything is ready?"

Ly nodded.

Kon strode through the shattered glass door and stood on the stone balcony overlooking the square. The street was encircled by Khmer Rouge soldiers holding automatic rifles. More soldiers manned machine guns along the front of the hotel.

In the street a group of forty men, women and children squatted on the pavement. Many of them wore white lab coats. The scientists and their families were the audience for the coming attraction.

In front of them stood a young man in his early twenties and a beautiful dark-haired woman not yet out of her teens. A party of soldiers held guns at their backs.

From the balcony, Kon signaled to the garrison commander to begin the show. The commander turned to the assembled crowd and addressed both soldiers and scientists. The crime was explained. And the penalty. He motioned to some soldiers. Quickly they threw a rope over the arm of a street lamp, securing one end around the post and the other to the man's hands. Then his arms were yanked up over his head.

While he waited the woman was dragged forward and thrown to the ground. Four soldiers with wooden clubs moved up. They raised their clubs.

The woman screamed once, twice, and moaned in agony as the first blows came down on her head.

A low whimper of fear and revulsion rose from the assembled scientists and their families. But no one dared to turn away. When Angka Loeu ordered an execution everyone was expected to watch.

The clubs came down hard and fast, and the young woman's pain was short. Her head was pounded into a bloody pulp on the pavement.

Now it was the young man's turn to die. His death would not be as quick, however.

The rope was jerked tight, forcing his arms up over his head and allowing him only enough slack to move in a small circle under the streetlight.

The rest was simple.

A Khmer Rouge soldier moved forward with a knife and made deep cuts into the tender undersides of the man's upper arms.

Angka Loeu's unfortunate victim screamed as incredible pain rippled through his body. His arteries severed, blood gushed forward from the wounds. He howled and jumped in agony.

The man would dance to his death in a little circle around the streetlight.

From his ringside seat, Kon smiled.

It was a pity, he thought, that this death would not be witnessed the way such protracted deaths usually were. They provided invaluable lessons for the populace he ruled. And the endless variety of executions he used taxed his imagination. Today's method was a favorite of his. The one he had used last week on a recalcitrant Buddhist monk had also been excellent.

"Where is my daughter?" Kon turned suddenly to Commander Ly to ask the question.

"Upstairs, General Kon. In the usual room."

"Since the Vietnamese are launching their attack tomorrow, we will return to my headquarters in the northwestern mountains. You will come with me. We will leave a hundred soldiers here to defend the city. They will have the honor of dying for Angkor Loeu. Have the soldiers execute the scientists and their families."

"It shall be done as you have ordered, General Kon." Ly pointed to the metal drum on the table. "And this?"

"Load it into the trunk of the red Mercedes," said Kon. "I go to see my daughter." He picked up the box containing the test tube and left the room.

A minute later, the warlord entered a second-floor suite of rooms that remained undamaged. The room was stifling from the sun's heat. The sealed windows looked over the square. His daughter stood by them, looking outside where the execution had just taken place.

She didn't turn as Kon entered.

He crossed the room and knelt beside her, placing a hand on her shoulder.

"My daughter, we must return to the mountains, immediately."

Her voice came back to him, strangely muffled.

"Now, daddy? But we have only just come. And it's such a long ride."

"My child, we must. But do you not like the mountain village of Radam better, where you are surrounded by people like yourself?"

"Yes. I like it much better there. I hate it here. Here all the people are the same. They don't like me when they see me. I can always tell."

"But I love you, my daughter. I love you more than anything in the world. That is why I built Radam, in the mountains and brought people there from all over Asia. People who do not laugh at you, or recoil in horror, because in some way they are like you. I did this because I love you."

"Yes, father, I know." The little girl turned from the window to put her arms around her father's neck. The growth covered her face like a giant white fungus, bloating and distorting it, swelling out on the left side and almost blocking an eye. Half the child's mouth disappeared in the spongy mass of tissue.

Kon's eyes wandered sadly over the tumor and tears came to them. He put his arms around his little daughter. "But I have a plan," he told her. "Soon, no one will laugh at you or be afraid of you. No one, ever again," he whispered.

He held up the little wooden box and took out the vial of deadly blue chemical. "Because of this," he said. "I will explain everything in the car on the drive to Radam. But

you will see. I will change the whole world. Just for you.''
He held his daughter tightly in his arms and rocked her
gently back and forth.

In the square outside the window, the young man
danced in incredible agony. The body of his loved one was
already bloating under the hot Cambodian sun.

11

In the mountains northwest of Kiri, Radam baked in the afternoon heat.

Kon's secret mountain headquarters was small. On one side of the little town, cliffs rose above the luxuriant jungle and a waterfall poured down into a deep pool where the river began. It was the dry season now, and the river meandered lazily, barely spinning the rickety bamboo waterwheel that had been built at the water's edge.

A collection of thatch-roofed houses stood on stilts along the banks of a muddy river. The houses farther back were shaded by the high lush growth of jungle vegetation. The warm breezes that moved down from Laos fanned the long leaves of the verdant palms, and boughs of trees hung heavy with flowers. In the center of Radam was a temple compound, where an elegant gold-trimmed pagoda sat among elaborate gardens. It was surrounded by other, sturdier buildings with red tile roofs and stucco walls.

On the banks of the river, men and boys fished with nets and baskets while in the baked-earth streets between the houses, women dried pepper, washed clothes in big enamel basins or lit the coals in small hibachis to prepare dinner for their families.

It was a typical, peaceful Cambodian village. Except for three things.

First, Khmer Rouge soldiers in their sinister black uniforms were scattered throughout the village. Seemingly unoccupied, they lounged against the stilts of the houses and walked through the streets. In the gardens of the pagoda, a gallows was hung with straw dummies, and young soldiers practiced with bayonets. Their blood-curdling shrieks perforated the air. It was their duty to ensure that none of the villagers in Radam left. But duty was casual because few wanted to leave, even though they were prisoners.

The second unusual thing about Radam was that few of the villagers were Cambodian.

Many were unmistakably Vietnamese. But some of the men were much too big to be Asians. Some of them had white skin, tanned and leathered by the sun and the elements. Others had darker skin of African origin. Some had blue eyes, some green or hazel, all uncommon colors in Asia.

There was one more thing about Radam that was unusual.

The disease.

A man with long sandy hair and a stubbly beard of the same color stood beside the post of a house away from the riverbank. A tattoo on his shoulder told his history. The colors had faded with the passage of years spent under the Asian sun. But the message was still there. "U.S. Marine Corps. Da Nang 1971. Give 'em Hell!"

He looked casually in both directions. The coast was clear. He turned and went under the house.

The conveniences of dwellings built on posts six or seven feet above the ground were obvious. The houses stayed above the floodwaters of the river during the monsoon season. And the space underneath doubled as a barn.

The blond man made his way among a rabble of chickens and ducks and squeezed carefully around a pair of oxen who moaned in annoyance. The person he was meeting was already there. Far back in the darkness and obscured by a dung heap, a tall thin man with long brown hair squatted on the ground. The oxen snorted loudly and kicked their hooves at the earth.

"It's our smell," the darker man said to his visitor. He was fiddling with something in his hands. "The oxen don't like the smell of Westerners."

"I didn't know we smelled any different than Cambodians or Vietnamese."

"We do. We don't notice it, but they do. The women here notice it, too." He looked up at the visitor with a smile, but the smile only covered one side of his face. The other side remained limp, as if the skin had somehow melted. It was paralyzed. "It's ready," he said. "Hand me the wire."

The visitor reached over his head with his hands, gently moving them under a beam of the house and brought down a wire. The darker man took it and hooked it into the small, handmade radio unit he had just snapped together. He tried to wind the thin filament around its connector, but his hand trembled uncontrollably. He stopped for a few seconds, and tried again with an immense effort at concentration. The visitor waited wordlessly for the man to finish. Finally he slipped the circle of wire over the screw and wound it down.

"It gets worse, sometimes," he said.

"Worse for all of us."

The dark-haired man looked at the visitor. The blond ex-Marine's chest, from his waist to his neck, was covered with red boils and flakes of peeling dead skin.

"You look a little better actually," he commented.

"My wife made an herbal balm from a jungle plant. It helps. I wonder if this stuff will take the tattoo away?" He looked at the faded design on his biceps.

"'Give 'em Hell.' That's one piece of ID that General Kon can't take away from you."

The blond man shook his head. "Instead of giving 'em hell, we got it. We live in it."

"Hey, come on. That's not entirely true. This valley is a tropical paradise for one thing. And we're pretty much taken care of. We have our wives here. And we have lots to do taking care of the people who come here for help. We run the hospital. It's true we're all—'' he paused and looked up, giving a lopsided grin "—monsters...." Then he shrugged. "But that's not Kon's fault. Hey, it's coming in!"

He was excited as he rubbed the wire along a tiny rock crystal in the box. Static emitted from a crude speaker torn from a car radio.

"Voice of America." The voice of a woman news reader assembled itself from the static, and the two men stopped their conversation. In the dark shelter under the bamboo house, away from the watchful eyes of Kon's guards, they listened to the voice of their homeland. A voice that might as well come from another planet. The announcer read through a number of items of international news, then the lead for the next story.

"This is it!" the man who had built the radio whispered excitedly. Both men leaned closer to the speaker.

"Seven major chemical companies have agreed to pay a record liability payment of one hundred eighty million dollars to veterans who were exposed to Agent Orange during the Vietnam War. The poisonous chemical defoliant causes a wide range of maladies ranging from nerve diseases to rare cancers. It also causes grotesque birth defects in children. It is the largest liability settlement in history. Approximately fifty thousand American veterans are said to suffer from...."

The dark-haired man pulled the wire away and the radio died. "I told you. Agent Orange exposure is the one thing everyone in this village has in common. The Americans, the Vietnamese, even General Kon."

"Fifty thousand," said the blond man in awe.

"If there's that many soldiers affected, imagine the numbers of Vietnamese peasants."

"And a few hundred manage to find their way here."

"And more every day. Slowly the word spreads that there are other people suffering from these terrible diseases and that here they will be taken care of. And the children..."

The blond man nodded. No further words had to be spoken. They both knew, and neither wanted to speak the unspeakable. The chemical poisons dropped years ago on the jungles of Vietnam were creating a generation of children with terrible deformities. Perhaps many generations.

"That's why General Kon created Radam," said the dark-haired American. "He was exposed to Agent Orange and his daughter's deformity is the proof of it. Radam is his gift to her, and at the same time his obsession. He's like the Chinese emperor who fell in love with a woman with deformed feet. He married her and decreed that all the women in China had to bind their feet to make them look like his beloved wife's. For hundreds of years afterward the women of China mutilated themselves so they could barely walk. All in the name of fashion because some ancient emperor loved a cripple. And today, General Kon created Radam so no one can laugh at his little girl."

"Remember when we were brought here," said the blond man. "Twenty American prisoners of war. All of us suffering somehow from this chemical poison. Nerve disorders like you. Skin diseases like me. The cancers that some of the guys have. Remember what it was like? The hospital run by Khmer soldiers who'd been brought from the rice paddies and given Western medicines. They put sterile solutions in Coke cans and fed people from penicillin bottles. Anytime anyone had a complaint they'd grab a handful of the first pills they could find and force-feed the patient.

"We cleaned all that up. Now that we run the hospital people here are getting proper treatments. And we're learning new treatments from the herbal remedies our Asian wives have taught us," added the other man.

"But how much longer can we go on this way?" The ex-Marine clenched his fist in anger and frustration. "Already the children here are...they're so easily influenced. Last week when Kon ordered the death of the Buddhist monk..."

"I know." The monk had committed the crime of teaching the children how to read and write. In the new Khmer Rouge society, only Angka Loeu could give permission for such teachings. Kon had ordered the monk's death by hanging. A rope had been placed around the unfortunate man's neck and thrown over the branch of a tree. The other end was given to the children. Together they pulled the squirming monk high into the air, dropping the rope from time to time to jerk him painfully as he asphyxiated. It was a gruesome death made more macabre by the reaction of the children. They had enjoyed it.

"I know, it was terrible," the darker man said. "You know, all of us have been affected by the Agent Orange contamination in some physical way."

"Except Kon."

"No, I think Kon's been affected, too."

"How?"

"I think he's insane." The American whispered it like a secret.

"And we're his prisoners," said the visitor. "Stripped of our identities, told we must forget our past upon pain of death. Our lives, everything, everyone here is at the whim of Kon. And his little daughter."

"It's true Kon has the power of life and death over us. But not forever. Let's face it. We have no life left for us in America anymore. But we'll have our chance here. Something's going on here right now. I can feel it. The Vietnamese have taken over much of the country and the Khmer Rouge are on the run. Kon heads off to Kiri this morning, and I hear he's coming back today as well. He seems to be making preparations for something," replied the man with the darker hair.

"What could it be?"

"I don't know. But I'll tell you one American right

they'll never take away. The right to rebel. To fight back. And we will. When the time is right."

The blond American looked at his friend. "I always feel better after I talk to you. All of us do. You keep us going, you know. You keep us fighting."

The dark-haired man smiled. "Go on. I'll put the radio away. We keep each other going. That's the truth."

The visitor left as quickly and silently as he had come. The oxen snorted as he passed. The other American hid the radio in the beams of the house.

He sat and removed his sandal. It was a sandal typical of the kind worn by peasants in Southeast Asia, carved from an old rubber tire and sewed with rattan thongs. He dug his fingers into the rubber heel and, with his nails, removed a small piece of crumbled paper. It was an ancient IS card, faded and tattered almost to the point of disintegration. It was from a U.S. college, and in one corner there was the washed-out photo of a man, smiling happily as this man had once smiled a lifetime ago.

It was all he had left. Even the birth date had been obliterated. But the name was still there. John Scott.

Suddenly his face crumpled into sorrow. He stifled a sob in his throat and held a hand tightly over his eyes, squeezing his forehead and wiping the tears out.

It passed.

He breathed sharply and deeply, stood straight and put the card back into its hiding place in his sandal. He composed himself. Captain John Scott, U.S. Special Forces, missing in action, prisoner of war and victim of Agent Orange contamination was once again a block of granite. He was the man who kept the other American prisoners who had fallen into Kon's hands alive and gave them hope.

12

The ancient twin-prop airplane rattled and shuddered in the night sky over Cambodia. Bishop maintained altitude to avoid detection. Nile Barrabas sat silently in the copilot's seat, looking occasionally at the ground for recognizable features. The inky darkness yielded nothing, not even lights marking towns and cities that should have been there. It was as though the country was deserted.

Sometimes the plane bucked when a strong current of wind lashed out of the north. But for the most part, the sky was clear, whitened in places by a myriad of stars. The moon, almost full, cast a brilliant ground light to guide the soldiers when they reached their target, the dead city of Kiri.

By then, assuming there were no hitches, Bishop would be back into Thai airspace. More than anything, he wanted to go down there with the SOBs and fight on the ground. But he'd signed on as a pilot. That was the deal, and that was what the colonel needed. He would have the chance to fight another time. He didn't know when, but as long as he had a job with Barrabas, opportunity was going to knock. In the meantime, his next rendezvous was to exfiltrate them in two days' time at Angkor Wat.

Everything had gone smoothly since the morning briefing at the hotel. While O'Toole, Nanos, Beck and Hayes caught up on their sleep after the transoceanic airplane ride from the States, Barrabas, Hatton and Bishop had put together the hardware. They found the firepower in one of Bangkok's underground weapons bazaars with little difficulty. Southeast Asia was full of goodies left over from

Vietnam. With what Barrabas saw in a two-hour shopping spree he could have outfitted a good-sized army. But in a covert operation that involved getting in fast and getting out faster, he was limited in his selections. He needed weapons that inflicted a maximum amount of damage while being extremely portable.

The choice for this mission was the Colt Commando. The Commando was almost the same as the M-16, or Armalite. It was light and fired a 5.56mm cartridge at seven hundred fifty rounds a minute to a range of half a kilometer. It was kill power that all the SOBs were familiar with.

But the Commando had a few other features that came in handy on this job. It had a shorter barrel than the M-16, and a telescopic butt as well. This meant it was the kind of gun to take along on a parachute drop and on any other kind of close-quarter action they might find in an urban battle. They could add four-inch flash suppressors for night fights without making the rifle unmanagably long for passage through the jungle. Flash suppressors made a big difference. Night gave them an advantage, but tracers blew it. Suppress the muzzle-flash and increase the odds.

There was one other major consideration in Barrabas's choice of weapons. The Colt's 5.56mm ammo was the same as the M-16s. And according to his intelligence briefings from Jessup, most of the armies of Southeast Asia, whatever their political persuasion, used material abandoned when the United States pulled out in 1975. That included M-16s and 5.56mm ammo. If they needed to restock, Barrabas figured the supplies would be lying around somewhere. They might have to knock off a few Vietnamese or Khmer Rouge soldiers to get it, but that was like liberating the stuff for its original American owners.

The automatic rifle's firepower was supplemented by the 5.56mm Mecar antipersonal rifle grenades. When fired from the Commandos, they blew three hundred fragments of steel punishment in a radius of about a hundred feet.

Very effective. The graduated grid sight made them easy to aim, and they didn't need separate launchers or ballistite rounds to fire. The disadvantage was the smaller range. They weighed about a half pound each, the same as a hand grenade. Unfortunately they were longer and bulkier. But you can't have everything.

Finally, there were kudos for Bishop, who spotted the Heckler & Koch light machine gun designated the HK-13. The Canadian pilot really knew his guns. The HK-13 had all the features of the HK-21, a sixteen-pound machine gun that blew 850 rounds per minute with a range of half a mile. But finding the HK-13 was a brilliant stroke of luck. It had a barrel, bolt and feed-mechanism change that converted it to firing 5.56mm with a magazine feed, instead of the 7.62mm NATO round used by the HK-21. The advantage was obvious. It used the same ammo as the Commando.

Packing the added weight of the HK-13 was well worth it. The rate of firepower was about the same as the Commando, but it had twice the range. It could soften up the enemy while the other men went in closer with grenades and autofire to finish them off.

Barrabas didn't mind taking risks, but he liked to reduce the odds. Firepower selection was the most important part of that. In Bangkok he found what he wanted. The equipment was rounded out by accessories standard for jungle warfare. Machetes to cut through underbrush or for silent kills, salt tablets, water-purification tablets, decon kits and snake-bite kits were part of each soldier's pack. The chemsuits added some weight, but with luck they'd be able to drop those somewhere along the way. After they eliminated the source of the problem. General Kon.

In the metal belly of the old Otter, the dim bulbs hanging along the fuselage ceiling swung nervously with the dull vibrations from the engines. The soldiers sat back on their haunches against the wall, their packs and parachutes by their sides.

Alex "the Greek" Nanos, ex-U.S. Coast Guard navigator and ex-gigolo, was a great shot with a variety of weapons. Right now he played with his Commando, pulling the mag out and jerking it back in, with the rhythmic slide of metal on metal. Nanos was a wild card, especially when it came to members of the opposite sex. When lightning struck or Cupid pulled the trigger on his Magnum Special, Alex was beyond help. He thought with his crotch. Occasionally Nanos looked up to glance at Lee Hatton, who sat across from him.

Lee had gone through basic training in the women's services, trained as an M.D. and then worked her way through most of the intelligence agencies in Washington. She was brainy, sophisticated, beautiful and deadly. Her expert training in Escrimo, the Philippino art of self-defense, was matched by her Olympic-level marksmanship. Lee Hatton could have gone as far as she wanted, anywhere she wanted. But fate twists and turns.

Her father, a war-hero general in the American Army, had bought a dilapidated ranch on the Spanish island of Majorca as a retirement paradise. A fatal heart attack deprived him of the chance to enjoy it. Lee was hit hard by the tragedy. She secluded herself on the ranch, turning her grief into a one-woman effort to fix the place up. Jessup, an old intelligence connection, phoned one day and asked to borrow the old place for a few weeks to train a dirty-tricks team targeted for an African operation. By the way, Jessup added, would she mind infiltrating while they were at it? The leader was a guy named Nile Barrabas, and even though he didn't know it yet, his mercenary force needed a doctor. Lee took the job on whim, and she'd been a soldier of Barrabas ever since. It was the challenge she had needed to live again.

Lee sat against the wall of the plane with a pumice stone in one hand and a seven-inch knife in the other. The knife was razor sharp. She was making it sharper.

Across the aisle from Lee, Nate Beck stared off into

space. The Jewish high-tech wizard had worked his way through the intelligence departments of the U.S. Army inventing codes good enough to be ripped off by the Washington agencies Lee Hatton worked for. He got into the computer business when it was a brave new world, a frontier of discovery and invention. Then the multinationals took over and turned it into assembly-line humdrum. The man was a bored genius. Why does someone climb Mount Everest? Because it's there. Why did Nate Beck rip off a million dollars by using computers to skim the nickels and dimes out of hundreds of thousands of bank accounts? Hell, why not. He would have gotten away with it if his wife hadn't squealed. Barrabas had arrived at the door of his Swiss hotel room a few minutes before the Interpol boys with their arrest warrant. Now Nate Beck was sitting in a creaky airplane winging through the night skies of Cambodia. Surprise, surprise. Who knew what life had in store these days? Nate didn't think far ahead. No anymore. He was having too good a time living each moment as it came.

Across from him, lost in a silence so deep it echoed outward, Claude Hayes sat. The other soldiers knew and respected Claude's distances. They didn't know where he went, but they knew when he came back he was a savage and relentless soldier. Hayes was the dark and mysterious SOB. He began as a radical intellectual and worked his way through the civil rights movement. Anger took him on a one-man destruction binge in a small Southern town, and he paid for it with a couple years on a chain gang. He escaped to Africa with a new name and fought on both sides in the guerrilla wars that ravaged that continent. He got so famous that when one country finally seized independence from their colonial masters, they wanted to make him minister of defense. That was when Claude Hayes realized what he was really running away from, what he was really fighting. Routine. It was slow death no matter how you looked at it. One day Barrabas showed up out of the blue and offered him a job. Claude Hayes never looked back. Not then, not now.

Liam O'Toole pressed against the side of the plane and turned his head to look out the tiny window. The glass radiated the cold air against his cheek. They were flying without lights. Below, the land was a mass of blackness. Above the horizon's line, the sky scattered into stars. They flew above it, tiny, vulnerable in the little airplane, the propeller engines giving off orange sparks like bullet tracers to tell them they were still going. O'Toole was Barrabas's second-in-command. He'd been the colonel's sergeant when they both saw active duty in Vietnam, and now he was the man's sergeant again, keeping these mothers in shape and in line.

He looked around the cabin at his soldiers as each man and the lone woman sat wrapped in thought. His own thoughts haunted him. They were too painful to hide in. The little stint in the IRA made him an outlaw in his native country—and in the eyes of his mother. She had told him to his face that as far as she was concerned, he was dead. She wanted none of his blood money, as she called it, when he offered to share generously the fortune he was accumulating in the colonel's employ. So when there was work with Barrabas, he took care of the boys. And in between wars, he took care of the bottle. No, it was better not to have thoughts. He pressed his cheek against the cold window and stared out at darkness.

Up front in the cockpit, his face illuminated by the lights from the instrument panel, Geoff Bishop checked the readings. He spoke to the colonel in a low whisper.

"Five minutes to the drop zone, Colonel. There's our guide." He nodded ahead through the window.

The low curves of the mountains that hugged the Laotian border were a black line on the horizon.

Barrabas looked at his chronometer. Right on time. He pulled off the radio headphones and pushed himself from the seat. "Good work, Geoff. I'll see you at the next rendezvous in two days. I'll get Nanos up here to help you with navigation.''

"That's all right, sir, I can handle it myself," Bishop said a little sharply.

Barrabas looked at his pilot. It was obvious from the tone of voice that two of his men weren't getting along. It was natural on a mission, or over a number of missions, for tensions to arise between men. But it was also dangerous because such emotions clouded the reflex response to danger. Bishop was new to the team. Nanos was a little crazy. He could see conflict coming out of the two personalities. He'd have to deal with it or drop one of them. In the meantime, it wasn't a problem because Nanos was jumping and Bishop was going back to Thailand.

He left the cockpit without saying anything.

In the cabin, the SOBs had strapped their gear on and were doing last-minute checks.

"Parachute do your thing," Hayes said in a low hopeful voice, adjusting the folded pack on his back.

"Is that a prayer?" Nanos asked.

"Nope. An order."

"I've always hated high places," said Beck.

"Well, now you got your chance to get over it," said Hayes.

"Can the chitchat," O'Toole commanded. "You guys double-check each other. And hold on to your rifles on the way down."

Barrabas slung the last piece of equipment over his neck and fastened the case to his belt. They were NV passive night binoculars, the kind used by the Dutch army. They intensified minimum available light through a special fiber-couple image intensifier, giving the viewer astonishingly clear night vision. It was unlikely that any ground forces would have such sophisticated equipment. It gave the SOBs maximum advantage of night movement.

"Ready, sir!" O'Toole pulled back the door of the air

plane, and the last word was drowned by the howling rush of turbulent wind.

Barrabas felt the blast push him and gripped the handles on the wall. He patted his belt. Last chance to check it out. The flares were in place. Then he jumped.

His body pitched down with the dead weight of a stone in the cold night air, as he maneuvered into a spread-eagle position and breathed slowly and deeply in and out. He took thirty seconds to enjoy the jump, the free-fall and the rush of adrenaline that comes with defying the law of gravity and every human instinct against jumping at ten thousand feet.

He timed it to maximum descent before pulling the string. The parachute billowed out above him, jerking his arms and shoulders as it caught the cushion of air like a cupped palm. His body swayed at the end of the ropes, and the ground rose up like a black hole below him.

He hit and rolled to distribute the G-force onto the ground. Savanna grass absorbed some of the weight. Then he was up and stripping the parachute off. The twin-prop buzz of the old Otter was a faraway sound, but he could hear it growing louder as Bishop brought it in for the next drop. Barrabas dug the flare from his belt and jabbed it into the ground.

It sputtered to life, then threw its orange glare into the night. It was a low flare, which glowed rather than cast bright illumination. It was visible from the air where the SOBs could see it on the way down, but not highly visible to anyone on the ground.

Barrabas saw the airplane as a small black shape cutting across a star. One by one tiny black dots fell from the belly. When they hit the air, they ballooned into bigger dots as the chutes opened.

Barrabas stripped his chute off and crammed it into a bundle. He moved back from the flare, checked the mag on his Commando and stripped the case away from the night binoculars. He surveyed the landing sight.

He was in savanna, the transition zone between th
northern mountains on the Laotian border and the jungl
that led to the rice paddies in the fertile central basin o
Cambodia. The land was broad and flat there, but on a
incline running south.

He could make out a distant tree line where the jungl
began. The wind was blowing from the northwest, whicl
meant they could be smelled downwind. Barrabas ha
spent enough time in Vietnam to know this was important
Guerrilla armies of Southeast Asia recruited from peasan
stock. Lacking the sophisticated equipment of moder
armies, the soldiers used senses that well-trained America
soldiers from modern societies just didn't have. More tha
once the odor of after-shave blown downwind to a Con
encampment had meant surprise death for every man in
platoon.

He heard a thud and scramble some distance off to hi
left. He went for it. Two hundred feet away, Nanos ha
already stripped the parachute off and was running fo
him. In a few minutes they made the rounds of the landin
spots, pulling in Hatton, Hayes, Beck and finally O'Toole
who toted the HK-13. The men moved silently, communi
cating by the sixth sense that soldiers have in battle situa
tions in unfamiliar territory. Their bodies locked int
responses as they shucked the parachutes and checked thei
packs.

"Let's move out," Barrabas ordered, extinguishing th
flare. According to his calculations, it would take then
about an hour to march down the long incline of savann
until they reached the jungle bordering the Mekong River
The semitropical Cambodian jungle was almost impene
trable because of undergrowth. And Barrabas knew tha
unlike Hollywood's romantic notions, the jungle was n
place for heroines in high heels. It was filled with tigers an
pumas and about thirteen kinds of deadly snakes, in
cluding boas, cobras and kraits.

But the jungle led to the highway, and barring Khme

Rouge checkpoints, they would move fast there. If all went well, they'd get to Kiri in two hours, just in time to launch an attack under the cover of night. The natural body rhythms of the enemy would be at their lowest ebb. With six soldiers, Barrabas was intent on maximizing the odds any way he could.

The white-haired warrior took point and led southeast down the long savanna incline to the Mekong River. At times the grass grew five feet high, closing in on the line of mercenaries. They parted it like scythes, Barrabas pushing it apart with the barrel of his Commando, or hacking it with his machete when it got above eye level.

In half an hour they suddenly stepped through the towering grass and found themselves on a cart road of beaten earth. Barrabas put his hand up to stop his soldiers and swiftly went down on one knee.

The tracks on the dried-mud road were old and worn by the wind. No one had passed this way in days. He put the binoculars to his eyes and spotted through the night in a one-hundred-eighty-degree circle. The land on the other side of the earth road descended sharply amid rocks and boulders to a stream a hundred feet below. The stream flowed rapidly to the southeast. To the Mekong. There was no sign of animal life. But the jungle, which began on the other side of the stream, promised treachery.

O'Toole pulled up beside him.

"We'll go down there. Follow the stream on this side and stay off the road." Barrabas put down the glasses and moved on.

The mercs jogged silently, lifting their feet high, down the rocky hillside to the stream, and turned right to follow it. Soon it descended more steeply, the sound of the water became louder as it flowed rapidly over rocks and small falls in its rush to the Mekong. The jungle had jumped the stream in parts, too. Trees and vines grew from crevices and small shelves on the rocky hillside.

Footing became more treacherous and the column of

soldiers slowed down. Barrabas glanced at his chrono
meter. The glowing dial showed an hour had elapsed. H
glanced at the stars overhead, allowed for their movemen
and with some swift mental calculations compared thei
positions now with what he'd seen at the landing site. If hi
conclusion was right, they should hit the Mekong ver
soon.

But there was something else. Barrabas sniffed at the ai
blowing down the hillside. Charred wood. The smell of
dead or dying fire.

He put his hand out behind him and touched Lee Hatto
on the shoulder, motioning for her to be silent.

She pressed herself back against the hillside an
crouched with the Commando barrel out and ready
Quickly down the line behind her, Nanos, Beck, Hayes an
O'Toole followed suit.

Barrabas backed up, moving around a tree. With lon
powerful strides he climbed up the rocky hillside toward
copse of shrub brush that blocked the slopes in the direc
tion of the wind.

He turned and signaled to Hatton and Nanos by jerkin
his head and the butt of his rifle. The two mercs silent
ly left their positions and pulled themselves up the hil
behind their leader. The other three soldiers moved for
ward. They stayed low, keeping their knees bent and thei
backs down.

The rustle of wind and leaves and the furious insec
warbles of the jungle night knit a fabric of sound aroun
them. Barely had Hatton and Nanos got to the colonel'
side when there was a different sound.

Somewhere in the darkness ahead of them the ai
twanged. Barrabas threw his entire body left, bowling int
Hatton and Nanos and knocking them over. The soldier
flattened themselves on the ground as a shower of har
projectiles spun through the air and stabbed hard into th
trunk of a tree. At heart level. Another landed in th
ground centimeters from Nanos's and Hatton's eyes

Others shot past them, landing farther down the hill just a meter short of the other SOBs.

They were arrows.

Somewhere out there in the darkness there were men with bows. And they weren't being nice about it.

Nanos and Hatton pulled their Commandos from underneath them.

"Don't shoot!" Barrabas whispered hard and furiously, stretching out his arm to hold down the barrels of their rifles. "It's friendly fire!"

Hatton and Nanos stared ahead at the arrow, its tip deep in the ground five centimeters from their noses. One thought hit them both at the same time. Had the colonel gone crazy?

13

Kon paced inside his quarters in the temple compound o
Radam. Despite the encirclement of northern Cambodi;
by the Vietnamese army, he felt calm. The project ha
taken him years. Now he was only hours away from its suc
cessful completion.

Poisoning the oceans was an act of love for his littl
daughter, just as the creation of Radam had been whe
she was born with her terrible deformity. The doctors—th
finest in Cambodia, all prisoners of Khmer Rouge at th
time—had advised Kon that the disease was due to his ex
posure to Agent Orange in the battlefield at Ban Do River
It was happening to thousands of Southeast Asians, the
had told him. Most of them were peasants, all of them ha
suffered exposure, all of them were victims of strang
diseases or parents of deformed children.

This was what the Americans had done. Kon found him
self clenching his fist and gritting his teeth in danger. The
had come to Asia with their sophisticated weapons of war
and the guerrilla armies, in bare feet and with primitiv
weapons, had victoriously driven them out.

But the American devils had left a hideous legac
behind, one that General Kon was forced to see every tim
he looked at his daughter's face. Why, he had demande
from the gods he did not believe in, why must my daughte
pay the price for a war fought before she was born? Ther
was no answer, of course, from the gods, who did not exis
anyway. Kon created the village of Radam for her. H
gathered Vietnamese and Cambodian people and thei
children who suffered as his daughter did. He brough

American POWs who had been exposed to the chemical. He made a world where everyone suffered from some bizarre deformity and no one would dare laugh at his daughter as he had once been laughed at, at school in Phnom Penh and Paris. The little village of Radam was a world where his daughter would never feel out of place.

Slowly, imperceptibly, other ideas had come to General Kon as the years went by and his daughter grew. If he could create his own world in Radam, then he could also make Radam a model for the world at large. Since fate had decreed that Kon would sire a monster, Kon decreed a destiny of his own for the entire world. The scientists in Kiri were given their instructions. He was on the threshold of success at this very moment. The Americans would pay for what they had done to his child. They would pay with children of their own.

The brooding Cambodian warlord heard the door open behind him. He turned. The garrison commander of Radam waited patiently.

"General Kon, the prisoner has been brought to the courtyard," the commander informed him. "He awaits your presence."

"I will attend to him immediately," said Kon. "But first, repeat the information from my agents in Bangkok. I wish to hear it again."

"Sir, your agents sent word that the final shipment of relics from Angkor Wat will take place in two days' time. The Frenchman Raoul will make his payment in diamonds, as you requested."

"Not that, Commander. Repeat the information involving the assassination attempt."

"Sir, agents of Heng Samrin attempted to eliminate the Frenchman Raoul, and the Dutch woman who is brokering the Angkor Wat relics in Europe. The attempt was defeated by the woman's business partner."

"His name again?"

"Nile Barrabas, an American citizen who appears to have a special relationship with the Dutch woman."

"And they are coming to Angkor Wat with Raoul to receive the last shipment?"

"That is our information, General Kon."

The warlord turned to the window and rubbed his chin with his hand in a pensive gesture.

Once again the battle of Ban Do River reached out from the past to darken the future. Was this Nile Barrabas the same young white-haired colonel who had come after him in Vietnam? It must be, he thought. Then why was he in Bangkok now, a businessman brokering stolen archeological treasures? Perhaps it was a coincidence. But something told Kon it was not. It didn't matter. At Ban Do River he swore he would someday kill the American colonel. In two days' time, Barrabas would deliver himself right into Kon's hands.

The warlord turned back to the garrison commander. Once again he was a brisk and efficient Khmer Rouge general. "I will see the prisoner now," he said. "You are certain of his identity?"

"General, two of your own elite soldiers saw him emerge from the house. There can be no mistake."

Kon picked up an object that rested on a desk near him. It was the handmade radio his soldiers had found hidden in the floor beams of a house.

"He shall pay for it with his life," said Kon. "The only question I must decide is the method of execution. Bring him in." The Khmer Rouge officer walked from the room.

As he waited, Kon had another of his inspired moments. The box containing the blue vial of chemical poison rested on the desk beside the illicit radio. It was an interesting idea.

The door to the room opened again. This time a party of soldiers entered, pushing the prisoner ahead of them. The American man with long dark hair stumbled forward, caught himself and stood straight and tall before his Cambodian captor. One side of the man's face tilted and drooped into a mask of tragedy. On the other side, the eye was bright, the lips firm, the expression defiant.

"Is this yours, Captain Scott?" The warlord picked up the radio and dangled it in front of the prisoner.

Scott looked at it and said nothing.

"No matter," said Kon. "I have heard enough to judge. Angka Loeu is merciful and warned the people of Radam about criminal acts involving contact with the outside world. I have kept you alive since your capture at Ban Do River because you have proved useful in a variety of ways. This shows you have outlived your usefulness."

"You may have power over us here, Kon," said Scott, deliberately omitting the title of general to show his contempt. "What will you do when the Vietnamese army have wiped the Khmer Rouge out? What will you be lord of then? This village of mutants and monsters? You may be judge in this village, Kon, but someday the world will judge you."

Kon caught his breath at the prisoner's insolence. In a way he could not help but admire these Americans. He had never known men who had such pride, who were so difficult to break. But break them he would.

"Tomorrow morning, the village will assemble to watch your execution, Scott." Kon pointed his finger. "It will be the most unusual I have ever devised." The warlord nonchalantly lifted the vial of blue poison from its cushion in the little box. "I have had my scientists refine this for me," he told Scott, looking into the prisoner's eyes for some sign of fear to take pleasure in. "It is the deadliest chemical poison invented. This vial, sprayed over one acre of land, will spread and destroy thousands of acres of jungle. The tiniest drop on a man's skin, a drop so small as to be invisible, will kill you. Tomorrow I will point my finger at you and you will die. You and I will know how it is done. The watching villagers will only wonder." He placed the vial idly back in its holder.

"As for being judged, Scott, your words mean nothing. Radam, it's true, is not the world. But perhaps someday the world will be like Radam." His enigmatic words sounded playful—a riddle the prisoner was being tempted to solve.

"Take him to a cell," Kon ordered abruptly. There was still no hint of fear in the American soldier's eyes. Kon turned his back to signal the end of the interview.

The guards threw Scott into a cell, propelling him forward by a solidly planted kick in the ass. They laughed heartily when he crashed headfirst into a corner. The door to the cell slammed shut, closing off light from the corridor.

He heard the sound of the key in the lock, then the fading laughter of the guards. He was alone.

He took a deep breath and stood up. The cell was in a small building inside the temple compound. There was a window set with iron bars on one wall. Through it Scott could see stars in the night sky. He went over and pressed his face through the bars as far as he could. He took a deep breath and gazed upward at the stars. He thought about dying. It was not the first time since he'd been captured by Kon at Ban Do River.

The American soldier remembered Barrabas, remembered how proud he'd been to fight side by side with the legendary colonel. He knew that the white-haired man had followed relentlessly through the jungle. But he had known there was no way they could catch Kon. Scott had prepared for his death then.

Fate had intervened. Two of Kon's men stepped on a land-mine booby trap that they themselves had set days earlier. Scott's paramedical training had come in handy. Kon decided to keep him alive a little longer.

Then two things had happened. The Khmer Rouge won the Cambodian civil war. Kon was now one of the leaders of the new regime, and very powerful. His newfound power seemed to sate the warlord's lust for blood and death, perhaps because he gloried in it when the Khmer Rouge emptied the cities and carried out wholesale massacres of the civilian population.

The second thing was the birth of Kon's daughter. The infant had been horribly deformed. The mother rejected the child. Kon ordered her death. To Scott's surprise, the bloodthirsty warlord became utterly devoted to his misshapen offspring. He gathered together the entire medical research establishment of Cambodia—not a difficult thing to do since the Khmer Rouge were holding them prisoner. They advised him on the appearance of his child. On the appearance of thousands of children being born in Southeast Asia, especially in Vietnam. People were giving birth to a race of monsters. And all the evidence pointed to Agent Orange as the chemical that caused the genetic mutations.

Kon launched his great project, the village of the mutants. From all over Asia troops sent the victims of Agent Orange to Radam. The village's new inhabitants included ten American POWs who were brought from camps deep in the jungle. It was at the same time that Captain Scott began noticing the trembling. He'd lose control of a hand, an arm, a leg, an eyelid. Parts of his body would suddenly begin to tremble uncontrollably. Then the side of his face became totally paralyzed. He was lucky. Some of the POWs suffered from worse things.

Scott noticed that he was not trembling now. He was quite calm and relaxed. It was amazing how imminent death relaxes a person, he thought ironically, still gazing at the stars.

He heard another sound in the cell. It was the sound of labored breathing, and it was coming from the door. He recognized it immediately. It was Kon's daughter.

A patch of bright light threw itself into the cell as a small window on the door opened. The space was filled by the little girl's face, the bloated tumor hidden in shadow. She giggled suddenly and stared at him.

She's come to gloat, Scott thought. He had never liked her. Her powerful father gave her everything she wanted, and the little girl had soon learned that her smallest whim could mean life or death for another human being. And she often took advantage of her whims. If anything, she was worse than her father. Kon usually had a specific reason for killing—even if it was only to terrorize or make an example of someone. Scott had seen the little girl cause the death of others out of sheer boredom.

"Tomorrow you die, Scott," she whispered into the cell, then giggled uncontrollably. He heard her breath again, the air harsh as it slid out through the bloated tumor. This time she breathed faster, as if the thought of death excited her.

Scott turned from the window and faced the dark figure at the little window. "You little bitch!" he said impassively. It was hard to believe a child could be so malevolent. But this child was.

"I will like to watch you die tomorrow," the little girl said in her hoarse voice. "It will be fun."

"Why?" Scott asked. "Will it make you feel better? Will it make you feel less ugly?" He wasn't talking to the girl anymore. He was thinking out loud and staring off into space, sad that the world, which was so beautiful, could create such evil.

"Soon, everybody will be like me. My father has told me. He will make them so."

"And how will he do that?" Scott asked absentmindedly.

"The scientists in Kiri gave him a chemical to pour into Tonle Sap."

Scott looked up and took notice of what the child was saying. He remembered Kon's boast. Radam is not the world, Kon had said, but someday the world will be like Radam.

"A magic potion?" Scott said with derision. "Little girl, don't be foolish. Your daddy's just telling you things."

"He is not!" the child shouted angrily. "I know because he told me. It is the strongest chemical in the world, and it will go into all the water of the world and everyone will drink it and so all the new children that are born will be just like me. He will make this village the world, my father says."

"Go away, little girl. I don't like you."

The shadowy face moved at the little window. He heard the labored breathing again and the little window snapped shut.

Then he heard her voice again as she gleefully called out, "I shall like to watch you dying, Scott. I am glad you die. I hate you." Her footsteps faded as she ran down the corridor.

Scott sank back against a wall. It can't be true, he thought. But he knew it could be. It was possible because Kon had also suffered from his exposure to Agent Orange.

The Cambodian warlord was mad.

Scott turned to the cell window and pulled at the bars. They were immovable. He felt along the sill to see if one might come out. They were set in wood. Maybe he could chew his way out, he thought ruefully. But maybe he didn't have to.

He felt deep into his pants pockets. They were empty. The guards had searched him earlier. Then he felt something way down at the bottom of one. He knew what it was—a small remnant of his life as an American so many years ago. Nail clippers.

He folded them into position and clipped at the sill. The wood was dry and splintered easily. With only a little nail clipper to work with it would take all night. As if he had a choice. Captain Scott started clipping.

14

Barrabas lay flat on his stomach and slowly moved his hands out from his side. He cupped them to his lips and blew into them, fluttering his hands and creating an odd warbling sound.

Then he called out in a strange foreign tongue. Only O'Toole and Hatton, with their own experience in Vietnam, recognized it as Cham, the language of the Southeast Asian mountain people.

There was no response. The soldiers waited, breathing slowly and silently, their bodies tensed. Barrabas called out again.

This time an answer came from the tree ahead. A voice demanded in Cham to know who it was.

"Friends," Barrabas said in Cham. "We are Americans. We have come to fight here again."

Barrabas stood up, hitched his rifle over his shoulder and held his arms out in a gesture of peace. The trees rustled, and one by one from along the hillside, the diminutive warriors emerged into the open. In the darkness they were visible mainly by the glowing whites of their eyes.

"My name is Barrabas, Nile Barrabas. I fought with your people in Vietnam. Now I have come to fight your enemies again."

Nanos and Hatton stepped up to their leader's side as one of the Rhades moved forward.

"You did not fight with our people, Nile Barrabas. You fought with us."

Suddenly pitch torches held by warriors burst into flame, casting a flickering light along the hillside, illuminating the faces of the soldiers from different cultures who now confronted one another, soldiers who also remembered different times. The Americans wore camouflage suits, and the light glinted dully on the metal edges of mags and belts and the barrels of their rifles. The Rhades were dressed only in sarongs, their bodies covered with tattoos and paint. Ivory ornaments dangled in their elongated earlobes, and bangles gleamed on their wrists and ankles.

"Blah po gia, Barrabas. We remember you," said their leader.

Barrabas burst into a smile. He couldn't help it. He was smiling at luck. This man in front of him was the Rhade warrior-shaman who'd trained him in his jungle fighting skills when he had first arrived in Vietnam, as a lieutenant. *"Blah po gia,"* he returned the compliment, "I never thought our paths would cross again."

"Fate speaks many mysteries," said the shaman-warrior. "It is for us to accept, not to understand." He pointed to the night sky overheard. "The stars told me I would meet an old friend tonight. We have been waiting."

"With arrows?" Barrabas asked in disbelief.

"If we wanted to kill you, we would have aimed at you," said the Rhade.

The American warrior smiled. He had learned that lesson well.

Liam O'Toole joined the torch-lit circle with Beck and Hayes. None of them could help staring with wide-eyed amazement at the primitive warriors. Barrabas turned to his soldiers and translated the conversation. Then he faced the shaman leader again.

"You have come far from your home in the mountains south of here."

The Rhade nodded. "There has been much fighting in the north, in Laos, by our brothers. The skies bring rain that is yellow, and the yellow rain spreads a strange disease. There is much death. We go to help them. The journey has been long. And we have encountered many enemies. And you, our first friend. You, too, are far from home."

The American nodded. "We have come to destroy our old enemy, the Cambodian warlord, Kon. We are going to the city of Kiri to find him, and we must hurry."

The Rhade leader turned abruptly away and began shouting rapidly at some of his men. They answered just as rapidly, too fast for Barrabas to understand.

Then he turned back to his American friend.

"It is a city of death, and Kon has become more evil in the passing years. His evil covers this land. We will take you to Kiri, but we will not go in. You do not have much time, Nile Barrabas. The Vietnamese army has invaded this region. They are poised to attack Kiri after sunrise."

"Then we have to get in and get out before that," said Barrabas.

"It can be done. We will show you the way."

The Rhade warrior shouted orders at his men and quickly the torches were extinguished. The Rhade men set off along the rocky banks of the stream in the direction they had come, with the SOBs following behind them. The smaller Rhades, who were more familiar with the terrain, seemed to have vision that could penetrate the dark. They went fast, at times almost losing the Americans who followed.

The line of soldiers soon moved away from the stream at a cleft in the rocky sides. They turned onto another channel, a streambed that had run dry because of the season. was littered with small round boulders and brittle rock, but it gave them a faster route in the darkness than the jungle that grew up on all sides.

Half an hour later, a silver coin of a moon rose above the treetops and cast a brilliant light down the path the soldier had taken. The mercs simultaneously recognized what they were walking on.

"My God," said Lee softly, looking down at the ground where she stood.

The dried-up stream was a mass grave, several years old. The remains of victims of a Khmer Rouge massacre had been dumped here and had rotted away in a river of flesh. Their bleached and broken bones were a testimony to the atrocities committed in a gentle land.

Barrabas and the Rhade warriors stopped and turned to the mercs. "Let's move it!" he ordered. "Or we'll end up down there with them!" It was a hard order, but in the circumstances necessary. And hard as it was, the mercs knew he spoke the truth.

Soon they climbed the hillside out of the old stream and went a short distance through the jungle. Passage was easier now with the light of the moon. They passed several peasant houses, the roofs caved in and abandoned. Finally they were on a paved road next to a small river, which ran toward the Mekong some distance farther.

The side of the road was strewed with junk. Rusting machines and bits of broken furniture lay sprawled among gutted cars lying in a shallow ditch.

"We leave you here," the Rhade leader said to Barrabas. "The city is not far. You must hurry. The Vietnamese army is on the other side of the Mekong River, and they will come when the sun rises."

Barrabas looked at his watch. That gave them about two hours. He turned to thank the Rhade warriors, but already they had melted back into the forest along the road, leaving the mercenaries alone on the outskirts of the dead city.

"O'Toole, you, Hayes and Beck take that side of the highway," Barrabas ordered. "Go for the ditch if there's any sign of Khmer Rouge. Lee and Alex, we'll take this side."

The two lines of mercs separated and went quickly forward, walking on the shoulders close to the edge of the jungle. The junk scattered in the ditches increased, and occasionally the bone mixed with the rotting ruins of some abandoned household item. Soon houses appeared, and they were on an avenue leading into the heart of the city.

It was empty. There was no sign of life. Even the tree that lined the street seemed dead and rustled eerily in th night wind. Occasionally a squeaking hinge or hollow slar of wood sounded as the breeze passed through an empt building. The mercs walked quickly up the sidewalks of th dead city.

"I never seen nothing so creepy," said Nanos softly.

Barrabas and Hatton didn't answer. They felt the sam way.

On the other side of the road the only living soun O'Toole, Beck and Hayes heard was their own breathing It alone reassured them of their sanity in the midst of th broken hollow buildings, where they could almost hear th rattle of death. For Claude Hayes, creepiness gave way t anger. He tensed, his hands on his rifle and his eyes nar rowed as though strained to send lasers out across the cit to find the madman responsible for creating this horror For Hayes could see beyond the night, the abandone buildings, the rusting junk littering the boulevard. He sav a hundred thousand people whipped from their house: beaten and forced from the city. War was his business, an he accepted the risks. What he couldn't accept was the su fering and murder of innocents. He wanted to kill for this Whoever had done it deserved to die.

A few yards across the street, the image of misery cam to another man's eyes. In the surreal junkyard, Barraba also saw the cruelties forced upon the people who ha once called Kiri their home, the old and the children, th sick and the dying. They passed a hospital. On the browr overgrown lawn by the front doors sat a line of rustin beds, the chrome peeling off the metal legs. There wer skeletons tangled in the rotting mattresses. No one ha been spared.

Suddenly a sound reverberated through the city. The heard distant machine-gun fire in the east. A light filled th sky, then a long whistle and the far side of the city wa rocked by an explosion. The Vietnamese were shelling Ki to soften it up for the impending invasion. They'd picked a hell of a day to call on Kon.

Barrabas listened to another sound buried under the guns. It was a truck gearing up on the long avenue, coming from the same direction they'd just walked. It was still some distance off, its noise audible in the lulls between explosions in the eastern part of the city.

Barrabas looked around and saw an abandoned Peugeot with its doors hanging open and its tires stripped away.

Barrabas spoke rapidly to Nanos and Hatton. "We take the truck. Use the artillery noise to block the sounds of our gunfire. But if they stop the barrage, we go for the truck anyway. Get the car on the road to block it!" He ran across the street to fill in O'Toole and the other two soldiers.

Nanos and Hatton pushed frantically, the sudden action pumping adrenaline into their muscles. The car had sunk into the earth and barely rocked. They pushed again, straining and sweating against the tail end and the frame until, with a sudden lurch, it rolled forward, the metal rims screeching on their rusted axles. The truck slid off the curb into the middle of the road. Barrabas joined them, and they pushed it farther into the road until it was centered. Just far enough to narrow the lane on both sides and slow the oncoming truck. A wide swath of headlights splashed up the pavement just as the mercs scattered into the cover of doorways along the sidewalks.

The truck sped quickly up the street, not braking even when the lights caught the old car lying in its path.

More explosions boomed and the eastern sky flickered. Then there was silence. The shelling had stopped. The sounds of distant machine-gun fire faded. The truck came on.

Suddenly it swerved and braked, pulling off to the left. Six soldiers jumped from the back of the covered two-ton. Quickly they ran to the car and began pushing it to the side, shouting to one another in Cambodian. The driver stayed in the cab and idled the engine. Still the city was quiet, a calm from the storm of invading forces.

Barrabas tightened his grip on the Commando and watched the Khmer Rouge soldiers haul the vehicle aside. Whether or not the shelling started again, the SOBs were going to have to open up. If the noise gave them away they'd have a harder fight on their hands farther up the road. But this was a fast chance to get to command central, and with the Vietnamese army chomping at the bit a few kilometers away, Barrabas wasn't going to pass it up.

He heard a shrill whistle far in the east.

A momentary silence. It was a rocket. Barrabas aimed his Commando.

The enormous explosion shook the ground. It landed close. The faraway chatter of machine-gun fire began again. The six Khmer soldiers had the Peugeot out of the way.

The SOBs opened up.

The enemy soldiers were running for the truck.

None of them made it.

Screams were clipped and short as bullets stitched their jagged lines across the torsos of three of them, while a fourth turned, bringing up his own weapon to fire back. The rifle fell from his hands as his head blew into a gory mass and his body spiraled dead onto the ground.

The last two made for the truck, clambering over the tailgate and pulling it up behind them.

Beck grabbed a grenade from his belt and was about to ram it on the end of his rifle when O'Toole clutched his arm. "Never can tell what's in back there with them," the Irishman said. "Let's try it with bullets first."

Holding his Commando at hip level, O'Toole darted out from the sidewalk in a zigzag run. He fired 3-round bursts at the targets behind the tailgate.

One caught it, standing up to scream with pain. Standing was a big mistake.

O'Toole pumped a couple of rounds into his chest. The man pitched forward into the street.

Meanwhile Hayes had swung out in a circle around the truck and was racing in from the side. He shoved the Commando into his left hand and leaped for the bumper. He grabbed on to the frame to pull himself up so he could see over the tailgate. With his other hand he pumped the trigger of his rifle, sending rounds into the back of the truck. With a heavy clang, the tailgate fell back down. The body of the last Khmer Rouge soldier tumbled after it and sprawled on the street, seeping blood.

At the other end of the truck, Barrabas and Hatton were neutralizing the situation. The colonel ran for the passenger door of the cab, and Hatton took the driver's side. The man at the wheel slipped the truck into gear, and the vehicle was moving forward.

But the truck jerked suddenly and stopped as the driver pushed on the brakes. He had to.

The barrels of two Commandos were pressed against his temples. Hatton held on to the door handle outside the cab as Barrabas opened the other door and climbed across the seat. The autorifle was in his left hand, not moving from the Khmer soldier's head.

The soldier froze in terror.

"Kon," said Barrabas. "You take us to Kon. Or you die." He ground the barrel of the rifle hard against the man's head. The soldier didn't understand a word but he got the message. He nodded frantically and gulped in fear.

O'Toole appeared at the side window. "Back's full of ammo, Colonel, 5.56 rounds for M-16s."

"Tell the boys to replace what they just blew off and take whatever else they can carry. We're going downtown. Now."

O'Toole grabbed the as yet unused HK-13 and threw it into the back of the truck after the SOBs climbed in. In the front seat, Barrabas jabbed the driver with his rifle. "Kon," he said again. "Now."

Quickly the soldier put the truck in gear and drove up the street, turning right at the end and heading up a broad processional boulevard strung with monuments and empty fountains.

The bombardment to the east had fallen off again, and there was a temporary stillness in Kiri. But as they approached the end of the boulevard, Barrabas could see lights on in a building ahead and movement in front of them.

"Slow!" he ordered the driver, raising his free hand and bringing it slowly down. The driver understood and pulled the truck into the square at a low speed.

Barrabas peered through the windshield. The activity was centered around a grand old building on one side of a large central square. A few jeeps and a truck were pulled up out front, and Khmer soldiers ran back and forth from the vehicles to the trucks without much apparent purpose. The truck in front of the old building suddenly pulled out and drove quickly around the square to the far side. There Barrabas could dimly make out the outlines of a colonnade that marked the bridge over the Mekong River. He could see sandbagged machine-gun positions on each side. This was the last stand of the Kiri garrison.

In the back of the two-ton, the five mercs loaded up on ammo from the metal crates. None of them failed to notice the stenciled letters on the boxes that read U.S. Army.

"Good thing you stopped me from throwing the grenades," Beck said to O'Toole.

The red-haired Irishman nodded as he stuffed more grenades from a crate into the pockets of his bush jacket. "It's a rule of thumb, Nate. Don't use the big guns when the little guns will do."

Beck looked at his Commando. It wasn't so little. And it sure was deadly.

Hatton pulled her knife from her belt and made three slits in the canvas along one side. Hayes and Nanos peered out beside her as the truck entered the square. The soldiers quickly sought out and noted the positions of Khmer Rouge soldiers around the hotel and the jeeps out front.

There weren't a lot of them, but enough to keep them busy.

O'Toole pulled open the small window separating the back of the truck from the cab and stuck his face through. "What's the plan, Colonel?"

Barrabas turned to the terrified driver and applied a small amount of persuasive pressure on the cold steel rifle barrel against the man's head.

"Kon. Where is he?" Barrabas demanded.

The man sputtered out a mouthful of Cambodian. Barrabas didn't understand a word.

"Kon?" he said again, this time his tone clearly indicated a question. He pointed repeatedly with his free hand toward the building they were slowly approaching. The driver nodded frantically. Barrabas turned to O'Toole. "I'll keep the driver quiet. We'll take out whoever's in front of the hotel, then go in. I want Hayes up here in the driver's seat after I pile out to drive getaway. Inside we find Kon. He's our hostage. We leave Kiri the way we came in."

The SOBs could feel the truck slowing a hundred feet from the hotel. In the last seconds a single thought struck all of them. They'd followed the colonel to hell and back a few times already, and they were going to do it again right now. That was the deal. Risking their lives made their lives worth living. It was an irony that struck each of them, made each soldier wonder about it in his or her own way. But no one tried to figure it out. Ever. When they were fighting with Barrabas, they were too busy to stop and ask why. All they knew was that they had to do it.

The truck was almost in front of the Khmer Rouge headquarters. Barrabas could make out the name of the old hotel in broken letters across the stone front. Outside, in the square, he saw something that sickened him. The bodies of dozens of civilians, including women and children, many of them wearing white technicians' clothing, lay heaped up like islands in a lake of blood, which ran off

the square into a storm sewer. The bodies were riddled
with bullets.

Something wasn't right there, and it hit him hard in the
pit of his stomach. These soldiers were making a last stand
against the enormous Vietnamese army poised on the outskirts of the city. It was definitely a last stand because there
wasn't enough of them to survive a battle and live to fight
again. Not enough to defend the headquarters of a powerful Khmer Rouge general. Not enough to be commanded
by him if he was in charge.

Kon wasn't here.

But, it was too late to back out now.

The truck stopped in front of the hotel. Barrabas looked
at the driver. His eyes deadly, he muttered slowly, again
putting pressure on the rifle. "You make noise—" he
pointed to the man's mouth "—you die." He gave the rifle
a little dig to make his point.

The driver shifted into neutral.

Then he screamed and clenched madly at the door handle, pulling it up and swinging the door open. He
desperately tried to throw himself down and away from
Barrabas's rifle. Barrabas pulled the trigger. Three rounds
mushed out the driver's cranium.

A line of Khmer soldiers who had been guarding the old
hotel jumped to alert and ran toward the truck.

Barrabas threw himself across the seat, kicking the dead
body out of his way.

The driver went out the door spraying blood. Barrabas
came out spraying bullets.

15

Barrabas's bullets chewed through the night and slammed into the encircling Khmer soldiers. Their hands flew up in surprise, their rifles clattering to the ground as gore lines were drawn across their chests. They fell back, collapsing in death on the steps of the grand hotel.

At the other end of the truck, the SOBs were finishing the job. They jumped out of the back of the two-ton, sending autofire in steady lines back and forth across the front of the stone building. The Khmer soldiers who had stepped forward to check out the approaching vehicle had a big surprise. They died.

In less than a minute, the SOBs regrouped by the cab amid the fallen bodies. From the east the sounds of the Vietnamese bombardment rose steadily, and buildings along the far side of the square near the bridge burst into flame. A shell landed in the center of the square, blowing bits of stone and pavement into a spray of chips. Caught in the maelstrom of explosions, the mercs turned against the blast to protect their faces and eyes.

Barrabas cut the orders out fast. "Hayes, drive getaway. Be ready when we come out of there. The rest of you follow me."

He ran across the sidewalk and loped up the half-dozen steps in two long strides, jumping over the bodies of a couple of soldiers. He slid in the entrance of the hotel, going down on one knee and sending a zigzag line of bullets across the ruined lobby. Two soldiers bursting through a doorway on one side caught slugs in the chest and slammed back the way they came. Dead.

Barrabas was up, with Hatton, Nanos, Beck and O'Toole beside him in the lobby. They checked out the four corners with their backs to one another.

"O'Toole, Hatton, check the upstairs. Beck, cover Hayes and the door. Nanos, come with me." Their leader ran for the doorway the two dead soldiers had come out of.

O'Toole and Hatton took the stairs. Nanos went after Barrabas into the ruined ballroom where, a few hours earlier, Kon had watched the executions outside on the square.

The room was deserted.

"Check out the other rooms around the lobby," Barrabas ordered Nanos. The Greek followed the colonel back and they split up, pushing through piles of junk and debris around them and kicking in the doors of offices behind the main desk.

One door resisted. Nanos and Barrabas rushed it together with two solidly planted kicks. They booted it in. It was the radio room. A Khmer soldier jumped back from the shortwave set swinging a pistol. Barrabas and Nanos opened up together. The twin stream of autofire sliced him in two. The upper half of his torso fell backward, plunging through a window in a shower of glass and landing on the steps outside. A trail of bloody guts led down the wall onto the floor. The bottom half wavered a few seconds before falling over.

"Shit," said Nanos in disgust.

Barrabas picked up the headset dangling from the radio. Heavy static almost drowned out the thin excited voice somewhere on the receiving end of the interrupted transmission. Then it went dead.

Hatton and O'Toole came running down the long staircase. They pulled up beside the colonel and Nanos.

"Empty upstairs," said Lee.

"Geez." Liam O'Toole saw what was left of the dead man. He was as disgusted as Nanos.

Barrabas looked quickly around the room. A desk was strewed with papers, four telephones and a tiny Khmer Rouge flag. The commander's office, but no commander.

They'd just taken a deserted hotel.

"Let's get the hell out of here." Barrabas turned and pushed through the lobby in a blind rage.

Outside, Hayes had the truck idling and the SOBs ran for the tail end. Barrabas climbed in the passenger side.

More buildings along the river were burning now, and the rain of artillery was steady. The whistling of incoming shells and the explosions drowned out all but the loudest shouts. Orange tracers striped the eastern sky like fireworks.

Hayes put the truck in gear and it rolled forward just as O'Toole and Nanos pulled Hatton and Beck into the back. Lee looked back when the truck drove away from the hotel.

The sky lit up a brilliant orange. Shells landed across the square on the machine-gun post guarding the bridge. The screams of maimed and dying Khmer soldiers stretched through the noise of demolition. The rapid chatter of machine-gun fire stopped. The artillery barrage ended at the same moment.

Hatton could see flames licking away at the destroyed machine-gun post. The dry leaves of the trees along the square burst into flaming torches. The tiny shapes of fleeing soldiers, some of them on fire, were silhouetted by the orange backdrop of the burning city.

The battle was over. The tiny garrison of Khmer Rouge soldiers was wiped out. Another sound poured out of the east—the sound of engines and tires and marching soldiers. The Vietnamese army was on the move.

The truck gathered speed. Hayes turned it toward the boulevard that led out of the city. Then Hatton saw something move.

"Stop, Hayes!" She shouted at her comrades behind her and leaped from the back of the moving truck.

"Stop the truck!" Beck shouted into the cab, banging on the window. "Hatton's jumped!"

"What the hell. . .?" Barrabas turned to look out the tail end of the truck. Hayes slammed on the brake. Barrabas pushed the door open and jumped out.

O'Toole hopped from the back of the truck and ran after Hatton.

The woman ran toward the bloody pile of slaughtered civilians lying in the middle of the square. She stopped before she came to them and knelt by a single body slumped at the foot of a streetlight. Barrabas and O'Toole ran up beside her.

The man's knees had collapsed, but his body was held up by the rope wrapped around the arm of the overhead light. Great swaths of dried blood ran down his arms in a thick crusted coat. But one thing was obvious from his eyes. They were open. He was alive.

"I saw him moving as we went by," Hatton said, hacking at the rope with her knife. It cut with one swift slice and the tortured youth crumpled, too weak to hold himself up.

Barrabas and O'Toole caught him as he fell, and the colonel wrapped his arms under the limp body, gathering it up.

"We take him with us," he said, and the three mercs ran for the truck. Barrabas handed Kon's bloodied victim up to the waiting hands of Beck and Nanos as Hatton and O'Toole clambered back in.

Hayes had the truck moving already. Barrabas ran alongside, grabbing the open passenger door and swinging into the seat.

Hayes floored the accelerator, depressed the clutch and popped it into gear. The truck careered madly across the pavement toward the boulevard they had followed into the square.

The sky was turning from black to dark blue, and the stars fled the approaching sunrise. The noise of the oncoming army grew louder, intermingled with sporadic rifle fire in different sectors of the dead city.

Hayes swung around the square keeping the speed steady. He slipped into high as the boulevard opened up in front of them.

Then he braked. Hard.

In the back the SOBs slammed up against the wall of the cab, while Hayes and Barrabas bounced on the seats in front. The truck screeched and slid in a long rubber burn to a full stop.

The reason was obvious. A mile down the road a brigade of the Vietnamese army marched straight at them.

Hayes steered the truck into a three-point turn and took off in the opposite direction. Once again, the truck sped across the square as he aimed for a street that led into the southern part of Kiri.

Before he got there he knew it was too late.

The entrance was blocked by burning rubble from the shelled machine-gun post and a building that had collapsed into the street.

"The bridge!" Barrabas shouted over the noise of the grinding gears as Hayes shoved it into reverse. "Go for the bridge!"

Last chance. If they could get across before the Vietnamese got on it, they could deke down a street on the other side of the river.

The tires screeched and smoked as Hayes reversed and pulled forward. He drove it toward the entrance to the bridge and made a fast right turn at the colonnade. Then he stomped on the brake again, hurtling his passengers forward once more.

It was too late.

Ahead of them, across the quarter-mile stretch of the Mekong, the headlights of the Vietnamese main army surged relentlessly forward.

THE ROSY PINK LIGHT OF DAWN wandered in through the cell window as General Kon picked at the splintered wood that had once held the iron bars of Scott's cell in place.

"How did he do this?" Kon asked the guards who stood around him. They looked at each other guiltily. No one offered an answer. "With his teeth?" Kon demanded. Still no answer. "These Americans," said Kon, as if that explained everything. "Search the village. Leave nothing unturned. But likely he has gone to the jungle where the tigers will feast on him."

He strode from the cell. As he crossed the courtyard to the temple living quarters, a messenger rushed from an operations building.

"Great Kon!" the man said, his face nervous and fearful. How easy it was to tell bad news before it arrived.

"What is it?"

"A last broadcast from Kiri, General."

"The city has fallen to the Vietnamese, then."

"The Vietnamese are bombarding the city and approaching from the east and the north. But there was something else."

"What is it? Hurry up!"

The man gulped nervously. "The radio operator said the headquarters was being attacked from within the city. By mercenaries. European mercenaries."

Now Kon stopped and gave the man his full attention. "What else? I want to know the exact words."

"That is all he said, General Kon. There were shots and then the broadcast ended. But he said one other thing. He was very frightened and did not make sense. He was babbling nonsense."

"What nonsense? Tell me!"

"About white hair, General Kon. He said the white-haired one was leading them into the headquarters. That the white-haired one killed everyone in sight."

"Go back to your radio and continue to monitor for further messages."

Now Kon walked slowly to his quarters, deep in thought. It was incredible. What were these Americans made of? The white-haired one could only be this Colonel

Barrabas. But instead of delivering himself to Kon's hands at Angkor, he was coming after the warlord. He had found Kiri. There was no way he could find his way to Radam. Or was there? Kon now knew better than to underestimate the talents of this strange white-haired warrior. These Americans were incredible.

The sun was rising, burning off the low dampness from the night and presaging a hot new day. Kon made a decision. They would leave for Tonle Sap with the chemical immediately.

He would take no more chances on the white-haired warrior named Barrabas.

16

"Over there!" Barrabas shouted above the roar of th[e] burning city.

Hayes looked to his left, past the burning machine-gu[n] positions. Three silhouettes darted along the concret[e] balustrade where the bridge opened into the square. Bar[-] rabas recognized them before Hayes did. "It's the Rhade[.] They've come to take us out of here."

"How in hell. . . ?" The black man stared in disbelief.

"I don't know, either," said Barrabas, "but let's mov[e] ass!"

The two men bailed out of the cab and ran to the back o[f] the truck just as the Rhade got there.

"*Blah po gia*. Our leader has sent us. Follow quickly[.] We have a boat," one of them told the white-haired wa[r-] rior in a rush of words. He was pointing to stone steps tha[t] led down to the river from the side of the bridge. The othe[r] SOBs were pouring out of the back of the truck with thei[r] rifles and packs. Nanos hoisted the HK-13 machine gu[n] onto his back, while Beck and O'Toole carried the wound[-] ed Cambodian. Hatton had already started the patch-u[p] job by binding his arms in gauze.

"Go with the Rhade," Barrabas ordered. "I'll follow i[n] a second."

The mercenaries obeyed, running across the road towar[d] the steps to the river. Barrabas headed back for the cab o[f] the truck. He threw his rifle onto the driver's seat an[d] climbed in after it. He slipped it into first gear and presse[d] the gas.

The truck rumbled forward again as he drove it towa[rd]

he entrance of the bridge. The front line of the Vietnamese army was halfway across. At the sight of the truck bearing down on them the first vehicles were braking.

Barrabas slipped it into second as the truck picked up speed. Timing was everything now.

He pulled a grenade off his belt, floored the accelerator and ducked down behind the dash as the windshield exploded into fragments from machine-gun fire. The Vietnamese were shooting back. Holding the steering wheel steady with one hand, he reached over, pulled the door handle up and opened the door. Then he pulled the pin with his teeth and counted slowly to three.

With one fluid movement he tossed the grenade through the little window into the back of the truck, grabbed his gun and flew out the door. He landed on his feet but rolled sideways to break the fall.

The truck kept going. Straight toward the Vietnamese army.

The grenade blew. Shrapnel ripped through the canvas top. Flames began licking at the fabric. Barrabas pulled himself up and ran at lightning speed for the stone steps down to the river.

The first box of ammunition exploded in the back of the truck like a roll of firecrackers. He could hear the regular reports of gunfire coming from the Vietnamese army. But still the truck didn't stop.

Soldiers on the bridge began screaming. There was no time to turn their jeeps around, so they bailed out and started running. The truck bore down like a metal monster breathing flame.

It blew when it hit the first jeep.

There was the wrenching sound of metal slamming into metal, smashing glass and an explosion that blew Barrabas forward.

He felt the heat wave licking over him as he picked himself up and swung around the corner of the bridge. A

Rhade was waiting for him, crouched low behind the concrete balustrade.

The center of the bridge burned bright in a roaring conflagration. The gas tank of the first jeep blew up and the flames moved on to consume the second. Soldiers ran from the fire but the fire followed. They were living torches. They went for the first water that came to mind. The Mekong River.

They blazed over the sides of the bridge to their deaths in the water below.

It was a hell of a way to stall for time. But time was what they needed to get out of there.

"Come," the Rhade whispered. Barrabas followed him quickly down the stone steps that led to a concrete embankment along the water. The river was pink with a false dawn from the reflections of the holocaust on the bridge.

Bits of burning debris plunged down and sizzled with loud hisses as the water snuffed the flames. The screams of death gave way to the consuming roar of the fire.

There was a long boat against the embankment, the middle part covered by a flimsy canvas roof. It was a typical peasant craft, the kind poor families lived in or that farmers used to bring their produce to market. Now it held the SOBs.

Barrabas and the Rhade got in, and another Rhade pushed off from the side of the embankment. The swift current of the river quickly took hold and swept them under the dark arch of the bridge.

Silently, and with speed, the boat moved along the edge of the darkened city, the fire fading behind them. The sky ahead grew pink with the rising sun.

The mercenaries were silent. In the aftermath of battle each soldier sat alone to collect his thoughts. Soon the river carried them past the edge of the city into countryside where the jungle grew to the edge of the water.

Hatton busied herself with the wounded Cambodian under the shelter of the thin canvas roof. Already the morning sun was beginning to press its heat. She bound the wounds in his arms and injected him with morphine and adrenaline.

Barrabas moved over beside her. "What's the story?"

"He's lost a lot of blood," she said. "I dressed the wounds but they'll keep seeping unless the arteries are stitched. We need a hospital for that. He'll probably die."

"You can't save them all."

"No."

"Can he talk?"

"Try him."

Barrabas leaned over the young man and spoke slowly and clearly. "Can you give us information?"

The young man nodded weakly, saying, *"Français, français."*

"He speaks French," Hatton said. "Of course, that was the second language here."

"Hayes!" Barrabas called to the black man who sat in the narrow stern of the boat. "French is your department. Can you try to get some information out of this guy." Claude Hayes crawled on his hands and knees toward the middle of the boat. The little craft was too flimsy and unstable for him to stand and walk.

"Find out if he knows where General Kon is," Barrabas told him.

Hayes leaned over the dying man. An anguished look crossed the Cambodian's face as he explained his story. And Barrabas could sense the disbelief in Hayes's voice when he asked the questions.

Finally Hayes turned to Barrabas and Hatton.

"He was a lab technician at the Agricultural Research Institute in Kiri. He says Kon did this to him as punishment because he was caught making love to his girlfriend. The girl was killed. The rest of what he's saying is incredible. I don't know whether to believe it or not."

"Tell us," Barrabas said.

Hayes cast a slow look back at the dying man, who in turn eyed the black man eagerly.

"He says General Kon brought all the captured scientists of Cambodia together in Kiri, with the families as hostages."

"The people massacred in the square?" guessed Hatton.

Hayes nodded. "Apparently Kon supplied them with the required ingredients and commanded them to manufacture an environmental poison similar to Agent Orange, but more powerful. The scientists, under threat of death, came up with the formula for the deadliest chemical herbicide ever made. A few molecules on the skin will kill a man, he says. And they tested it as a spray in the dead forest the satellite pictures picked up."

"What does Kon plan on doing with the stuff?" Barrabas asked.

"That's where his story gets really crazy," Hayes said. "And what he knows is only rumor. But apparently Kon wants to poison the irrigation system of Cambodia."

"Does Kon have this chemical now?"

Hayes nodded. "They presented him with a twenty gallon drum of it yesterday. Then he killed them all. Twenty gallons is enough to poison the oceans."

"Does he know where Kon is?"

Hayes bent over the Cambodian again and spoke to him. The man nodded and answered. Hayes looked up at the colonel. "He says Kon has a secret headquarters in a small town called Radam in a mountain valley in the north central region."

Barrabas thought a moment. Then he spoke to Hayes and Hatton. "It sounds crazy, but we better believe it. This General Kon has been around for years, and I saw his tricks in Vietnam. He's a madman. He'll do anything."

"We walked on skulls last night," said Hayes. "I believe it."

Barrabas pulled a plasticized map of Cambodia from his pocket and opened it on his lap. The two men scanned the north-central region of the country. Hayes saw it first. "Radam, there," he pointed.

"And we're here," said Barrabas pointing to a spot on the Mekong just south of Kiri.

"No roads and about a hundred kliks overland to get there."

"With twenty-five kliks of defoliated forest to walk through. That's the dead zone." Barrabas ran his finger around the area of the great blue spot he'd seen on the satellite pictures. He stared a couple minutes at the map before making his decision. Then he spoke to the Rhades. They nodded. What he suggested was possible.

He turned to his soldiers and briefed them. They had to go to Radam. If they traveled on the Mekong for a few more hours, they could cut forty kliks off the overland journey.

"It means we'll start marching in the worst heat of the day," he told them. "But if we're lucky maybe we can get to Radam in time to attack under cover of night. Any questions?"

There were none.

"In the meantime," he said with one eye on the sun, "try to grab some sleep."

By noon the current of the Mekong had swept them far south of Kiri. The living jungle ended, and they came into the zone of defoliated forest. The sun pounded down onto the dead land. Gaunt branches of trees hung with brittle brown leaves, and the ground was strewed almost knee high with crumbling foliage. There was nothing green, nothing alive. Without the cooling effects of tropical vegetation, the land captured the heat and held it. The forest baked. The reeking bloated bodies of dead fish rotted along the shore. It was like a wilderness in hell.

The mercs put on the silver chemsuits and adjusted the respirators on their foreheads, ready to pull them down when they stepped onshore. Barrabas wasn't taking chances with contaminating his men on the twenty-five-klik journey through the dead zone.

One of the Rhades poled the boat to the shore. It jarred as it hit the land. Nanos and Beck stepped off quickly and held the prow for O'Toole, Hayes and Hatton. Barrabas was the last to go. The wounded Cambodian was left in the care of the Rhades—to live or to die. It was out of their hands now.

Barrabas turned back to the Rhades to say goodbye. "Thank you. And thank your leader for delivering us from Kiri."

"He say to tell you he is doing great magic for your protection," said one of the warriors.

The second Rhade gave a wide, gap-toothed smile. "And beware of tigers, also, great leader."

"Tigers? In there?" Barrabas couldn't help a smile as he waved toward the dead forest.

"Farther on," the Rhade said. "The stench of death is on the jungle, and the tigers have grown fat on human flesh. They have had so much of it they have a taste for it now. So beware of tigers, *blah po gia*." The man smiled.

Barrabas laughed. "If they're bold enough to come for me I'll give them something to chew on." He patted his Commando. Then he stepped off the boat and turned with his arm up in farewell. The Rhades pushed away from the riverbank, and the current carried the boat into the river.

It was back to business.

The other mercs adjusted the respirators over their faces. Barrabas looked around. The party of soldiers in their silver chemsuits and with the respirators and goggles covering their faces looked like aliens set down on a dead planet.

Lee Hatton handed him some tablets. "Salt," she said. "We're going to need it."

Barrabas nodded and popped them into his mouth before lowering his mask. He took a compass bearing and led off.

The sun seemed to plod across the sky with agonizing slowness, matching the progress the mercs made in their march toward Radam. The brown, crisp sameness of the dead jungle obscured any sense that they were moving. Their passage was anything but silent as they slipped past the gaunt remains of trees, their boots crunching and snapping against the brittle debris underfoot.

The tropical heat beat down on their heads, magnified not only by the baking forest, but also by the suffocating chemical-protection suits. Sweat ran in rivers down their faces, backs and legs until it reached the point where their boots were soggy from their own fluids.

They stopped frequently to take water and more salt. At one point, Barrabas thought of letting the men abandon the stifling clothing. Then they came to the edge of a brackish pond. The surface was covered with an oily blue sheen. Defoliant. They kept the suits on, but the colonel gave up all thought of reaching Radam by nightfall.

It was not only the temperature that slowed their journey. The drifting debris from the dead vegetation covered all traces of any animal paths they might have used to pass through the heavy brush. Brittle fronds of dead palms snapped as Barrabas parted them by shoving his rifle ahead of him through the forest.

Four hours later he estimated they had covered twelve kilometers. Halfway through, and they had not seen a single living thing since they had entered the forest.

The sun was lowering in the west, and soon it would begin to cool. They were soaking wet from their sweat now, and with the cool of evening, the wetness would become as much a danger to them as the excess heat was now.

He ordered his men to rest for half an hour in a long shadow cast by a high rock that rose above the clogged bed of a dry stream.

Then he pushed them on. Just as the light grew gray with the approach of evening, Barrabas saw something that made him pull up short. A single blade of grass grew out of the earth in front of him. And it was green.

The worst was over.

He motioned to the others and pointed. They moved faster now, rejuvenated by the prospect of leaving the dead zone behind.

The single blade of grass soon gave way to clumps, then small shrubs only half-blighted, then trees with bits of leaf sprouting on the highest branches. Even the arrival of black flies buzzing at the sweat-soaked soldiers was a relief.

Half an hour later the dead zone ended. They were in jungle. The air, cool from the onset of evening and moist vegetation, rushed around them like air conditioning. They yanked off their respirators and drank in deep lungfuls of cool air, scented by the thick smell of jungle greenery.

They stripped off the silver chemsuits. "Remember to leave your gloves on until the last," Hatton reminded them. "So when you roll the suit up and pack it you don't have to touch it." Finally they stood there pulling their clammy sweat-soaked fatigues away from their skin.

Barrabas sniffed at the air. There was another smell, too. Faint, but unmistakable. It was the smell of something dead and rotting.

O'Toole came up beside him.

"Do you notice it?" Barrabas asked him.

O'Toole sniffed at the air. He did. "Dead animal?"

"Maybe. But something tells me that's wishful thinking. How're the men?"

"Exhausted. Soaking wet. But feeling a lot better since we got out of the dead zone."

"We have an hour of daylight left."

O'Toole nodded. "Let's do it. Let's get as far as we can from what's back there." He announced it to the mercs, who stood without hesitation, ready to push on.

"Who's turn on the HK?" Beck asked, lifting the sixteen-pound machine gun.

"I'll take it now," Lee volunteered. She finished putting away the carefully obtained leaf samples and a small bottle of polluted water she had gathered in the dead zone. All the mercs had taken turns carrying the gun except her.

"Uh-uh, Lee," said Nanos. "You got enough to carry with your extra medical stuff. This gun gets heavier as you go along."

"I'll take it," said Hatton firmly, and gave them a look to say the discussion was finished. She took the gun from Beck. "Let's just hope one of us has a chance to use it after all this carrying," she concluded.

The colonel led them into the dense undergrowth of the jungle. He used his machete to hack away at leaves and branches to open a way through the forest. The jungle broke abruptly at a narrow path a few minutes later. A quick examination revealed no signs of recent use. But at least it would afford them faster passage. The foul smell of carrion continued and with it the subtle fear that there was a trap ahead.

Barrabas felt something tug at his foot. They heard a tearing of leaves in the branches overhead.

"Move!" Barrabas shouted, throwing himself back at Lee Hatton, next in line. An eighteen-inch-square board weighted with bricks landed on the path where he had been standing. It was suspended a foot off the path by the barbed iron spikes that impaled the ground. It was a device known as a tiger trap, and it had killed often in Vietnam.

Barrabas moved forward, the other SOBs following. This time he kept a careful eye on the path ahead of him, looking for variations in the texture of the ground or wires strung across the path.

A few dozen feet later, the path joined another one. The stench was becoming stronger. There were human footprints in the baked mud, but they were old. Fifty feet farther, the path widened and was littered with leaves. Barrabas took his machete and hacked a branch from a bush. He lopped off leaves and turned it into a long staff. Then he edged forward, tapping the ground ahead of him, and listening carefully to the wood knock on the dry earth. Ten feet later, the wooden pole came down soft. Barrabas pushed at the ground. It moved. One end went down, while the path farther along erupted upward from the leaves. Then it slapped back into place.

"Pivoting-lid pit," Barrabas told the mercs who came up around him. He pressed on the earth again and once more the lid on the spike pit tilted down. This time, it went far enough to see that the trap had already swallowed its victims.

It was about eight feet deep and six feet wide. A heavy stench rose out when the lid was opened. Barrabas caught a fast glimpse of bloated bodies impaled on two-foot spikes. He didn't count the number. There were a lot.

"Colonel, take a look around," O'Toole said to him. The Irishman pointed farther up the path to where the undergrowth of the jungle thinned. In the dying daylight, Barrabas saw what they had walked into.

The forest was dotted with skeletal remains enmeshed in various kinds of booby traps. He could make out a few that were obvious by the way the remains lay. Some had been killed by bamboo whips edged with spikes. Others lay half in the ground, the spikes of sideways-closing traps piercing their rib cages. The landscape of death seemed to go in every direction the mercs looked now. In jungle clearings through the trees bones lay strewn about haphazardly, the pitiful remains of people who had walked into minefields.

The entire jungle was a death trap. And the SOBs had walked right into it.

Lee Hatton turned to Barrabas. "Colonel, if the Khmer Rouge took this much trouble to lay booby traps all through here they must be protecting something. Or trying to cut off these people's escape route."

"But the maps show this entire region to be deserted jungle," said Claude Hayes. "We're supposed to be in the middle of nowhere."

Barrabas nodded. "When the Khmer Rouge emptied the

cities, they forced many of the people into the jungles to build new settlements with their bare hands.''

"And they wouldn't be on the maps," said Beck.

"Right. We must be near one now.''

"Which means," said Nanos, checking the mag on his Commando, "we may have a fight on our hands.''

"We'll try to avoid it if we can and get straight to Radam," said Barrabas. "But none of these bodies are new. Even the decomposing remains in the pit are weeks old. We may not run into anyone.''

"If we do, I got a few pounds of hot lead for them," muttered Hayes.

"Colonel, if there is one of these new settlements around here, it may mean a road, too," said Lee.

"So let's find it.'' The colonel took another look through the trees at the grisly relics of Khmer Rouge barbarism. The light was fading now, which made the jungle even more dangerous. They had maybe a half hour left.

He led them around the pivoting-lid pit, and farther through the jungle, traveling at a snail's pace as he continually pounded the ground ahead and sighted in the bushes on either side and above for traps.

Five minutes later they came to a stretch where white bones lay scattered. A land mine had gone off, months earlier. Another fifty yards down the path yet another skeleton stood impaled to a tree by a pivoting spike board that had swung down from the trees.

These lives had not been lost in vain. In death, they had triggered most of the booby traps, making passage safer for the SOBs.

Finally Barrabas saw the jungle underbrush thin and end. The soldiers crept quietly up to the edge of the jungle and looked across a field to a small gathering of thatched buildings a hundred yards away. Everything was deserted. The field was parched and dry. The roofs of some of the houses had already collapsed. The village and fields were ringed by jungle except for an opening on the far side where a crude road snaked out.

"That's why none of the booby traps have claimed any recent victims," said Hayes.

"But why?" said Hatton. "Why would they build these new settlements and abandon them?"

Barrabas shook his head slowly in disgust. "We've seen enough in the last day to show us that the Khmer Rouge are madmen. Everything is dead here."

"They turned the entire country into a concentration camp like Auschwitz," said Beck softly.

The mercs moved through the jungle around the edge of the fields until they came out behind the village. There was still no sign of life. Finally Barrabas gave the order to break the forest. They strode across the dry mud of the paddies to the abandoned houses.

Dusk closed in. After the morning battle in Kiri and the long hot march through the defoliated zone, Barrabas's soldiers suffered the petty things that all mortals must suffer—even warriors. They were hungry and exhausted.

Barrabas estimated it was another ten kliks to Radam. If they rested for the night, they could do it in a couple of hours the next morning.

He pointed to one of the thatched roofed houses that stood on stilts above the ground. "We'll go in there and rest for the night."

His soldiers nodded. No one cheered, but he could see in their faces that they needed it.

Tired soldiers who didn't rest before battle all too often ended up with more sleep than they bargained for. The sleep of the dead.

Tomorrow they would take Radam. Tomorrow Kon would pay for the hell he wrought in this gentle land. Barrabas swore that Kon would pay in blood.

17

While Barrabas and his soldiers settled in for the night in the abandoned village, General Kon and his little daughter climbed into the red convertible Mercedes. The driver tore from the compound in a cloud of dry yellow dust. Another long convoy of jeeps and trucks headed for the highway that led to Tonle Sap.

General Kon settled back for the duration of a four-hour ride. The excellent suspension of the expensive car cushioned them from the ruts and holes in the earth road. His daughter slept beside him. He put his hand on her and stroked her.

The general's mind wandered. For the first time in a long while, things were going wrong. The Vietnamese, once loyal allies, had turned against the Khmer Rouge and invaded the country. Soon they would control all of Cambodia and Kon would be forced to flee. And in Radam, John Scott had escaped from his cell. Soldiers had searched the village for an entire day and were unable to find him. Kon had been denied the pleasure of the morning execution.

His breathing came fast and sharp as he considered the failures. He ground his teeth. And then he thought of Barrabas, the white-haired colonel who somehow had the audacity to come after him in Cambodia. And miraculously almost find him. He wondered how far away the American devil was. Or if he was closing in.

The thought of failure caused the warlord to stiffen. He put his hand to his mouth and clenched his teeth on a knuckle. His eyes grew wide. He whimpered.

It was all so apparent to him. They wanted to laugh at him again. They wanted to make fun of him, to push him around and beat him up the way they had so many years ago in school. He had bided his time and waited for revenge. He would not fail now. In the Cambodian night, the car tore across the muddy plains of rice paddies to the Great Lake. Kon's resolve strengthened. He looked at the little girl beside him and caressed her.

Kon's breathing became light again as he focused on the precious cargo in his truck, the steel drum of poison chemical that he would pour into Tonle Sap. From there it would flow into the tributaries of the Great Lake, and thence into the oceans. The Organization on High had decided. Everyone must be equal. If that meant equally miserable, so be it.

But what if the white-haired warrior was really coming? The fear struck the general again like a chilly wind that warned of death and defeat. He must stop him, leave a warning of his power in the colonel's path.

The convoy slowed only slightly as it came to a peasant village straddling the highway. Kon leaned forward to speak to the driver. "We stop here. All of us. I have business here to take care of." The driver began to slow, honking to alert the rest of the convoy.

In the trunk of the Mercedes, Kon's precious cargo lay on its side and rolled heavily with the bouncing movement of the car over the road.

But it did not roll far. The precious cargo was cushioned by the unexpected addition of a load that not even Kon suspected.

Captain John Scott crouched on his side in a fetal position, his body curled in the narrow space around the steel drum.

It had taken hours to chew away the wooden frame with the little nail clippers, and as the eastern sky grew orange with its premonitions of dawn, he had almost given up. It would be impossible to escape by light of day.

He burrowed with his fingers into the beam and found the center of the wood softened by insects. He was able to tear splinters out with his hands, faster and faster until his nails tore and his fingers bled. Then the bar came loose.

He squeezed through the opening onto the ground.

It was almost sunrise. He had managed to escape from his cell into the deserted courtyard of the compound.

Scott stayed in the dark shadows along the side of the building and edged toward the front gates. He had so little time. His mind worked madly. He needed a hiding place. In all the time he'd worked to set himself free, he'd had no chance to think out the next step.

He heard the voices of two soldiers talking as they walked along the other side of the building. He had to hide. Fast. He saw the Mercedes was parked just inside the gates of the compound. He ran to it and peered in the driver's window. The keys were there. He opened the door softly and grabbed them. He ran to the end of the car and ducked down below the bumper just as the Khmer soldiers came around the corner.

He waited breathlessly. One bade the other farewell and walked through the gate. The other leaned up against the wall to take up guard duty.

Scott peered over the trunk of the car. Looking through the windows, he could see the man in his black uniform smoking a cigarette and watching the sun rise.

Scott carefully inserted the key into the lock of the trunk and opened it slightly. On his hands and knees he took the keys back to the driver's door that he had left ajar. He squatted below the level of the window, reached in and pushed the keys back into the ignition. Then he closed the door as far as it would go without making a noise. He crawled back to the trunk of the car and looked up over the bumper. The guard was still smoking and watching the sunrise. Scott opened the trunk a foot and a half and slipped inside.

There was a metal drum there. He was certain it was the

chemical the child had talked about. He curled beside i
and closed the lid. He wasn't sure what would happer
next, but instinct told him he was doing the right thing. No
one would find this hiding place. At least not for now
Then he realized something else. He hadn't trembled in
hours. Not once.

More than twelve hours later, Scott still lay in the trunk
of the car. The Mercedes hadn't moved. He heard in the
morning the soldiers run back and forth with anxiou
shouts when his absence was discovered. He also hear
Kon cross the courtyard, and the troubled messenger tel
his master of the fall of Kiri. There was the strange in
formation about the white-haired mercenary, which for
few seconds made him think of the colonel he'd fough
with in Vietnam. If only, he thought for a second, bu
dismissed it. It was impossible. There was not going to be
any rescue. Not now, not ever. Whatever was going to hap
pen, it was something Scott had to do himself.

By noon the heat was so severe that the American soldie
was lying in a pool of his own sweat. He fiddled with th
inside of the trunk lock, using the nail file on the little clip
per to trigger the release. He raised the lid only enough t
allow a crack of light, and a bit of fresh air.

Scott waited, his body cramped and his muscles aching
Finally, darkness fell. The activity in the courtyar
presaged departure. He heard the sound of trucks idling
The car sunk as the warlord, his daughter, and the drive
climbed in.

The car drove into the coolness of night, but now th
heavy metal drum rolled and bounced, increasing Scott'
misery. After three-quarters of an hour, the car left th
earthen road from Radam and turned onto a paved high
way.

Half an hour later the convoy stopped. Scott waited. H
prayed the trunk would not be opened.

It wasn't. He heard Kon shouting orders. They were in
village and the inhabitants were being turned out into th

center of the square. He heard shots, screams of terror and pain.

He heard the warlord tapping his fingers on the lid of the trunk and ordering his soldiers to kill. Nearby, closer than the screams of dying people, he heard the sound of a little girl giggling uncontrollably.

18

Each soldier took a turn at keeping watch for an hour, Barrabas last. He awoke as the sky heralded a new dawn with a glimmer of gray. Claude Hayes stood by the door of the abandoned hut. Barrabas moved quietly toward him.

"Look," said Hayes in a soft voice. He indicated something on the ground below the house.

Barrabas stood in the doorway and looked down. It was a tiger. The enormous cat's yellow eyes glowed through the gray light. It stopped and eyed them. Low deep growls rolled from its mouth.

"It's sizing us up for breakfast," said Barrabas.

Hayes nodded. "He does look well fed, doesn't he?" Barrabas knew what Hayes was referring to. They had seen evidence that the corpses in the jungle had been feasted upon.

The tiger bared its long, sharp teeth in a giant yawn, stretching its mouth wide enough to swallow a man's head. Then it turned and ran from the empty village to the jungle.

"One look at you, Colonel, and it gave up," said Hayes. "Too tough."

Barrabas smiled. "Sleep, Claude." Hayes nodded and went inside. Barrabas stood by the door breathing the fresh morning air as the eastern sky brightened from gray to bone white, and finally admitted the low spreading carmine of the sun. He lit a cigar, and pulled the map out. Six kilometers away there should be a dirt road, leading to Radam. They could be there in less than two hours. There was one other major concern. Erika and Bishop were flying in to Angkor Wat today. The SOBs had twelve hours to get to Radam, take care of Kon, and rendezvous in the ancient ruined city.

The soldier looked out as the world began its new morning. He envied nature its peace. A little while later he woke the others. They climbed down from the house, ate a quick breakfast of high-energy rations and made their way across the paddy to the break in the jungle.

It led west, in the direction of Radam. Several kliks later they came to a gravel road. It was the one Barrabas had seen on the map. It led north, rising toward low-lying hills. The jungle gave way to scrub trees and high savanna grass. The mercs split in two, traveling along each side of the road, close to the savanna. Finally the cover broke. The gravel road ascended a low foothill. It opened into a narrow valley with terraced paddies on one side.

Barrabas stopped the mercs from going farther and motioned them into the savanna on the other side of the hill where the slope continued upward. Crouching in the high grass, he scanned the paddies with his binoculars.

For the first time since they had jumped into Cambodia, he saw something that bore a resemblance to normal life. Peasants in wide straw hats worked the paddies.

But the resemblance was only superficial. Black-uniformed Khmer Rouge soldiers with automatic rifles stood guard along the edge of the valley.

They had crossed into the territory of the warlord.

The colonel examined the terrain. The slopes rose high above the gravel road, and the crest of the hill promised a wider view of the valley, perhaps even Radam itself. It also offered a back way in.

He led the soldiers in a low run through the grass. Just below the crest he stopped and surveyed the surroundings yet again. The morning sun still hovered at nine o'clock in the east, burning the moisture off the land into a fine blue haze down the long valley. The road hugged the hillsides. A kilometer or so farther along, poised on the edge of the

next hill, stood a collection of buildings beside a waterfall
Radam. The Cambodian warlord's mountain headquar
ters.

Directly below the mercs, where the road swooped along
the curvature and where two hills rubbed shoulders, wa
the first guard post.

Barrabas raised the binoculars, and brought a few
Khmer soldiers into focus.

Obviously they weren't expecting anyone.

Three of them loitered around a little shack of woven
palm fronds. They carried their rifles loosely in their hand
or over their backs. Easy targets, but the point was to tak
them out silently. That meant Hayes, Hatton and him
self—the three best knife soldiers in the unit.

"Lee, Claude," the colonel whispered, "all of you
Listen up. There are three of them and three of us." H
looked at the woman warrior and the black man, pulled hi
knife from his belt and shook it in his fist. "We take ther
out. The rest of you—" he was talking to Nanos, Beck an
O'Toole now "—when we take care of the three guards
cross the road and set up for the rest of them down in th
paddies. Hold the shooting until I give the command."

He stopped, scanned their eyes. They knew what to do
He turned and led off down the hill.

By the time they got to within sight of the guard post
was cat and mouse. Barrabas, Hayes and Hatton moved i
from two sides. Hayes circled away from the colonel an
Lee. They darted closer, moving from tree to rock to th
cover of bushes.

Barrabas peered through the web of branches an
leaves. The guards still sauntered about, bored and u
alert, talking casually with one another. They could b
easily distracted.

He knew a trick. He had used it so many times it was a
most a reflex. He picked up a rock and hurled it over h
head across the road so it bounced on the roof of th
guardhouse.

They looked. Instantly. The oldest trick in the book, and they fell for it. Dumb.

Barrabas, Hayes and Hatton sprinted across the road. Hatton got to her man first. She ran up behind the Khmer soldier, grabbed his hair, pulled his head back and jabbed her knee into the small of his back. The knife sliced long and clean across the man's neck. His jugular blew like a garden hose in a spray twenty feet across the road. His body jerked forward, the head hinging backward on the spine. Those who fall for tricks fall dead. A smile went from ear to ear, the death grin still spurting blood.

The fate of the two other soldiers was similar. O'Toole, Nanos and Beck tore across the road, while Hatton, Hayes and Barrabas dropped the bodies.

Now they controlled the hillside view of the paddies below. The mercs crouched behind big boulders along the edge of the road.

Barrabas scanned again with the binos.

"Twelve guards down there," he said.

"Great. That means it's two to one this time," O'Toole commented wryly. Considering the odds they were usually up against, it wasn't bad.

"We can jump six of them from along the road and take them out quietly," Barrabas moved the field glasses slowly back and forth over the field of toiling peasants. "But when we come up, we shoot if we have to. There's six guys with rifles another hundred feet down the hill. "O'Toole, check this out." Barrabas handed his second-in-command the binoculars.

O'Toole put them to his eyes and peered at the rice terraces, the guards and the workers toiling in them. Something about the workers was different.

"Some of them look Vietnamese," Barrabas said.

"Colonel, even after all those years I spent in Asia I could never tell the difference between Vietnamese and Cambodians. But some of those men down there aren't even Asians. They're Europeans or Americans."

"POWs?" It was obvious. Who the hell else would be in the mountain headquarters of a Khmer Rouge warlord in the middle of Southeast Asia.

O'Toole shrugged. "I don't imagine any of our boys would voluntarily enlist out here, Colonel."

"Okay, let's take out the guards." Barrabas pointed along the edge of the field. "Nanos, Beck. That way with O'Toole. Hayes and Hatton, you come with me. We move in on them in one minute." They checked their chronometers.

He led his two soldiers along the edge of the road and positioned them one at a time on the hill behind their targets. He took the last one, farthest up the valley.

The hand on the chronometer swept toward zero. He spun around a boulder and in three running leaps he was down the incline. He dropped six feet onto the first terrace.

Clumps of earth and gravel spilled down where his feet kicked ground. Just as Barrabas came in sight of the guard, the guard turned to see what was coming down the hills.

Barrabas. Feet first, right in the face.

The Khmer soldier bucked backward. The American landed on his haunches and bounced up. He flung himself on top of the surprised guard with his knife out. The man tried to rise. The knife plunged straight into his heart. Blood gushed over his bottom lip and down his cheeks. He looked at Barrabas and saw a white-haired demon. Barrabas saw the man's eyes register defeat. The head fell back, and the body flopped.

He yanked his knife out and wiped it on his pants before rolling off the body into the muddy rice plants. He could hear shouts coming from the bottom of the hill. The other guards had seen it. It was inevitable, but at least the odds were better now.

Barrabas snaked twenty feet through mud and water before coming up to have a look.

The two-second surveillance. Enough to see the guards

were rushing up the wooden steps that led from terrace to terrace. One was shouting orders to the others. They'd made a stupid mistake. The enemy soldiers had divided up into groups. Two and three. The one with the mouth was alone. That was the one Barrabas wanted.

He jumped up and hurled himself over the edge of the terrace onto the next one down. A 3-round burst echoed from the other end of the hill. The boys were fighting back.

Barrabas came down with his knees bent like a cat on the prowl. He looked up into the amazed eyes of a peasant woman holding a hoe. She took one look at the white-haired warrior and ran, shouting, *"Neak taa. Neak taa."* Cambodian for "Devil!"

He hopped over the next edge and then two more, bringing himself a third of the way down the hill. The workers ran in all directions from him as he bounced from terrace to terrace. The Khmer guards were still running up. At the far end of the valley, three of them were playing hide and seek in the paddies with Nanos, Beck and O'Toole. Barrabas could hear more sporadic bursts of autofire as they fought it out.

He made one last jump. He landed on his haunches and sprang up with his Commando at hip level, firing.

The Khmer Rouge commander stopped shouting orders. A 3-round burst splatted across his chest. He looked down at himself. Three big blood splotches. He looked surprised. Then he fell down dead.

Now the colonel was below the level of the other two guards who were going after Hayes and Hatton. The guards ducked in and out of cover along the terraces, hugging the earth walls for cover while firing between the SOBs and the big *B* himself. A 3-round burst made one turn and the other dead.

Lee Hatton popped up from cover, wet from the muck in the paddies. She fired from the hip. The other guard bought it.

The three SOBs headed for the other side of the valley as a final 3-round burst came from that direction.

Around them, all hell had broken loose for the poor workers. They ran with panicked screams from all over the terraced hillside toward the bottom of the valley, where they fled into a wooded canyon.

Barrabas leaped up the steps connecting the different levels until he joined Hatton and Hayes. They ran wordlessly forward around the curve of the hill and came face to face with six workers, running from the bloody action.

They stopped in their tracks and eyed the mercs. Their faces were frozen in fear. Two were Asian. Four weren't.

Barrabas spoke. "It's okay. We won't hurt you."

The workers backed up. They looked at the man who had just spoken with apprehension. Barrabas looked at them. It was the first time he was close enough to notice that something wasn't right. They all had something wrong with them. Some had skin that was red and blistered or blemished by bruises where blood vessels grew over the skin. Others had enormous lumps at their necks, or near their hips.

"Looks like a goddamn leper colony," Hayes muttered.

"Uh-uh," said Hatton. "It's something else. I'm not sure..."

Then Barrabas saw something that confirmed his first suspicion. A blond man with blue eyes and a stubbly beard had a tattoo on his arm. Barrabas strode forward and grabbed the arm to look at it. "U.S. Marine Corps, Da Nang 1971, Give 'em Hell!"

"You're American, aren't you?" Barrabas demanded. "You speak English?"

The blond man snatched his arm back and eyed the white-haired soldier with total fear. His voice was frozen with shock. The workers kept backing away from the mercenaries like frightened animals.

"We're Americans, too. It's all right. We came to take you home," the colonel said. He walked forward again.

The blond man turned and fled as fast as he could run. The others ran after him, leaving the SOBs standing alone on the terrace.

Barrabas led them up the hill to the road where O'Toole was waiting for Nanos and Beck. They paced the highway with a burn to fight. It happens when the energy gets turned on and the battle's not over.

"Up the road!" Barrabas motioned them to follow him. "Into Radam!" They jogged quickly as the road veered away from the edge of the terraced valley and into dry scrub forest. They heard a vehicle approaching. A jeep. Barrabas motioned to go for cover. They melted into the scrub forest.

The jeep roared along the road, lured by the sounds of shots that had come from the valley. Barrabas waited until it came opposite him. He nodded to Nate and Hayes. The three men pivoted out from their hiding place, Commandos blazing. On the other side of the road Hatton, Beck and O'Toole took their cue.

The jeep was caught in the middle. They sewed up the ambush with stitches of 5.56 lead. The Khmer soldiers spilled onto the road. The driver instinctively braked before he took a bullet through the head. The body slumped over the door. The jeep hit a tree and came to a stop.

Barrabas yanked open the door and the body fell out. "Get in!" he shouted. He was already at the wheel of the jeep and slamming the gears into reverse. He booted it backward as the mercs scrambled to get in. Then he rammed it into forward and stepped on the gas.

He floored it to the gates of Radam.

In the back the mercs found a machine-gun mount. It lacked the gun.

"Goddamn," O'Toole cursed. "After lugging that HK-13 halfway across Asia we finally might use it." His hands flew as he set up the machine gun on the mount and secured it. Nanos already had a mag slammed in.

The road came out of the scrub forest and back onto the rim of the hill. The low thatched buildings and the plume of the waterfall that made up the town of Radam grew larger. Half a klik off they saw a bridge over the narrow river. And some buddies of the guys who had just left in the jeep.

They were probably wondering why their friends were coming back so soon. They stopped wondering when O'Toole opened up on the HK-13. Then they knew. The jeep had changed hands. These weren't friends. But by then it was too late.

The hot 5.56 took a one-second trip from the jeep to the other side of the bridge. The guards were in the way. One by one they caught lead, spun, danced and jerked to the ground.

The bridge was clear.

The jeep roared over it and into the village. More opposition ran from a compound of white stucco buildings directly ahead. With Nanos feeding and Liam O'Toole aiming, the HK-13 came back to life.

This time there were enough Khmer to fire back. Bullets pounded into the metal body of the jeep. But there weren't too many for the HK-13 to take care of. Four more Khmer guards sprawled backward onto the ground. Barrabas braked the jeep sharply, and it lurched to a halt outside the gates of the compound.

The mercs piled out. Barrabas was there first, swinging around from the protection of the wall to pour a stream of hot lead through the open gate. Nanos ran from the jeep, firing from the hip. The two men caught a couple of Khmer guards in the courtyard. Their bodies flopped onto the ground. Nanos heard the sound of running feet behind him. He turned to see a Khmer coming out a doorway. The enemy soldier raised a submachine gun. He was dead serious.

Bam! Now he was seriously dead.

The mercs split off in different directions to search the

buildings in the compound, with O'Toole and Hayes outside in case of rear-guard trouble. The complex echoed with the sounds of shattered doors.

No one was there. A minute later they were back in the courtyard. It was too much to believe. Kon had evaded them again.

O'Toole came through the gates. "Captain, you gotta come outside and talk to this guy."

Barrabas went outside. Standing on the road near the jeep was the blond American he'd encountered in the rice paddy. The man seemed to shrink from the colonel's look. He bowed his head and wrung his hands nervously.

"Who are you?" Barrabas demanded.

The man looked up, then averted his glance again. He spoke, but his voice trembled with nervousness. "I'm an American."

"Why are you here?"

"We work for Kon. Kon brought us here."

"Are you prisoners?"

The man nodded.

"Prisoners of war? From Vietnam?"

Again the man nodded wordlessly.

"It's incredible," said O'Toole under his breath. "This guy's one of the missing POWs."

Barrabas nodded. "Yeah." Then he turned to the blond man again. "How many of you are there?"

The man looked unsure for a minute, as if he was counting. Then he said, "There were ten. Three are dead. Cancer. And our leader is missing. He's...he was taken prisoner. Kon was going to execute him yesterday morning."

"He's not in there," Barrabas said, motioning toward the compound. "We just looked. No one's in there."

The blond man looked down as if searching for words. Barrabas eyed him carefully, noting the ugly blisters and sores that covered much of the man's body. The man had been a prisoner in the Cambodian hills for years, and the

SOBs were the first contact he'd had with his past in all that time. No wonder he was so cowed by their presence.

From underneath the houses strung along the river, other people began to come forward, their faces reflecting both curiosity and fear of the strangers in their midst. Many were Asian. Some were Americans. No one spoke.

The women carried their children. Barrabas's face tightened. It was painful to see. So many of them had pathetic stumps for arms, strange rashes that covered their bodies, open cavities on their faces. What the hell was going on here? Radam was a village of monsters.

"Who are you? All of you?" Barrabas asked.

"Kon brought us here," the blond man told him. "Because. . .it's supposed to be Agent Orange that did it. Even Kon. His daughter was deformed. He made this village for her so she wouldn't be alone."

Kon's madness began to come into focus. The warlord had been poisoned. Now he was going to do it to everyone. It fit with everything the colonel knew about the Khmer general.

"Can you help us? We must find Kon. Do you know where he is?"

"He left last night. The guards told me he went to Praach, a town on Tonle Sap, the Great Lake."

Barrabas walked to the jeep. "Let's go!" he yelled at the mercs. He dropped his rifle into the front seat when Nate Beck spoke up.

"Colonel, this jeep's not going anywhere." He pointed at the radiator. The front was chewed up by bullet holes and three neat streams of water trickled onto the ground.

Barrabas swore. He turned back to the blond man. "We need transportation. We need a truck, a jeep, anything."

"Yes, yes," the American prisoner said. "Come with me. I'll show you."

They set off quickly past the compound and down a narrow lane between some of the thatched houses. At the end of the village another compound was surrounded by a fence of woven bamboo. Inside were a half-dozen bright, shiny, expensive sports cars.

"Kon. He likes these." The blond man opened the gate and let the mercs walk in. "They're his loot, from the cities. They're all in top condition and ready to drive. I'm the mechanic." He smiled proudly.

"Which ones?" Barrabas asked.

"The Trans Am and the Porsche are the fastest." A black Trans Am with red racing stripes and a blue Porsche stood side by side.

"O'Toole, get the machine gun and the mount out of the jeep on the double. Nanos, give him a hand." Barrabas looked at the blond American. "Do you have something we can use to knock holes in the roof?"

"That's the machine shop there." He ran under an open shelter on one side of the yard. Barrabas followed him and came back carrying eight-inch spikes and a steel mallet just as O'Toole and Nanos brought back the machine gun and mount. Barrabas climbed onto the roof of the Trans Am, positioned a spike and drove a hole into the roof. "Beck, Hayes, smash the back windows on both cars and get the glass out. Unless you wanna sit on it."

Beck looked a little confused. "Move it, Nate!" the colonel commanded.

A few minutes later the back windows were gone and the HK-13 was mounted on a bipod bolted to the dented roof of the Trans Am.

Barrabas and O'Toole tightened the last nuts around the thick bolt that held it in place.

"Incredible," Beck commented. "If anyone told me I was going to see a Trans Am with a machine gun bolted to the roof and the gunner sitting in the back window, I wouldn't have believed it."

"Seems a shame to wreck a beautiful car like this," said Nanos.

Lee Hatton laughed. "Uh-uh. This is a once-in-a-lifetime experience."

Barrabas climbed down from the roof of the car "Hayes, you drive the Porsche. O'Toole and Hatton g₀ with him. Beck and Nanos you're in the Trans Am." H₂ started to climb into the driver's seat when he remembere₀ the ex-Marine who stood patiently to one side.

"We'll come back for you. I promise."

The man was startled. He looked at Barrabas and shoo₂ his head emphatically. "No," he said. "No, please..." Then he turned and ran away.

Barrabas jumped back into the front seat of the Tran Am and slammed the door. "We'll come back. Let's g₀ the hell out of here and settle with Kon."

19

When Kon had finished in the village, the village was done for. It was a slaughter ground. Torchlight flickered across piles of butchered bodies.

"Burn them," the warlord snarled. He walked to the Mercedes.

Several hours later, in the middle of the night, the convoy arrived at the fishing town of Praach. Like every other urban center in Khmer Rouge-occupied Cambodia, Praach was empty.

Curled up in the trunk, his body aching and weak with hunger, Scott listened carefully. The Mercedes came to a final halt.

He heard Kon tell the soldiers to have the steel drum carried to the boat and ready for him first thing in the morning. Then the warlord walked off to retire for the night.

Scott tensed, waiting for the sound of a key in the lock.

Instead, the noises outside died down. Soldiers took up guard positions around the town or turned in. Scott twisted the nail file in the lock. It occurred to him that he could write a book about a hundred one uses for nail clippers, and then he found himself laughing softly at the absurdity of the thought. It was a genuine laugh, though. For the first time in years he felt he was alive.

The lid came up. It was dark outside. He peered through the opening. No one was about. He slipped out and crouched behind the rear bumper. He could hear the sounds of soldiers playing some kind of dice game in the back of a truck up the street.

The convoy had come to stop along the waterfront

where a long pier jutted out into Tonle Sap. He could make out the silhouette of a gunboat. The stars in the night sky were reflected in the wide waters of the enormous lake. French colonial buildings four stories high lined the wide street that ran along the shore. Lights came from one where the facade was draped with a huge Khmer Rouge flag. Kon was in there.

He made out guards along the waterfront. Otherwise the street was deserted. Very quietly, Scott opened the trunk of the Mercedes. He grabbed the lip of the steel drum and rolled it toward him, cringing at the noise it made. He tried to lift it from the trunk. It was heavy. He gritted his teeth and tried again. He remembered the old rule from weight lifting sessions, breathe out and blow the weight up. He expelled a deep lungful of air and tried again. His arms began shaking, first one, then the other. He couldn't do it. His strength failed him. His nervous system destroyed by the effects of Agent Orange, he could not get the metal drum out of the trunk.

Scott closed the lid quietly and slipped across the nearby sidewalk into the doorway of a building where the shadow hid him. Just in time. A guard strolled casually along the sidewalk, not noticing him. Scott tried to figure out another way. He was too close to it now to give up.

The barrel of chemical was to be put aboard the gunboat first thing in the morning. Scott guessed that Kon would order the boat to drive into the lake, open up the barrel and spill its contents. There was only one thing he could do.

Kill Kon. Kill the warlord as he walked along the pier the next morning. To do that, he needed a rifle.

The sounds from the gambling party became a little more raucous. The off-duty soldiers were drinking the foul but potent palm beer favored by Cambodian peasants. Scott stood in the doorway and waited.

An hour later a soldier left the party in the truck and lurched along the sidewalk. He hiccuped drunkenly. Scott figured out one more use for his nail clippers.

He took a deep breath and jumped. He swung his arms quickly around the soldier's neck and plunged the two-inch-long file into the man's throat. Blood and air gurgled noisily out. Scott clamped his other hand over his enemy's mouth, pulled the nail clippers out and stabbed again. He stabbed repeatedly, while dragging the man back into the doorway. Blood began to spurt from the soldier's neck and ran down Scott's arm. Finally, after what seemed like an eternity, the man's body went limp.

Scott opened the door to the building and dragged the body in. Exhausted, he dropped it onto the floor. The dead man's automatic rifle, which he wore slung over his back, clunked heavily.

Scott turned the body and slipped the weapon off. It was an M-16. The mag was full. He searched the man's clothing. He found a Hershey bar. Something else he hadn't seen in years. He ate it slowly, savoring the flavor, the nourishment and felt the sugar energy revive him.

He rolled the body out of sight into a nearby corridor and climbed the stairs, M-16 in hand, to wait until morning.

SLEEP TORMENTED General Kon. When he closed his eyes he dreamed he was being pursued by an unknown monster. He ran and ran and still this creature was behind him. The horror was that while Kon ran as fast as he could, he knew the creature was merely loping along at a comfortable gait, tiring his quarry, playing with him, waiting for the whim to make a final strike at his exhausted victim. Kon opened his eyes in terror and found himself breathing hard, as if he had just run an enormous distance at full speed. His heart pounded in his chest. The monster was a tiger with teeth and claws and glowing yellow eyes and white hair.

He propped himself up in bed and watched the sky lighten and the sun come up. At ten o'clock his guards came to his room. They reported that all was ready.

THE HOT YELLOW SUN woke John Scott with a start. He ha*
fallen asleep against the sill of a fourth-floor window
which gave him a clear view of the pier and the gunboat
He'd overslept. By the sun it must be at least ten o'clock.

He peered out over the street. The soldiers were rolling
the metal drum up the pier. For the first time, he notice*
there was a speed launch moored near the gunboat. Ko*
was watching the pier from outside the headquarters. Hi*
little daughter stood beside him, her body bent and th*
tumorous face lumpy and horrible. They watched the pro
gress of the drum as the soldiers lifted it onto the gunboa*
and rolled it toward the stern. A soldier waited there with
wrench in one hand, ready to open the drum. Scott slippe*
the M-16 on to full automatic.

Kon walked to the dock, the little girl running alon*
beside him. Scott drew a line on the warlord's body. H*
hands were steady. He prayed that they remain so.

Kon began the long walk up the pier.

Scott's fingers tightened on the trigger.

As HE LEFT the building and strolled across the street, h*
daughter beside him, Kon could not shake a feeling th*
something unpleasant was about to happen.

He looked around. Everything seemed to be as it shoul*
The sky was blue, the sun yellow, his soldiers stood *
attention along the street and down the pier. The met*
drum sat on the deck of the gunboat, and a soldier leane*
over it with a wrench in hand. He felt a steel shiver ripp*
up and down his back.

He looked north along the lake where the highway led t*
the mountains. Clouds of dust blew along it. Somethin*
was traveling their way at incredible speed.

"Wait," he cried to the soldiers undoing the met*
drum. He turned to his lieutenant. "Give me your binoc*
lars."

The general put the field glasses to his eyes and focuse*
them out along the dust clouds on the distant highway.

could not be! Two of his own cars hurtled toward the town. The black Trans Am had a machine gun mounted on top. He thought he was still dreaming.

Spellbound, he could not take his eyes off them. The two vehicles turned from the highway to the road that led into the town and along the shore to the pier. Finally Kon realized he had to act. He pulled the glasses away and shouted orders at the men in the gunboat. "Man the machine gun. We are under attack." Immediately the soldiers pulled away the canvas cover from the big MG mounted on a tripod on the deck of the gunboat. The gunner swiveled the barrel around toward the approaching cars. The street along the pier turned into bedlam as soldiers rushed for cover.

"To your positions," Kon shouted. "Stop those cars."

THE TRIGGER ON SCOTT'S M-16 was a hairline from firing when the warlord grabbed the binoculars from the soldier behind him. Scott looked to the north. He, too, could see the clouds of dust blowing from the rush of the oncoming cars. Their speed of travel quickly brought them into focus. He couldn't believe his eyes. They were Kon's cars. And the Trans Am had a machine gun mounted on the roof. A soldier sat where the back window should be, pivoting the barrel.

The Porsche had some guy sticking out the back, too, with an automatic rifle up over the roof. Other rifles were sticking out the side windows of both cars.

The guns opened up as the cars screeched off the highway toward the town. It wasn't a bon voyage party.

The black-uniformed Khmer soldiers along the pier fell like mechanical ducks in the rifle shoot at the midway. Other soldiers scrambled from the pier and ran for the cover of trucks. Scott aimed for the Cambodian warlord again. Kon had grabbed his daughter. He ran for the speed launch tied up beside the gunboat. Scott sighted. His hands trembled slightly. "Damn," he cursed. "Please don't fail

me now.'' Then he saw the barrel of the machine gun piv‹
around toward the Trans Am.

The two cars were circling. The Porsche poured fired
the enemy soldiers on the sidewalks behind the cover of t‹
trucks. The Trans Am was busy with a knot of soldie‹
behind a pile of crates at the foot of the pier.

The machine gun swung around until it was center‹
dead on the back of the car. Whoever was down the‹
hadn't noticed the MG. Scott swerved his M-16 away fro‹
Kon and aimed for the machine gun. His hands we‹
steady again. He squeezed the trigger.

IT WAS A THREE-HOUR DRIVE to Tonle Sap by the faste‹
possible means. Barrabas did it in two. The cars stopp‹
only once, at the smoldering ruins of a peasant villa‹
where charred corpses littered the highway. Barrab‹
surveyed the carnage. The colonel knew the warlord‹
madness well enough now to read the bloody message l‹
with the burned bodies. It was more than slaughter. It w‹
a warning. The radio operator in Kiri had got the wo‹
out. Kon knew Barrabas was closing in. This savagery w‹
an acknowledgment of Kon's impending defeat.

Finally the sun burned onto the expansive lake with‹
blinding silver reflection, and the buildings of the fishi‹
town came into view. Barrabas kept the accelerator of t‹
Trans Am floored, and it zipped down the long flat hig‹
way at a hundred seventy. The Porsche kept up.

He started to slow a little as a turnoff approached. F‹
could see the town, the pier leading out into the lak‹
soldiers moving and the gunboat at anchor. He hoped th‹
weren't too late to stop the warlord's chemical war again‹
planet Earth.

The only strategy he had in mind was to roar into tow‹
at full speed and shoot the shit out of everything th‹
moved.

''Nanos, get ready to feed Beck some bullets. We're g‹
ing in there now, and we aren't slowing down.'' He veer‹

he car off onto the Praach turnoff. The road led straight
along the lakefront to the pier. The Trans Am's tires
screamed but held the curve. Nanos scrambled over the
seat and out the back window, pulling a belt of mags with
him. Barrabas crossed his left hand under the right one on
the steering wheel and grabbed his Commando. He pulled
it up and held it out the window with one hand itching on
the trigger.

They were a half mile away. On top of the car the
machine gun opened up. The vibrations shook the Trans
Am. A row of Khmer soldiers along the pier went down
like tenpins and splashed into the water.

The scene had turned into madness. Black-uniformed
soldiers ran helter-skelter across the road and the pier
looking for shelter.

There was no shelter from Barrabas's storm.

The colonel aimed his gun up and fired full-auto at a
group of Khmers who rushed from a building. They caught
lead and fell back inside.

He heard the roar of the Porsche as Hayes floored it and
passed, burning down the road past the pier. Hatton
leaned from a side window and O'Toole stuck out the
back. They blew mags off into the soldiers along the street.

Barrabas heard a hard knock on the Trans Am's side
panels as bullets dug through the passenger door and
chewed into the seat. He braked. He saw the autofire coming from some soldiers hidden behind a pile of crates on
the pier. The car screeched as it fishtailed and fanned
around in a circle.

He dropped his gun and put both hands back on the
wheel, straightening it just as the vehicle passed the pier.
Now Beck and Nanos had a clear shot behind the crates.
At the same time, Barrabas saw the Porsche turn and chew
its way up the sidewalk, spitting bullets at the soldiers who
ran behind the trucks for cover.

There was no cover. There was no retreat.

The Trans Am shook as the machine gun fired, and one

of the bolts tore through the roof. The Khmers behind th
crates turned to fire from their exposed positions. The
didn't make it.

Dance boys.

The HK-13 spat its last bullets.

They twitched and jerked and dropped dead.

The Trans Am slid to a stop. Barrabas opened his doo
and grabbed his rifle. He propelled himself from the ca
just as the windshield exploded into spiderwebs.

He rolled onto the ground and came up. Then he saw th
machine gun on the boat. The gunner was firing at Nan(
and Beck at the back of the Trans Am. And he wasn't g(
ing to miss.

Barrabas came up firing the autorifle, but the gunn(
wasn't exposed. Death for the boys was certain.

Suddenly the gunner flew back and the machine-gu
barrel swiveled free on its mount.

Barrabas wondered who killed the guy, but there wasn
time to figure that out. A speed launch tore away from th
side of the pier. In the back was a man in a black uniform
Another Khmer drove. Barrabas knew without asking. I
had to be Kon. Getting away. Again.

He emptied the mag in his Commando across the lak(
jammed another one in and fired again. Bullets poppe
along the water.

The speedboat was out of range. Kon had eluded cap
ture once again. Barrabas stood at the edge of the pi(
watching the boat disappear. He couldn't believe it.

"Colonel, thanks for taking out that machine gun on th
boat." It was Beck walking up behind him. The battle wa
over. Barrabas turned.

Nanos was smiling. "They just about got the two of u
if you hadn't got them first."

"I didn't get them." The two soldiers looked surprise(
Hatton and O'Toole ran up and Hayes sauntered slowl
across the street behind them.

"Kon?" said Hatton first. "Is he...?"

"Got away," said Barrabas. His voice was cold with rage. He snapped himself out of it. "Did you get the machine gunner?"

"What machine gunner?" said O'Toole. He looked over at the gunboat and saw the idle MG. "Didn't even notice it, sir. We were too busy on the other side of the street."

Barrabas looked at his soldiers, then back at the machine gun. He flicked his eyes across the buildings that lined the street. He pulled out a cigar and started to unwrap it. "Well, someone shot him," he said slowly.

He stuck the cigar in his mouth, bit off the end, spat it out and pulled a match.

The mercs looked at one another, then back at the colonel. Hayes shrugged. "I dunno, Colonel."

Barrabas lit the cigar and blew out a mouthful of smoke. "Maybe it was him," he said, looking past them. The soldiers turned.

A tall American with long dark hair walked slowly from the entrance of a building. He carried an M-16 in one hand. Something was wrong with his face.

The man raised his hand and smiled. "Hi!" he said nervously. "I'm Scott. John Scott. I'm an American."

Barrabas walked past the mercs and eyed the strange-looking man.

Scott saw the man with the white hair standing tall in front of him. He stopped. They looked each other in the eye. "Barrabas?" Scott said, his voice filled with disbelief.

Barrabas nodded.

Scott walked forward, slowly at first, then covered the remaining distance quickly. His lips formed the name "Barrabas" again, but no sound emerged, until he stood in front of the white-haired warrior. "Colonel Nile Barrabas, 5th Special Forces Company C?"

Barrabas nodded again, and smiled at the missing soldier.

Scott saluted weakly. "Captain John Scott reporting, sir." Then he collapsed.

Barrabas caught him before he fell, and the two men embraced each other. Scott wept. The colonel held him for a minute. "Come on, let's sit," he said quietly, helping the man over to the seat of the Trans Am. "Lee," he called to the company doctor. "Check this guy out."

SCOTT WAS ALL RIGHT. Hatton looked him over quickly, gave him a small injection of adrenaline and some energy concentrates to eat.

He told them his story, and the story of Radam.

"It's pretty crazy of me, blubbering like a baby about all this. It's just that...you're the first Americans from the outside I've seen since Ban Do River. And I didn't think I could stop Kon. I had to try, but I didn't have much to work with."

"You saved the lives of a couple of my men," said Barrabas.

"But you stopped the warlord."

"What do you mean, we stopped him? Kon got away."

Scott nodded. "But you stopped him from pouring the chemical poison into the lake."

Barrabas gave him a questioning look.

"That's it," Scott said, pointing to the metal drum on the deck of the gunboat. "That's the chemical defoliant. I was going to try to kill Kon from up there before he dumped it over. You got here just in time."

"Goddamn," Barrabas said under his breath. "You mean that twenty-gallon barrel on the deck is what we're after?"

Scott nodded. "I'm pretty sure. He had a small vial of the stuff, too. It's a blue liquid. He showed me. I was supposed to be executed with it. Apparently a very small drop will kill a man."

"Well, let's just take the barrel with us," Lee said. "I don't want any of you guys opening it up to have a look. Leave that to the guys in the lab."

"Sounds good to me," O'Toole said with a nod. "Pity

we didn't get the warlord himself. That's a score we still have to settle."

"At least we stopped his current mad plot," said Barrabas. "We have to exfiltrate real soon, though."

"How," Scott asked. "If you parachuted in?"

"We set up an exfiltration rendezvous with some people smuggling treasures out of Angkor Wat. I want you to come, too—" His words broke off. He and Scott shared a look of understanding and horror.

"Kon," said Scott.

"That's where he's gone. Angkor Wat. He knows today's the last shipment. He's gone to use our exfiltration."

Everyone understood the unspoken message. Erika Dykstra and Geoff Bishop were going to be sitting ducks unless the SOBs got there first.

20

On a landing field two miles east of the ruins of Angkor Wat, Erika watched the Cambodian laborers hoist another crate of artifacts aboard the twin-prop airplane. It was already noon. The sun was relentless, and the humidity from the surrounding jungle oozed through the air.

"Raoul," she said to the Frenchman beside her, "it's too hot to work anymore. Let's wait for a few hours before we load the rest of the shipment."

"But, Madame Dykstra, I advise you earnestly. It is better for us to be gone. Every moment here is a moment of danger," Raoul replied.

He meant what he said, but Erika's problem was to delay departure until the SOBs arrived. She also wanted as few things loaded aboard the airplane as possible. The added weight of six big mercs was something Raoul didn't know about yet.

"Well, let's go back to the site of the ruins. I'm not sure I want all the things that your benefactor has picked out. I'm more interested in some carvings and statuary from the Temple of Ta Prohm."

Raoul mopped his forehead with his scented handkerchief. He could not conceal his exasperation with Erika. "But *madame*, I don't understand why you didn't decide this before you arrived."

"Raoul, the English have a saying that I once learned. He who pays the piper calls the tune."

Raoul nodded reluctantly. He understood.

As they walked across the landing field toward the car,

Erika realized she had to think of another delaying tactic, and fast.

Geoff Bishop had flown Erika and Raoul in four hours earlier. Their welcoming party at the landing strip was a company of Khmer Rouge soldiers. All of them were heavily armed, and extremely brusque and unpleasant. The atmosphere of danger was tangible. These men could go off at the slightest provocation. Raoul was not exaggerating.

Immediately on landing, they traveled to the site of the ruins. Angkor Wat was breathtaking in its splendor. The ancient temples, still largely intact after a thousand years lost in the jungle, stretched on, seemingly forever. This had once been the capital of the wealthy Khmer empire, and succeeding generations of emperors had built the intricately carved temples with high conical domes that were like man-made mountains. They were surrounded by long rows of ornate columns and balustrades and mile-long walks lined with statues of Khmer warriors or friezes of dancing maidens. Erika beheld the wonder for the first time with awe. Then it was down to work.

She examined the damage done by the removal of the artifacts already in the warehouse in Bangkok. The plundering of the ancient city was a tragedy, but not irreparable. Someday she would return what she had bought, and the city could be restored. Then she began to supervise the final selection of artifacts, their packing and shipping to the airfield. She took her time, trying to appear as indecisive as possible. But she could only procrastinate so long. Finally Raoul insisted they load the first shipment. They returned to the airfield. Bishop stayed at the temple to supervise the rest of the packing.

Now, as Erika and Raoul walked to the car again, a Khmer Rouge army jeep drove into the airfield and circled around until it stopped by the two Europeans. A messenger in the sinister black uniform of Kon's soldiers jumped out.

"The warlord Kon awaits you at the Great Causeway of the temple of Angkor Wat," he announced. Raoul and Erika exchanged looks. They hadn't expected this. It immediately occurred to Erika that it would hold them up. But she wasn't sure if it was exactly the delaying tactic she had had in mind. Then it struck her. If Kon was here in Angkor Wat, where were Nile Barrabas and the SOBs?

"Say nothing," Raoul told her as they climbed into the jeep. "Nothing at all. I will say everything. This Kon..." The Frenchman rolled his eyes and twirled his hand at the temple a few times in the universal sign for "he's nuts."

Ten minutes later the jeep deposited them before the stone causeway that led across the dried-up moat that had once reflected the facade of the magnificent temple. A warm breeze played in Erika's long blond hair as she gazed across at the ancient splendor.

Angkor Wat was the largest temple ever built in the history of man, bigger than the pyramids of Egypt. It had six miles of carved steps along the moat, ten thousand pinnacles rising up to the elaborately carved five-peaked domes and thousands of life-size carvings along the walls.

Erika and Raoul walked to the stone causeway that led across the six-hundred-foot-wide moat. At the end, under the great conical stone towers, which rose behind the outer wall, stood a tall Cambodian in a black uniform. On one side stood a little girl. On the other side was another Khmer soldier.

"That's General Kon," whispered Raoul to Erika. They began to cross the causeway. "The one in the middle with his hands behind his back."

"Where's Bishop?" Erika whispered back. "He's supposed to be here."

Raoul shrugged. Erika sensed something behind her. She looked back. Half a dozen Khmer soldiers walked behind them. They had rifles, and the rifles were pointed at their backs.

The warlord watched them as they approached. His face

showed no emotion. His eyes were cold, his lips set in a rigid line of cruelty. Erika shivered. He looked evil. He looked mad.

The little girl beside the general also watched. Dark eyes glinted beadily in the hideous face.

When they were three meters away, the warlord suddenly beamed and extended his arms. "Welcome to Angkor, the ancient city of the Naga Kings," he said smoothly.

Raoul bowed. "Allow me to introduce Madame Dykstra, a businesswoman who has purchased the artifacts that you have supplied."

Kon inclined his head graciously. "And allow me to present my daughter." Erika averted her eyes from the ugliness. There was something chilling about the child that had nothing to do with her face.

"Is this your own business venture, Madame Dykstra, or do you work with others?" Kon asked.

Raoul answered quickly. "Madame Dykstra has a partner. He was unable to come, sadly. A change of plans at the last minute."

Kon looked at Raoul attentively. "And who might that be?"

Again Raoul jumped in before Erika could say a word. "Monsieur Barrabas. Nile Barrabas. A wonderful man. You must meet him."

"Nile Barrabas," Kon mused. He began to pace. "And what were his change of plans?" He looked at them. "Would it have been a secret mission to Cambodia? An attack on the city of Kiri? Would he have come in pursuit of me, Madame Dykstra?"

Erika froze. Raoul looked at her, his eyes both puzzled and fearful. Kon continued pacing and talking.

"And is this not merely a setup, Madame Dykstra, this venture to Angkor Wat? Is it not really intended as a rendezvous to take Nile Barrabas and his soldiers out of Cambodia?"

"B-b-but I knew nothing. . ." Raoul sputtered.

"Shut up!" Kon shouted at him. "Yes, Barrabas wil
rendezvous here. I will be waiting for him. He will hav
quite a surprise won't he, Madame Dykstra." Kon spok
to the soldier behind him. "You may round up all th
workers now and kill them. I have instructed you on wha
to do with the bodies."

Suddenly the little girl raised her arm and pointed ;
finger at Erika. "Kill her, Daddy. She thinks I am ugly.
know she does."

Erika refused to look at the child.

"All in good time, my little darling," Kon assured hi
daughter.

"Kill her with this!" The child held up the vial of blu
liquid. It was all Kon had left of the chemical poison h
had had made. It was enough to kill a thousand people.

"Yes, my dear," the warlord said. "We will."

BISHOP SUPERVISED THE PACKING of the last crates in th
inner courtyard of the great temple. The job done, h
waited for Erika's return. He was edgy and restless. Whil
the colonel took the SOBs into the jungle to fight, he ha
to wait in Bangkok for the exfiltration rendezvous. H
knew his skills as a pilot were extraordinary. Otherwise h
wouldn't be on the team. It was ironic, then, that it wa
those same skills that disqualified him from the fight. The
needed him to fly them out later and that was that. But h
knew what else was bugging him. Lee Hatton. She was ou
there.

He watched the morning light play over the exquisit
walls of the ruined temple. He decided to look around.

Angkor Wat was merely the largest among a complex o
many temples that had once formed a city. He saw th
craggy domes of another temple rising over the treetops ;
short distance away. He crossed the road and found a pat
through the forest. He had barely started along it when h
smelled a thick musky odor blowing downwind. He hur
ried along the path and came to the steps of the temple. H

climbed it, scrambling over some carvings where the steps had crumbled with age, until he stood on a stone terrace above the trees. He could see the road, the forest and the great temple of Angkor spread out below him.

And something else at the foot of the temple.

Two tigers walked together out of the forest. Their powerful feline bodies were long and husky, the fur thick and richly colored. Well fed, thought Bishop. The two cats prowled and sniffed until they caught Bishop's scent. They followed it to the temple, where they looked at him greedily. They lay down and waited.

There was no way they could climb up after him. But in the meantime, Bishop had to stay put and outwait them.

A few minutes later he saw the jeep carrying Erika and Raoul to the main causeway of Angkor Wat. He watched them cross the great moat and talk to the black-uniformed soldiers who had appeared at the entrance to the temple.

Suddenly he caught his breath. Something was wrong there. Some of the soldiers had grabbed Erika and Raoul and were tying their hands. Bishop wore his Canadian-made Browning in a holster at his side. He looked down. He didn't want to, but he'd kill the cats if necessary to get away. The tigers jumped up and listened for something in the jungle. Then they ran off with graceful feline leaps into the underbrush.

Bishop scrambled back down the temple and ran along the path toward the main road. He was still downwind from the direction in which the tigers had gone. But he kept his gun ready.

As the forest thinned, he heard harsh voices coming from the road. He stopped and stepped behind a huge blanched root of a silk-cotton tree. Khmer soldiers had rounded up the workers who had packed the crates in the temple.

The workers stood in a tight group. The soldiers around them aimed their submachine guns and opened fire. The workers fell amid screams of death and chattering bullets.

Silence returned when the bodies lay in a pile, peppered re[...]
with holes.

The worst was yet to come. The Khmer soldiers bega[...]
picking up the bodies and throwing them into the back of [...]
nearby truck. Except for one.

The last body was held up against a tree. A soldier with [...]
mallet drove a long iron spike into the neck of the corpse[...]
pinning it to the trunk. The soldiers got into the truck an[...]
drove down the main road toward the airfield.

The body hung on the tree, a gruesome signpost.

Before he could move, Bishop heard a low blood[...]
curdling growl. The two tigers burst from the undergrowt[...]
onto the road. One grabbed for the body and ripped [...]
down. It held the corpse by one shoulder between its grea[...]
teeth. The other tiger growled angrily and pawed for th[...]
body. The first dropped the body and roared back. Th[...]
two cats fought for it, tearing it limb from limb and ru[...]
ning back into the forest with the pieces. Only a trail thi[...]
with blood remained behind.

Bishop wrapped his hand around the reassuring steel [...]
the Browning. He ran past the carnage and across the roa[...]
into the forest on the other side. He headed for the mai[...]
causeway where Erika and Raoul were prisoners.

WITH THE AFTERNOON SUN HANGING at four o'clock, th[...]
dust of the Cambodian plains, blown up by the hot dr[...]
winds coming out of the northwest, turned the sky grayis[...]
yellow. The Trans Am and the Porsche sped down th[...]
highway that followed the shores of Tonle Sap before tur[...]
ing inland for the city of Siemreap. Angkor Wat was only [...]
few miles away where the jungle began again. Soon the[...]
could make out the tips of stone towers poking above th[...]
tree line. On the other side of the highway a twin-prop a[...]
plane waited in a long field lined by hangars and sheds.

Nanos drove the Trans Am now, and Captain Scott ro[...]
'n the back with Beck. Barrabas looked at the airfield [...]
*y approached with his binoculars. He saw soldiers b[...]

no sign of Erika, Bishop, Raoul or Kon. It didn't look good.

"Fly by the guard post," Barrabas instructed Nanos. He shoved a Mecar rifle grenade onto his Commando and handed one back to Beck who sat in the open back window. Khmer soldiers were running for the gates along the road.

Barrabas steadied the rifle by leaning hard against the door. The grid was useless for aiming in the moving car. He waited until they were within three hundred meters. He felt his finger on the trigger a razor's edge from death. The enemy soldiers went down on one knee with their rifles up.

He fired. The grenade landed just behind the line of soldiers at the gate. On impact the grenade blew its metal fragments in a hundred-foot circle. The soldiers in front were hurled forward into the road. The Trans Am was headed straight for them. It was too late to stop now.

Two heavy clunks and a couple of wild bumps rocked the car as the wheels flew over the bodies. Beck fired his grenade from the back window just as the car was opposite the gate.

Right in the faces of the next line of Khmer Rouge.

It blew them backward, cleaning out the area. Nanos brought the Trans Am to a screeching halt and dug up the road by ramming the car into reverse and whipping it around so it faced back the way it had come. The Porsche had reached the gate. Hayes was at the wheel. He veered sharply with a right turn at the entrance of the airfield, bouncing over the bodies that had caught grenade disease.

A couple of soldiers, covered with blood from their shrapnel wounds, had pulled themselves up from the dirt. The Porsche didn't stop. One dived out of the way with a scream of panic. The other flew into the air like a pop fly.

Hayes turned again, pulling the car to the right so it traveled beside the buildings on one side of the field. Hatton and O'Toole started firing from the windows. Soldiers

who rushed from the buildings to get the car got aut
bullets instead.

At the gate, the second Khmer soldier had just picke
himself up from the dirt again when Nanos vroomed th
Trans Am back and veered inside. He didn't stop, eithe
Thud! Out of the ball park.

The Trans Am ripped across the field and circled th
airplane. It was deserted. It whipped back to the hanga
where the blue Porsche had just finished its tour of duty
The shooting had stopped. A few soldiers fled toward th
jungle across the highway. The two cars circled, until the
drove parallel to each other, kicking up long lines of du
across the field.

Barrabas pulled himself up from the seat and sat on th
window, holding on to the roof.

"Where now?" Hayes shouted across from the driver
seat of the Porsche.

"The temples!" Barrabas shouted back over the high
revved roar of the car engines as massive clouds of du
spilled up from the wheels.

"Which way do we go?"

"Follow us!" the colonel yelled. He dropped back insi
the car.

"Which way do we go, sir?" Nanos asked as he steere
the car back over the bodies littered around the front gate
They were flatter every time.

"Hell if I know. Just drive."

Nanos turned back onto the highway and floored it. T
Trans Am shot down the road, picking up speed.

"There!" shouted Barrabas. Nanos saw it, too. T
route had been marked.

The Greek braked. Barrabas clutched the dashboard
prevent a transwindshield takeoff. An ear-wrenching ti
scream brought the car to a halt. Nanos backed it u
the gear whining as he floored the accelerator merciles

'e braked again and brought the car to half a foot fro

the front bumper of the Porsche, which was waiting at the turnoff.

"This is the way," said Barrabas. "Jesus Christ." The bullet-ridden body of a Cambodian worker was impaled on spikes hammered into a tree. The corpse's right arm was nailed in such a position that it pointed down the road.

Nanos turned and the two cars soared down the road. It led through the jungle where clearings on both sides opened into complexes of stone temples that belonged to the ruined city.

Every tenth mile another nailed-up corpse pointed. Barrabas scanned the road ahead with his binoculars.

"Slow down, there's something coming up," he told Nanos. The Greek geared down. The road ahead, near a turnoff, was covered with blood and bits of a dismembered corpse.

"Brake," the colonel ordered. Nanos brought the car to a halt at the turnoff. Beyond the trees on the right, the high stone towers of Angkor Wat turned a rich golden yellow in the late-afternoon sunlight.

"Turn here!"

Nanos turned right and drove the Trans Am along a dirt road that led through the trees. The Porsche followed closely behind. The jungle broke in an immense clearing.

Straight ahead of them, with all its magnificent symmetry of towers, steps, columns and the great stone gates, lay the temple of Angkor Wat.

The long causeway led a tenth of a mile across the dry moat. At the end, under the high stone gates that marked the entrance to the courtyards of the temple, stood their opponent. General Kon. The Cambodian warlord was defiant, his arms folded across his chest. To one side, gagged and bound on the stones of the causeway were his hostages—Erika and Raoul.

"There are no soldiers around," said Nanos.

"He doesn't need any," Barrabas answered. "Not with those hostages."

The colonel got out of the Trans Am. The other merc:
followed. They faced General Kon across the causeway. A
deathly silence lay over them. Only their heavy breathing
broke it.

"Let's go," Barrabas said, turning to his soldiers and
John Scott. He started walking up the long causeway, car
rying his Commando carefully in front of him.

He stopped three meters from the warlord. His eyes me
Erika's and locked briefly. She was all right. Frightened
but not hurt. So far.

"Finally we meet, Barrabas," the warlord said. Hi
voice was smug with satisfaction. "Permit me to introduce
my daughter." He motioned toward the child who stoo
over the prisoners. She held the vial of chemical poison i
her hands. She giggled and held it higher. The lid was off.

Scott whispered furiously. "That's it. That's th
chemical agent."

"Your little monster," Barrabas said to Kon, looking a
the tumor that covered the girl's face.

Kon's impassive expression changed suddenly to bruta
anger. He dropped his arms and pointed at Barrabas.

"You shall pay, Barrabas. You will pay for what th
Americans have done with their poisonous defoliants t
me. To my daughter." The general's voice rose and fe
with triumphant conviction.

"And what about you, Kon? How will you pay?" Bai
rabas could barely squeeze out the words. His voice wa
contemptuous. "In two days, I have seen a country tha
has run in rivers of flesh, and a people drowned in ocean
of blood. How many hells will you burn in to answer fc
what I have seen here? Tell me that, Kon."

The warlord said nothing. His eyes lit up. He smiled. H
was looking past the stone causeway into the moat. Ba
rabas heard the roar of an animal. He stepped sideways
eping his eyes on Kon and looking for the source of th
e at the same time.

ok!" Kon pointed, his voice light and pleased,

though Barrabas's words had had no meaning for him. "Look, they have come to feast." Two enormous tigers were crossing the dry, grassy moat below the causeway. They opened their enormous jaws to growl at the people they saw on the stone ledge above them.

"Look how sleek they are, how shiny their fur. They have fed well, these animals. Ask them, Barrabas! Ask them how they like the land I rule over. The tigers, at least, have eaten."

Barrabas looked. He also saw something in his peripheral vision. He dared not look directly in case he alerted Kon. There was movement in the stone carvings atop the immense gateway. He talked to Kon, trying to relax his eyes, to absorb and focus the movement.

"And you, I suppose, are also a tiger?"

"Yes!" Kon said it excitedly, his eyes large, as if the colonel had made a brilliant observation. "I am a tiger! Because that's what the world is all about, isn't it, Colonel Barrabas? There are those who are tigers, and those who shall be eaten."

"You forget one thing, Kon." Barrabas saw it now. Silently scaling down through the ornate carvings over the entrance to the ancient temple was a man. Geoff Bishop. And he had a gun.

"And what is that, Barrabas?"

"Tigers are beasts. They kill for nourishment. We are people."

"And I nourish myself on blood," the warlord said. "I eat death."

So chew on lead.

Bishop fired.

The Browning's 9mm parabellum socked into Kon's back and blew a gore hole out his chest. Kon bucked and coughed. His eyes went wide with shock. He tried to turn.

Bishop fired again.

A second bullet punched through the warlord.

"Daddy!" The little girl shouted. She ran for her father, holding the open vial carelessly in front of her.

"Noooo!" Kon screamed, seeing his daughter run toward him, the vial tipping in her hand as she went by the two prisoners.

Raoul stuck out his leg.

Barrabas had always thought that the little Frenchman had the potential to be deadly.

Kon's daughter tripped over the outstretched foot. She flew forward, putting her hands out to stop the fall. The vial fell onto the causeway and shattered. The blue liquid splashed across the stone. The little girl fell on top of it.

"Noooo!" Kon screamed, wide-eyed with horror as his daughter tried to pick herself up.

Bishop jumped to the ground from his stone perch on the gateway.

"Stay back!" Barrabas yelled.

Bishop ran to Erika and Raoul, grabbing each of them by their collars and dragging them away from the spilled chemical poison.

Kon's daughter pushed herself slowly from the ground. The good side of her face was streaked with the oily blue liquid. Her body jerked once and her eyes went wide. The skin on her face, arms and legs seemed to ripple as it turned red and erupted into massive blisters that oozed a runny yellow liquid. Then the blood happened. It spurted from her nose, dripped from her mouth and fingernails.

"My daughter," Kon cried in anguish as he circled the stricken child. His hands gripped his chest over the bullet wounds. Blood seeped from between his fingers. His legs began to collapse beneath him.

Barrabas darted in a wide circle around the stricken warlord and his daughter. He rushed to Erika and began to unfasten her bonds, as Bishop helped Raoul. When the hostages were free, they backed up against the stone, keeping well away from Kon, his dying daughter and the dangerous puddle of deadly contaminant.

The little girl started to jerk. It began slowly at first, with her hands and her feet. Then it spread—her arms and legs outward in spasms, then her head, back and forth.

The thing was hardly human now. It began to grunt as the jerks pushed air out of dying lungs. The entire life force inside the little girl had been unleashed into a hurricane of energy inside the body. The jerking grew wilder until her appendages were blurs. Still it did not stop. Triggered by the deadly chemical, concentrated death, the muscle spasms threw the girl two feet into the air, in a violent burst. She flipped and came down on her stomach, then flipped into the air again. The little girl was dead. But the body flipped like a fish out of water.

The mercs stared, speechless with horror. There was nothing anyone could do.

Kon collapsed, sitting heavily on the stone railing at the end of the causeway. He breathed heavily. He was dying. He stared at Barrabas, his eyes not believing what he had just seen.

"Believe it, Kon. She's dead. You're dead." Barrabas walked slowly across the causeway to the general, his blue eyes boring into Kon's unmercifully. The ex-warlord shrank from the piercing look, cringing back on the stone balustrade.

"There...are...tigers," stammered Kon. Barrabas walked at him, each footstep ringing judgment on the stone.

Kon shrank from the American warrior. His hands dripped blood from his wounds. Barrabas took another step.

"No!" Kon cried. He put out his bloody hand to stop the avenging colonel.

Barrabas stepped forward again, bringing Kon's final judgment closer. His eyes pierced into the warlord's.

Kon tore his eyes away and held his head down. "No!" he shouted in horror and panic. He scrambled farther back on the stone balustrade.

The tigers roared in the moat below.

Kon fell. His long pathetic scream followed him down. He hit the grass floor of the old moat. But he didn't die. Not then.

Barrabas walked to the edge of the causeway and looked down. Kon's leg was broken. He sprawled on the grass and pushed himself up with one hand. The other stretched up to Barrabas. The warlord whimpered. He was pleading for pity. He was begging for a merciful hand to reach down and pull him to safety.

Barrabas looked him in the eyes. There was no mercy.

The tigers ate.

EPILOGUE

The light and heat of day died. The sunset turned the sky purple and mingled with the dry yellow dust that rose in the winds above Cambodia. The mercs straggled across the landing strip to the airplane. Their fatigues were soiled with dirt and sweat, and their faces caked with dust. They were as exhausted as they looked.

A battle high can carry a soldier through days of fighting, and the soldier will not know physical tiredness. But when the battle's over, and the war is won, exhaustion is not merely a matter of sore muscles or weary bones—it is a tiredness of the soul.

"Colonel, those were the hardest shots I ever fired," said Geoff Bishop. He walked beside Barrabas. The colonel had his arm around Erika and held her close to him. The beautiful blond Dutchwoman leaned into his side, his warmth and the hardness of his body assuring her that the ordeal was over. Lee Hatton walked on the other side of the Canadian pilot. They concealed their affection. But Barrabas noticed. What Erika had said in the elevator at the hotel in Bangkok—it seemed like years ago now—was true. It was in their eyes, the way they looked at each other. The way they couldn't stop looking at each other now that they were going home.

"Because you shot him in the back?" Barrabas said.

"Yeah." The Canadian pilot nodded, a little shame-facedly. "I guess it's part of that code of honor that says always give the other guy a shooting chance."

They stopped as they reached the airplane. Nanos and Beck were lifting the heavy metal drum of chemical poiso into the fuselage. Barrabas turned back to Bishop. "If soldiers didn't have a code of honor we'd be as evil as men like Kon. But Kon had his chances, Geoff. Too many of them. He also had hostages." His arm tightened around Erika. "Get the plane warmed up. I've got some things to take care of."

Nanos and Beck came back outside.

"Hey, Lee," Nanos shouted. "How 'bout you and me taking off somewhere for some R and R for a few days when we get out of here?"

"'Alex!" Nate Beck cried with exasperation and embarrassment.

Nanos turned to his buddy. "It's okay, Nate. Just friends."

"That's right, Nanos. Just friends," Lee said warily. She caught Bishop's eyes and the two of them couldn't resist a smile.

Hayes rolled up beside them. The black man carried the HK-13 over his shoulder. "Nanos, you keep using your balls for brains, you're going to get in real trouble some day."

"Hey, don't talk to me about brains. Someone should tell you the war is over. You can leave the gun behind," the Greek teased.

"Uh-uh. After lugging it across Cambodia, I got attached to this baby."

From behind the knot of mercenaries, Liam O'Toole's voice belted out. "Come on boys, let's move it. We got to fly out of here."

Even Barrabas caught himself smiling at the drill sergeant's booming voice.

"What's your hurry, O'Toole?" Nate Beck asked.

The red-haired Irishman pulled up alongside and kept going. "There's a perky little blonde I started something with. And I never start things without finishing."

The mercs climbed aboard the old twin prop. Barrabas

turned to Erika. "You go ahead. I gotta see what's going on with Scott."

Erika left him and climbed into the airplane. Barrabas looked around. Scott and Raoul were walking across the landing strip together.

"Ah, Monsieur Barrabas," Raoul greeted him. "Monsieur Scott has told me of his experiences. Most fascinating. To have survived...all this." The Frenchman waved his ever-present scented handkerchief in the air. "And to think, I had a little role to play in such a scheme."

"Not so little, Raoul. You were the one who stuck your foot out."

"Ah yes. A tragedy for the poor little thing." Raoul shrugged. "But when one is fighting for one's life, the will to survive overcomes all scruples, it would seem."

"Perhaps," said Barrabas. "Scott, you're coming with us, aren't you?"

"I will leave you gentlemen to discuss this." Raoul walked quickly on his little legs to the waiting plane.

Scott looked at the tall colonel. He shook his head. "No, Barrabas. I can't."

"I don't understand. I can arrange to get the other POWs out of Radam later. But you can come now."

"I can't," Scott said again, glancing down quickly. "I'm sorry." His eyes met the colonel's. "I'm a freak, Barrabas, and nothing can change that. In Radam we're all freaks, and I don't think any of us want to come back anymore. It's where we belong, with our own kind." Scott's voice became suddenly earnest. "We can help those other people there. The Asians who are suffering because of Agent Orange. The children of Asia. You saw them, Barrabas. It's better for America to forget about us. We've been dead there for a long time. Our new life is in Radam. It's where we're needed."

Behind them, the propellers of the airplane sputtered to life, sucking the air away and raising low clouds of dust around them.

Barrabas shook his head. "I don't understand, Scott. How can you stay here in a country that created the evil of the Khmer Rouge and the warlord Kon?"

"You've freed us from Kon, Barrabas. But Cambodia didn't make Kon what he was." Scott looked the colonel straight in the eyes. "We create our own villains. Sometimes when men think they're doing good they overreach and do things without a single thought of the consequences. But you can't justify everything. You can't justify dumping millions of tons of chemical defoliants on a country. You can't refuse to accept the responsibility for what happens. This! This is what happens!"

Scott swept his arms out, motioning to the carnage around them. "Kon was our creation. What happened to his daughter is what we did to the children of Asia. All the anger, all the sorrow for that, came together in Kon's evil. It drove him insane. That's another reason why I'm staying, Nile. I'm going to stay with the people of Radam. Someone's got to make it up to them."

"Good luck, Scott." The white-haired warrior extended his hand. He was shouting over the noise of the airplane engines, and the roaring slipstream.

"Thanks." Scott shook. His hand trembled slightly. He looked at it. The shaking stopped. "Sometimes it's better sometimes..." He shrugged. Barrabas nodded. They looked at each other for the last time.

"Goodbye." The colonel slapped him on the shoulder and headed for the airplane home.

MORE GREAT ACTION COMING SOON

SOBs

#8 Eye of the Fire
by Jack Hild

Nile Barrabas undertakes a personal mission to find the young brother of a dead SOB and lands in the middle of a dirty job he wanted no part of. A notorious Argentine death-squad leader and former CIA operative is rotting in a Cuban prison, stuffed to the teeth with detailed knowledge of U.S. intel operations in Latin America that he's ready to sell for his freedom. The CIA wants him dead, but a group of American extremists want to bring him to the United States to train their own death squad.

With the Cuban army on their tail and an extremist death squad staring them in the face, the SOBs are caught between a rock and a hard place.

GET THE NEW WAR BOOK AND MACK BOLAN BUMPER STICKER FREE

Mail this coupon today!